Saratoga Letters

*To Linda & Sam,
Merry Christmas!
Elaine*

Elaine Marie Cooper

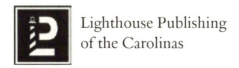

Lighthouse Publishing
of the Carolinas

SARATOGA LETTERS BY ELAINE MARIE COOPER
Published by Lighthouse Publishing of the Carolinas
2333 Barton Oaks Dr., Raleigh, NC, 27614

ISBN: 978-1-946016-00-3
Copyright © 2016 by Elaine Marie Cooper
Cover design by Elaina Lee, www.forthemusedesign.com
Costume Designer for 1777 photo: Laura Poresky
Interior design by Atritex, www.atritex.com
Photography by Nicole Young of Urbanwings Photography & Design, urbanwingsart.com

Available in print from your local bookstore, online, or from the publisher at:
www.lighthousepublishingofthecarolinas.com

For more information on this book and the author, visit:
www.elainemariecooper.com

All rights reserved. Non-commercial interests may reproduce portions of this book without the express written permission of Lighthouse Publishing of the Carolinas, provided the text does not exceed 500 words. When reproducing text from this book, include the following credit line: "*Saratoga Letters* by Elaine Marie Cooper, published by Lighthouse Publishing of the Carolinas. Used by permission."

Commercial interests: No part of this publication may be reproduced in any form, stored in a retrieval system, or transmitted in any form by any means—electronic, photocopy, recording, or otherwise—without prior written permission of the publisher, except as provided by the United States of America copyright law.

This is a work of fiction. Names, characters, and incidents are all products of the author's imagination or are used for fictional purposes. Any mentioned brand names, places, and trademarks remain the property of their respective owners, bear no association with the author or the publisher, and are used for fictional purposes only.

Scripture quotations from The Authorized (King James) Version. Rights in the Authorized Version in the United Kingdom are vested in the Crown. Reproduced by permission of the Crown's patentee, Cambridge University Press.

Brought to you by the creative team at Lighthouse Publishing of the Carolinas:
Alycia W. Morales, Rowena Kuo, Eddie Jones, Shonda Savage, Paige Boggs, Meaghan Burnett, Christy Distler, and Brian Cross.

Library of Congress Cataloging-in-Publication Data
Cooper, Elaine Marie.
Saratoga Letters / Elaine Marie Cooper 1st ed.

Printed in the United States of America

Praise for Saratoga Letters

Saratoga Letters is as beautifully titled as it is written. Poignant and suspenseful by turns and graced with an uncommon spiritual depth, this novel is historical fiction that truly grabs your heart and feeds your soul. My favorite Elaine Cooper story to date!

~ **Laura Frantz**
Author of *The Mistress of Tall Acre*

Saratoga Letters effortlessly takes readers into the Revolutionary War and beyond as strong-willed women put readers under their spell. As satisfying a historical novel you will ever find.

~ **Peter Leavell**
Award-winning author of *Gideon's Call*

Elaine Marie Cooper has written yet another compelling page-turner set in Revolutionary War times. Her skill in writing of the challenges during those years through the eyes, hearts, and lives of her characters is remarkable. An added plus—this novel offers two historical love stories, generations apart, that intertwine to surprise and satisfy readers. I absolutely loved *Saratoga Letters*.

~ **Beth Ann Ziarnik**
Award-winning author of *Her Deadly Inheritance*

Prepare for your senses to be fully engaged from page one of *Saratoga Letters* by Elaine Cooper. Not a history enthusiast, I was nonetheless riveted by the story of Abigail and William—their hopes, conflicts, sorrows, and joys. I *cared* for them and stayed up until the wee hours cheering them on as they fought against overwhelming odds. The author has a gift for placing you in the midst of the American Revolutionary War and introducing you to authentic characters with genuine life and death struggles. I look forward to reading more in this series!

~ **Leigh Ann Thomas**
Author of *Time Out, The Quiet Time Devotional*

Beauty or tenderness in the midst of violence can stir men's passion and devotion. Elaine Marie Cooper serves up an authentic "cuppa" flavorful brew for those who love history, suspense, and enduring romance!

~ **Denise Weimer**
Author of *The Restoration Trilogy* and *The Georgia Gold Series*

I love history. Especially American history. *Saratoga Letters* reminded me of how blessed I am to live in the greatest country in the world. We are unique in that we were founded on an idea. But the story demonstrates that there were heroes on both sides of the fighting. Men and women. It also shows that war can bring out the worst in us.

One of the things I particularly liked about the book was the love story. *Saratoga Letters* proves love can overcome what seem to be impossible barriers. Even time. My hat's off to Elaine Cooper.

~ **Marianne Jordan**
Author of *A Miser, A Manger, A Miracle*

Dedication

This book is dedicated to my sons,
Benjamin and Nathaniel Cooper,
fifth great-grandsons of a British soldier
who fought in the Battle of Saratoga.

Acknowledgments

I have so many to whom I am grateful for their help in accomplishing this novel.

My husband, Steve, first editor of every chapter, has been there for each of my novels to remind me of technical details that I too often forget. Thank you for your unending patience and support.

My team at Lighthouse Publishing of the Carolinas is incredible: Eddie Jones, Rowena Kuo, Alycia Morales, and Brian Cross. You are the best.

Thanks to so many in the Saratoga Springs, NY area who provided invaluable information and resources for this story: Eric Schnitzer, Park Ranger and Historian at Saratoga National Historical Park; Christine Valosin, Curator at Saratoga National Historical Park; Agnes Hamburger, Archivist, Saratoga Springs History Museum; Teri Blasko, Local History Librarian, Saratoga Springs Public Library; Mary Ann Fitzgerald, Saratoga Springs City Historian; Gregory Veitch, Chief of Police, Saratoga Springs Police Department; Linda Sanders, Deputy Town Historian and Village Historian of Stillwater, NY; Linda Palmieri, Stillwater Town Historian and Curator of the Stillwater Blockhouse Museum. Also, much thanks to Bill Buell, Features Writer, *Daily Gazette* in

Schenectady, NY; Doug Myers of the Albany Airport; and Nikya Pfeiffer, Public Relations, Redlands (CA) Community Hospital.

Thanks to author Peter Leavell for your helpful input.

Thanks to all of my readers and supporters who have faithfully read my historical fiction through the years and have been there to encourage me. Your enthusiasm helps to keep me writing. I am so grateful.

And thanks, as always, to my Lord and Savior Jesus Christ, from whom all blessings flow.

Part 1

Saratoga Letters 1777

Chapter 1

September 19, 1777: Saratoga, New York State

A dead soldier lay on top of him, but William was too weak to push him off.

Was the corpse an insurgent or his mate? The king's soldier couldn't discern regimental colors in the thick, black smoke.

And blood was blood—the smell sickened no matter the allegiance of its owner. The sticky fluid oozed from William's own leg and arm too. Perhaps his chest. Was his life ebbing closer to eternity? He tried to inhale, but the weight of the body squeezed the air from his lungs.

Dizziness overtook him.

Is this the end?

He could hear musket fire nearby. Then footsteps. The dead man was lifted from his chest, and William Carpenter breathed in air filled with spent gunpowder. Too weak to cough, he sputtered and choked then spit the acrid taste onto the ground.

"Are ya' all right, Corporal?" He recognized the voice, but William couldn't open his eyes wide enough to see the face.

"Don't know." His voice rasped.

"Over here," his rescuer shouted to someone.

As William was lifted onto a canvas stretcher, pain seared through his arm and he screamed.

"We'll get you to hospital quick enough. Hang on."

As a cannon sounded close by, the recovery team stopped short and hunkered low.

"We'll have to go through the woods toward camp." A face leaned low over him. "Corporal, it'll take a bit longer, but the trees will hide us. Can you hang on?"

"Yes. I'm grateful." He suddenly remembered his unit. Using the arm that wasn't in pain, he weakly grabbed at the man's shirt. "What about my mates?"

There was a pause. "All dead." Another pause, then he heard the man curse. "Come on. Got to get you to hospital."

William lost all sense of time. He occasionally woke up when the pain gripped him like a vise. Then darkness would overwhelm him again.

* * *

A voice woke him. An older woman washed his wounds while she shouted at another woman to "Get over to that one in the corner, afore he bleeds himself to death."

Where are my clothes? He tried to move, but the determined nurse forced him back down. Too weak to resist, he groaned, unable to stop the guttural moans from escaping his lips whenever the woman rubbed a wound.

Forcing his eyes open, William tried to focus on his surroundings. A large marquee rippled in the wind overhead. A pile of straw crumpled between his fingers.

The nurse poured a searing liquid over his arm, and he struggled to keep from screaming. Spots flashed in front of his eyes.

"That's a bad one, for certain." She dressed his arm in a bandage and scooped the dried straw bedding into a slight pile under his arm. "Have to have the surgeon check this one out."

At the word "surgeon," William's eyes opened wide. His breathing quickened. "No, not the surgeon." He reached for the woman's hand with his good arm. "Please, nurse. The surgeon will hack it off. I'd rather die."

"You might die if it's left to rot." Her wrinkled face drew closer to him. "We'll do what we can for ya', Corporal." Her words did not convince him that the fate of his arm was secure.

Indeed, nothing was secure right now. Not his health. Certainly not the success of the King's Army.

A cry from outside the hospital tent drew his attention. Nausea overcame William as the poor man begged the surgeon to spare his leg. Moans and cries of anguish sounded all around him. The women of the camp were in constant motion, washing men's bodies, giving sips of rum to the wounded, dressing holes in limbs and torsos.

As he focused on trying not to vomit, he remembered the words of his rescuers. "All dead." Tears stung his eyes. *All my mates gone. Why was I spared? 'Twould not have mattered if I'd died.*

If there was a God, there was no justice with heaven's decision this day.

Chapter 2

Abigail heard the musket fire in the distance, but she didn't move. She couldn't move. Heartache weighed her down.

Let the Regulars shoot me. I care not.

Had it only been a week since her father had died of the fever? Tears threatened again. *Poor father.* He could help so many others get well, yet his medicinals had seemed useless when Abigail administered them to her weak papa. Her dying papa.

She threw the quilt over her head, hoping the blanket, sewn by her mother so many years ago, would muffle the sounds of the world outside.

Yet even the multiple layers of material couldn't prevent the pounding on the heavy door from startling her. Abigail sat up so fast, dizziness nearly overtook her.

Perhaps the reverend was coming back to see how she was. At their last visit—when the man helped her bury father—he'd said he was taking his family and leaving the area. War was fast approaching. They needed to escape the coming battle.

Abigail had ignored him, preferring to stay. It was the only home she'd ever known and both her parents were buried here.

Relief flooded her as she threw a shawl over her shift and headed for the door. She was grateful for the reverend's return.

But the instant she lifted the door lock, she realized her mistake. The wooden portal flew inward, nearly hitting her head. Stumbling back, she gasped.

"Uncle Richard."

Unsettling memories stirred her thoughts. On her relative's last visit, Father had argued with her Loyalist uncle, brother to Abigail's deceased mother. Abigail had never cared for the man, as his manner was coarse and frightening. Now, his presence filled her with foreboding.

"What do you want?" She tried to keep her voice steady, but her throat had dried out and the words sounded weak and unsure.

"So yer father finally died, did he?" Richard looked around the room. "Where are your medicinals? There's hundreds of wounded at the camp and they need help."

"Wounded? At what camp?" She trembled at the thought of his reply. *The enemy camp?* Her legs weakened, and she gripped the edge of the door.

He glared at her. "The only army camp of importance, Miss Abigail." Her name sounded like a curse coming from his lips. "If your rebel father knew what was good for us all, he'd a taught you better."

She let go of the door and met his eyes with unexpected bravery. "Do not speak ill of my father."

She didn't expect the painful slap he inflicted on her cheek. Thrown off balance, Abigail grabbed the back of a chair and then plopped onto the hard wooden seat. The stinging elicited tears while her mouth and jaw stabbed with pain. Then the throbbing began.

"That'll teach ya to talk back to your uncle."

Weeping uncontrollably, she hated herself for revealing her weakness in front of such a hateful man. She could hear bottles clinking, and she turned to see him loading the entire shelf of medicinals—her father's precious supply—into a knapsack made of thick ticking.

"No!" Abigail screamed as a sudden burst of energy thrust her from the chair. She grabbed the pouch from his hands.

He gripped her arm so tightly she cried out. "Listen here, Miss Abigail. Ye'll release your grip on this pouch or I'll beat ya senseless. Do ya understand?"

Abigail looked into his cold eyes and saw the face of evil. She had no doubt he would carry out his word. Swallowing, she fought back more tears and let go of the bag now bulging with jars of medicinals. "Aye. I understand."

"Good. Now, you get your pathetic, rebel self dressed, 'cause ye're goin' with me."

"Going with you? Why?" Abigail's legs swayed, and she gripped the back of the chair.

"Ye're not the fastest in understanding, are ya? I said there's hundreds of the King's Army wounded and they need nurses. Ye're coming with me to help them. I'm certain your father taught you a few ways to heal a wound."

She shook her head slowly. "No. I … I cannot leave here. What if my intended comes looking for me?" She grasped at any possible excuse.

Uncle Richard threw his head back and laughed raucously. "That weasely insurgent? He wouldn't get three paces near where I'm taking you before his head'd be blasted off." His face lost all its humor. "Now get dressed."

Uncle Richard continued to confiscate all the dried herbs that her father had used. Father had been the local apothecary, supplying the surrounding communities with healing plants. Now all of his precious supplies would be used for the enemies of the Colonists. Abigail's heart broke at the thought.

Dear God, what is happening? Why do You allow this evil? Am I to face this alone?

The one-room cabin offered little in the way of privacy, but she did her best to dress discretely. Her fingers trembled while tying the cords that tightened her stays in the front. Donning her gown, she shook with a new fear as her uncle stared at her. She grabbed her woolen cloak, threw it on, and pulled it tightly around her neck.

I must get away from him.

Hurrying out the door, she stifled her tears as she glanced back at her family's cabin. Would she ever see her home again?

Her uncle stomped from behind her, carrying the bulging pouch of medicinals. He grabbed her arm and half-dragged her into the woods.

Abigail shuddered. "Where are you taking me?"

"Freeman's Farm."

Freeman. Another Loyalist.

Chapter 3

William lay on the cold straw for what seemed like hours when he heard a commotion at the door. Weakly turning his head toward the sound, he saw a burly man enter, escorting a young woman with hair the color of autumn leaves.

The man's voice was measured as he spoke with the matron of the nurses. William's blood heated at the tight squeeze the Colonist had clamped on the young woman's arm. Had he the strength, he would've dealt with the man.

"I am Richard Cawthorne, sergeant in the Loyalist militia. This is my niece, Mrs. Abigail Gillingham. She's been trained in the art of medicinals and should prove a worthwhile asset in healing these brave, wounded soldiers."

The matron looked at Abigail from her flaming hair to her mud-covered shoes. "Mrs. Gillingham, is it?"

The young woman looked at the ground and whispered so quietly one could barely hear her. "Aye."

The woman who had attended William hours before spoke again. "You seem young to be a 'Mrs.,' but as long as you've seen a man before, yer knowledge of medicinals will be quite useful. As you can see, this tent is full."

Mrs. Gillingham lifted her head. With widened eyes, she took in the scene. Dozens of wounded soldiers—some moaning, others lying deathly still—nearly filled the huge hospital marquee.

"So many."

"Those blasted insurgents." The matron shook her head.

William thought he saw Abigail's eyes narrow when the matron said "insurgents." But he forgot the brief expression when he noted the purple, swollen cheek marring Mrs. Gillingham's otherwise perfect face. Anger surged through him, but he had little strength to speak up.

Mrs. Gillingham stood as far away from her uncle as she could, but the beast drew her back to his side. "So, you'll be helping out these brave men fighting for our colonies, will you not, dear niece? Just remember your own husband fighting with the Loyalists to defend the king's honor."

Again, Mrs. Gillingham looked at the floor. Again, the soft "Aye."

"Well then, I shall leave you in the capable hands of your matron, Mrs. ..." Richard Cawthorne raised his eyebrows.

"Carberry. Sarah Carberry. I shall look after your niece, Mr. Cawthorne." She firmed her lips into a slight smile. "Fear not."

Cawthorne grinned. "I shall not fear. I'm certain she's in capable hands." He gripped Mrs. Gillingham's arm again. "Be strong, dear niece. I'll return for you when these wretched battles are over." He leaned down to kiss her on the cheek.

Mrs. Gillingham cringed and averted her face from him.

Cawthorne yielded a strained smile and tipped his farmer's cap at the matron. "Mrs. Carberry."

"Mr. Cawthorne."

The moment the uncle left the hospital tent, Mrs. Gillingham's mouth trembled and she covered her face.

Mrs. Carberry wrapped her arms around the young nurse's shoulders. The red-haired beauty collapsed into the matron's embrace.

The older woman spoke. "I have eyes to see." She held Abigail for a long moment. "You'll be safe with us, Mrs. Gillingham. Only man takin' you home from here will be your consort. God willing, he'll survive this war."

Chapter 4

As the painful cries of the wounded met her ears, Abigail wiped her tears away. There was work to be done. Regardless of allegiance to a cause, these men were in desperate need of help.

Mrs. Carberry released her motherly hold on her and pointed toward the corner of the sixty-man tent. "You can start over there with those new arrivals."

Abigail swallowed back the bile in her throat as she scanned over the many patients fresh from the battlefield. And they didn't stop coming. Bloodied men were either carried on stretchers or hauled over the shoulders of comrades.

The concern the soldiers had for their fellow warriors touched Abigail in unexpected ways. One young lad, bleeding from his own wounds, begged a surgeon to attend to his motionless comrade. The lad backed away from his friend and stared long and hard at him before he exited the tent. Audible sobs followed his leave-taking. Abigail's heart, so determined to hate, began to melt at the human misery.

There was no time to waste, but where to begin? Of course. Father's medicinals.

Grabbing the pouch her uncle had tossed at her feet, Abigail untied the twine knot and sought something—anything—that might be used to bring healing. Some of the bottles had shattered from her uncle's carelessness. Pounding blood rushed to her head. When a shard pierced her fumbling fingers, the pounding moved abruptly to her hand. She stifled a cry, then stared at the blood oozing from her right hand.

Such a small cut to cause so much pain. How much worse these men must be suffering.

She took the bottle of rum Mrs. Carberry had handed to her, poured a minuscule amount over the small gash, and tore off a portion of her linen petticoat. Wrapping the wound tightly to keep it from bleeding onto the soldiers, she forced herself to return to the task at hand.

As she hauled the heavy pouch toward the corner, her eyes fell upon three new arrivals. Her father had taught her years earlier that when there were many victims, whether of plague or disaster, always try to treat those who were likely to recover and save those with a death pall for last. Treat the treatable first. With medicinals and God's help, the soldiers would hopefully heal.

One of the newly arrived trio had an odd look—though he yet breathed, he stared with little movement of his eyes. She went to the next man with a severe leg wound. Grabbing a water bucket and soap from nearby, she intended to wash the wound. But the man's breeches were in the way. She tried tearing the heavy duck cloth to no avail.

"You'll have to take them off," Mrs. Carberry shouted to her from across the way.

Abigail swallowed. She knew this was necessary, but her father had always removed such articles of clothing.

The patient began undoing the buttons at his waist to help her. "It's all right, ma'am. I need my leg, ya see?"

His desperation forced all thoughts of modesty aside. "I'll try not to hurt you, sir." She squatted at his feet and pulled with all her might to remove his pants. His pained screams tore through her. "I'm so sorry."

His long shirt covered most of him, but now she was able to see the full length and depth of the wound in his lower leg. She cringed at the damage. She'd only seen a wound like this once before when a neighbor was accidentally shot while hunting bear.

I wish Father were here.

Grabbing an old rag from a bucket of murky river water, she carefully cleansed the area surrounding the wound. Clots of dried blood stemmed the flow, but it continued to ooze. When she poured rum onto the wound—Father always said "'twas better than water"—the young man seized with pain.

After recovering from the application, the soldier pushed up on his elbows. "I don't suppose you could put some of that to my lips instead?"

Abigail attempted a smile and offered him the bottle. He took a long swig, and she had to pull it away before he drank it all. "Your fellow soldiers are in need as well."

The man, who looked younger than herself, plopped back down onto the straw bedding. "Thanks, Mrs. …"

She swallowed. "Gillingham. Mrs. Gillingham." She bit her lip at the lie, yet knew better than to tell the truth. Her uncle had warned her that nurses must be married. If the troops learned she was not, she could be drummed out of camp—or worse. And then there would be the wrath of Uncle Richard to contend with. The thought sent shivers up her spine.

Before she could dress the leg wound, she heard male voices behind her, as well as Mrs. Carberry. "Gentlemen, this is Mrs. Gillingham. She is trained in the art of medicinals. Mrs. Gillingham, this is our surgeon, Mr. Braithwaite, and his two mates who assist him. I've told them they need to examine this man's leg." She pointed to the soldier in Abigail's care.

The surgeon nodded his head at Abigail. Squatting down, he lifted the wounded leg and looked at the back of the man's calf, eliciting more painful shouts from the patient. "I see no exit wound here." He reached his hand back, and one of the surgeon's mates handed him a probe. After inserting the probe into the wound, he began moving it around.

Abigail grew dizzy, but her attention was drawn to the poor soldier, who reached toward the surgeon and pleaded for him to stop. She knelt next to him and held his hands. When her strength wasn't sufficient to hold him still, one of the surgeon's mates helped.

Mr. Braithwaite gave a satisfied nod and reached back toward the other man, who placed long forceps into the surgeon's grip.

The young soldier cried and begged for mercy.

Abigail bit her lip so hard she could taste her own blood. Tears rolled down her cheek, and she noticed the surgeon's mate staring at her. She avoided his gaze and closed her eyes, praying silently.

Suddenly the soldier was quiet and his hands went limp. Opening her eyes, she sought the face of the man gripping the soldier's other hand. "Is he gone?"

"No." The man with straw-colored hair spoke for the first time. "Lost his senses from the pain. He'll come 'round."

Abigail released the patient's hand and laid it across his scarlet coat.

The gruff voice of the surgeon caught her attention. "Mrs. Gillingham, dress the wound." Looking at the next patient, the surgeon sighed. "Take this body outside."

The two assistants did so while Abigail searched for bandages.

Mrs. Carberry was already at her side with rolls of linen and a bowl of lint. "Here. Soak the lint in your medicinals to stave off infection. God willing, this lad will not lose his leg."

Abigail hadn't noticed how much her hands were trembling until she started to make the poultice. She dropped some of the linen onto the straw and silently berated herself for her clumsiness. At least the young soldier was unconscious and she could work on him without causing more pain. She added some of her own slippery elm to the oil and lint and packed it as gently as she could into the large hole in his leg. After wrapping a linen bandage around the wound, she sank to the ground. Her hand began to sting again from the laceration, but she tried to ignore it. There was too much work to do.

Pushing herself off the floor, she realized she still wore her gray cloak. As she undid the buttons, she felt like someone was staring at her. She glanced down the row of patients until she saw a soldier with a large bandage on his arm. The man who fixed his eyes on her shivered. After walking purposefully toward him, she knelt down by his side. "Are you fevered?"

The man tried to smile but shuddered. It was getting warm in this tent of death, so Abigail assumed the worst. "Here." She covered him with her cloak. "Let me get you some rum."

The man sipped it eagerly. "Thank you." His voice rasped. "Thank you … Mrs. Gillingham."

Abigail paused in her ministrations. "How do you know my name?"

The man tried to smile again, but he seemed so weak. "I heard your uncle introduce you to the matron."

His long, brown hair lay strewn over the straw and across his cheek. She slipped her finger under the strands on his face and drew them to the side. Abigail looked at her hands. "I see."

"Tell me, Mrs. Gillingham."

Her eyes met his.

"How did you sustain that bruise on your face?"

Covering her mouth with her hands, she turned away.

The soldier gently touched her arm. "Please. I did not intend to cause you distress. I only … I only wish you well."

His kind words melted her heart. "Thank you." Rallying her strength, she threw her shoulders back and ignored his question. "Let me see to your wound."

Blood had soaked through the bandage, necessitating it be changed. She also needed to discern why it was still bleeding. Carefully unwrapping the soaked bandage, Abigail recalled her father saying a wound would only heal when the blood flow was halted. Usually, a tight bandage sufficed. Obviously, it hadn't this time.

The soldier winced as she worked on his arm.

"You are very brave, sir."

The removal of the bandage revealed fresh, florid blood. Abigail inhaled sharply. She looked around the marquee, but there was no sign of the surgeon or his mates. "Sir, I must use some thread to stem the flow. Are you willing to let me try? My father has taught me the skill."

The soldier swallowed. "Yes. I place my life in your hands."

Abigail gently squeezed his uninjured arm. Then she carefully removed the bottle that contained waxed sutures and crooked needles from her knapsack. Threading the needle was awkward with her own wounded finger, but she ignored the sting and concentrated on her job. She must work quickly, as the man's lifeblood was slipping him closer to eternity. "Are you ready?"

"Yes." He closed his eyes tightly.

Abigail inserted her finger into the wound in his upper arm until she located the source of the bleed. Carefully singling out the blood vessel, she deftly sutured a stitch or two—enough to encourage clotting without impeding the flow completely. She removed her fingers as quickly as possible and placed a clean cloth over the wound, then she waited several moments before gingerly lifting the linen. The rapid flow had ceased.

Thank You, heavenly Father!

"I believe the wound should heal now."

Her patient had been silent during this task, but he was in obvious pain. "Thank you." His voice was barely a whisper.

"I'll put some medicinal into your wound and cover it again."

He nodded his head in agreement, but his face had turned red.

"I am terribly sorry for your pain." She placed a comforting hand on his wrist and was shocked when he gripped her hand with unexpected intensity.

"Thank you, Mrs. Gillingham."

Her surprise at his touch left her unable to speak for a moment. "You have the advantage on me, sir. I do not know your name." His blue eyes, the color of the sky, elicited the warmth of a summer's sun in her heart.

"William. Corporal William Carpenter."

Chagrined by the warmth that flooded her face, Abigail released his grip on her hand. "I must attend to the others now, Corporal Carpenter." She stood, careful to avoid stepping on the patient next to him.

The incessant cries of the wounded, as well as the near-constant volley of musket fire in the distance, sent ripples of despair through her. Weak from hunger and distress, she wondered how she would keep up her strength.

Just then the surgeon's mate, who had helped hold the patient's hands, walked through the opened flap of the tent and placed a chunk of bread in her open palm. "Here. You shall need victuals to sustain you." He turned and left the tent without saying another word.

"Thank you." Her words likely never reached the intended recipient as the sound of cannon fire grew ever louder.

* * *

As the heat of the day settled in, so did the routine of caring for the constant needs of patients. Abigail wondered if she'd grown accustomed to the frequent screams or if the men had weakened so much that their voices were shrouded by near death.

She worked automatically, moving from soldier to soldier, washing, giving rum, calling the surgeon when needed—hoping he was available. Sweat poured off her face as she labored in the stifling, overcrowded tent.

Feeling a hand on her shoulder, she turned. "Here. Drink this." Mrs. Carberry handed Abigail a tankard of ale and walked slowly back to the cook who stood in the doorway, delivering drinks to the nurses and surgeons.

She drank with an unquenchable thirst and thought of the casks of cider in her cabin to the north, praying she might drink it again. Someday. If she could survive.

At the moment, survival seemed as surreal as the morning mist over the river. The instant one tried to grasp it in their hand, it melted away like a ghost. A mere mirage best not counted on. What *was* real were the pain, blood, and fear surrounding her. Her energy could only be spent on these, without hope for anything more. She would work until her own life ebbed away without hope for anything more in this life. Not even cider from home.

The volleys of incessant musket fire had ceased for a time, only an occasional burst of gunpowder remaining. But by midafternoon, hell visited once again.

This time, the cries from a short distance away exploded with the vigor of many hungry beasts of prey finding their victims at last. Abigail trembled at the thought of the human carnage on both sides of the battle.

Minutes later, the expected deluge of blood-soaked bodies began their arrival. While Abigail and the other nurses waited with resignation, the sheer volume of pain that was carried or dragged through the door ravaged the core of her heart. She wanted to weep but could not afford the indulgence.

Scarlet-tinged straw that had earlier offered some comfort to the dying was quickly replaced with a fresh supply carried in by young boys. When a young girl, perhaps eight years old, carried in a fresh bottle of rum and handed it to her, Abigail's mouth dropped at the site of one so young in this place of wretched death. She hurried the girl outside when she saw her staring with horror at the patients.

Poor Mrs. Carberry. The woman's face was lined with weariness. Yet, like the soldiers who transported the wounded—often wounded themselves—the gallant matron of nurses carried on. "Start over there, Mrs. Gillingham." Mrs. Carberry pointed to two injured men who had just arrived.

Both were covered with so much blood, Abigail winced at the sight. *God help me. God help them.* Inhaling, she strode toward the soldier closest to her.

He looked like a boy. He also appeared extremely confused as he pulled at the bandages on his head. "Get it off. Get it off!"

She knelt on the straw-covered ground next to him. "There now, young man. Let's leave our dressings on. I'll re-do it for you so 'twill be more comfortable." She removed the blood-encrusted linen and covered her mouth lest she scream. There was a deep hole in his skull. Although she could not see it, there was likely a musket ball imbedded deep within that crevice. She gently laid a clean cloth over it and prayed. *Lord, do not let this lad linger for long. Help him in his suffering, Lord Jesus.*

"Mother?"

She jerked her head up from her prayers and found him staring at her.

"Mother?"

She grabbed his hand. She didn't even know his name. "Yes, son." Tears swam into her mouth, and she swallowed them with difficulty.

The boy smiled. "Mother. Your Charlie's come home. I told you I would."

"I'm ... I'm so glad you're here, Charlie."

Charlie smiled, closed his eyes, and slipped into eternity.

An audible sob burst from her throat. She stood and ran outside. "Lord, I've not seen death like this before. Help me, dear God!"

In the midst of pouring out her grief, an unexpected, invisible presence surrounded her. The peace she'd longed for in the last few weeks—ever since Father took ill—finally settled into her heart. Its calm came as unexpectedly as the knock on her cabin door had this morning. The resulting comfort that surrounded her contrasted with the fear and anger wrought by the presence of her uncle and this bloody war and all its death. This unseen spirit was the strength that she knew in her soul would carry her through this fiery trial. She could not explain—but she was grateful.

After a moment, she dried her face with her apron and her sleeve and resolutely stepped back through the canvas door. *Lord, with Your help, I can survive.*

* * *

William's emotions threatened to overwhelm him as he watched Mrs. Gillingham with the dying drummer boy. He knew the lad was not more than ten years old.

Rage over the death of one so young blended with sadness as the nurse stroked the dying boy's arm and pretended to be his mother. But he was completely taken aback when a wrenching sob escaped Mrs. Gillingham's throat. He didn't have the strength to follow her and bring her comfort when she escaped out the canvas flap door of the hospital tent. So he did the only thing he was able to do for her. He prayed.

It was something he'd not done in years. Something he'd vowed to never do again. But the pleas to heaven burst from his heart—unplanned, unexpected, and unhindered.

Chapter 5

Abigail hadn't slept all night. Whenever she started to nod off, something would awaken her. Usually it was cries of the wounded, prompting her to bring more rum. Otherwise, it was the chilling howls of wolves in the distance. Their incessant baying caused the hair on her neck to stand upright.

Wishing the surgeon had something stronger for the wounded, she wondered if the laudanum that would have provided relief to the dying men was being saved for injured officers. The surgeon had implied as much when she'd asked if there was any stronger medicinal to help with the wounded Regulars. It seemed that comfort was available only for those in power.

The cold night air crept under her clothing, eliciting shivers up her arms. Desperate for warmth, she uncovered a filthy blanket in the straw. It was stained with various shades of blood. Were she at home, she'd have picked it up by her fingers and tossed the wretched weave into the laundry kettle outdoors. In these early morning hours of despair and exhaustion, she embraced the small amount of warmth that stood between her and freezing to death.

Stiffened legs prompted her to get up and stretch. Longing for fresh air, Abigail opened the tent flap and, as she stepped outside, was immersed in the morning mist. She could barely see a rod in front of her. Peering into the low cloud, she realized she'd lost all sense of direction. Even if she tried to escape into the darkness, she'd likely never find her way home. She was as lost in this fog as a foreigner.

Walking carefully around stumps of trees, she found herself nearly tripping over a sleeping sentinel. Someone's grasp saved her from stumbling forward.

"Watch your step, Mrs. Gillingham."

She barely recognized the voice, but the man's face soon became clear in the mist. "You're the surgeon's mate." She didn't know if she should be grateful or afraid.

"At your service, Mrs. Gillingham." He bowed slightly, although she could not see his feet for the fog. "Come into the surgeon's tent for some tea and biscuits."

Entering through the flap he held for her, Abigail observed boxes of journals along the edge of the tent and numerous medicinals and tools spread across tables. Some of the instruments were filthy with dried blood. The surgeon had fallen asleep in a chair with his feet propped on a table. His mouth hung open as he snored loudly.

A lighted candle offered some illumination as the young man poured some tea into a cup.

Such finery in a war camp.

She took the cup of tea, wondering how long it had been since she had partaken of the delicious brew. Since the Boston Tea Party of years before, patriotic Colonists had settled for coffee. But her heart still thrilled at the aroma of tea, and the taste did not disappoint her expectations. She closed her eyes and exulted in the flavor.

"Such a pity the poor Colonists must forsake the king's brew, is it not?"

"Aye." She opened her eyes to find the surgeon's mate watching her with a steady gaze. "Of course, only the Colonists who have resisted the king have forsaken it." She attempted a smile, but her cheek still throbbed from her uncle's abuse the previous day.

"How did your face become injured?"

Her heart leaped erratically. She set the cup of tea down and averted her gaze from him. "I … I fell against a trunk at home."

"That is a lie."

Abigail's mouth began to taste like salt, and spots flashed in her vision.

The assistant gently touched her arm. "Mrs. Carberry told us about your uncle. You need not defend him or his despicable actions. Loyalist or not, the man's a horrid beast. No better than the savages."

The man's venomous assault on her uncle's character took Abigail by surprise.

He continued. "You need not fear that man. I'm certain if your husband were not at war against these rebels, your uncle would be a dead man." He paused. "Where is your husband's regiment?"

Her thoughts raced as she stuttered. "I … I believe near Canada, sir."

He sat back in his chair. "I thought as much." He stared at her with such intensity. "Have you heard from him of recent days? Is he well?"

She shifted in her chair. "It has been quite some time." She cleared her throat and took a gulp of tea, which elicited a cough.

The surgeon's mate got up and patted her back. Then he slowly removed the bloody blanket from her shoulders.

Abigail stiffened.

"I mean you no harm, Mrs. Gillingham. Let me get you a clean blanket." He searched for a quilt that he took from a pile nearby. "Here, the ladies donated these for the soldiers. Surely your service warrants some comfort."

"Thank you, Mr. …"

"Salyer. Thomas Salyer, at your service." He grinned and bowed, tossing his head slightly, which served to loosen even more of his hair from the ribbon he'd used to tie it back. He pushed the wayward strands behind his ear. "Forgive my appearance, Mrs. Gillingham. I fear I've spent too much time in hospital and far too little in front of the looking glass." His cheeks turned red, even visible by candlelight.

Abigail felt herself blush. "I dare not imagine my own appearance."

Mr. Salyer frowned. "Nothing could mar the loveliness of your flaming hair, Mrs. Gillingham." He stopped himself and looked away. After quickly downing the last of his tea, he abruptly stood. "Well then, the sun rises. Let us see what this day brings forth." He offered her his arm.

Abigail stood and hesitated. Then she took his arm and allowed him to escort her outdoors. The mist was still thick but beginning to disperse. In the emerging dawn, she observed what seemed to be sadness in his countenance.

"Off to hospital, then. Carry on." He bowed and went inside the surgeon's tent, where she could hear him waking his superior.

Abigail walked carefully through the fog back to hospital.

For just a moment, while drinking tea and sitting with the handsome Mr. Salyer, she'd been transported to a time long ago when tea was treasured and all seemed well with the world. It was an all-too-brief respite from her cares. For now, she must return to the mass of misery and the horrors of war.

Chapter 6

The last place Abigail Gillingham thought she would find an ally was in the enemy's camp. Yet here was a friend in the guise of a stern matron of nurses. Mrs. Carberry took on the role of mother figure to her—a relationship Abigail had long missed, since her own mother died in childbirth when Abigail was barely ten. Even now, ten years later, she longed for someone to hold her and assure her that all would be well, even if life had taught her otherwise.

Yet even in this new friendship, Abigail felt guilty. While it was true she could tend to the wounded Regulars, the young Colonist was definitely not married.

But the worst deception was in her loyalties. She hated these British soldiers. They invaded her country, and now the survival of their wounded was in her hands? Abigail shuddered at the thought. It was not as if she had sought to be a spy, although others would accuse her of such if they knew she was an ardent Patriot.

Had these anxious thoughts or the assault on her face induced the throbbing headache she now suffered?

Mrs. Carberry brought her to the section of the camp where the women bathed and did laundry. The smell was unforgettable. Not all the women had poor hygiene, but enough did that

Abigail's head swam with the stench. She tried not to inhale while Mrs. Carberry led her to clean aprons drying on a line.

As she tried one on, someone grabbed her arm and spun her around. A buxom woman spat, "Whaddya think you're doin', Miss Prig?"

The woman was barely clothed, and Abigail made every attempt not to gape at her bare skin. It was all the more difficult, seeing there was such an abundance of it.

Mrs. Carberry intervened. "Mrs. Cravens, this is Mrs. Gillingham. She's come to help with our wounded."

The rounded face transformed from bitter to sweet. "Is that so? Well, welcome to our bloody world, Mrs. Gillingham."

A male voice caught everyone's attention. "Lydia."

Mrs. Cravens turned toward the unkempt soldier standing on the edge of camp. She turned bright red and giggled like a lovesick schoolgirl. "Oooo! There's my Tommy! Back safe from battle!" The plump woman sashayed through the crowd of females, pushing aside corset-clad ladies as she went. Abigail's jaw opened wide when Lydia locked her lips onto those belonging to her Tommy. They tripped and danced their way into the woods without ever separating from their kiss.

She shifted her feet and cleared her throat. "Mr. Cravens, I assume?"

Mrs. Carberry gave an exasperated sigh. "Yes. For today, that is. Tomorrow, perhaps, 'twill be another."

Abigail opened her twenty-year-old eyes wide with astonishment but said nothing.

"Come on." Mrs. Carberry helped her tie her apron. "I'll show you what you'll need to do."

Before they left camp, a lad of perhaps ten years of age approached the women. "Miz Carberry, please ma'am. 'Eard father was in 'ospital. Can ya take me to 'im? Some says 'e's askin' for me."

Abigail's eyebrows furrowed and she twisted her apron between her hands as she sought the face of the matron.

The woman placed her hand gently on the boy's shoulder. "We'll find him for you, lad. I'm certain your presence will bolster his spirits."

While the woman smiled, Abigail could see that Mrs. Carberry's eyes were wider than usual and her smile was thin and tight.

The matron put her arm around the lad's shoulder and drew him toward the hospital tent. Abigail followed a few steps behind as though she were in a funeral march.

As the small group approached the tent—one of several—the incessant wailing of the ill and wounded greeted Abigail's ears. While visiting the women's camp had been a brief respite from this sound, the world of the camp followers and the "camp wives" was not without discomforts of a different sort. Abigail had stepped into new terrain, and she truly felt like a foreigner in her own homeland.

Stepping through the canvas opening, she saw that even more wounded had arrived in the brief time she'd gone to get the apron. Scouts had dragged them in. This time they weren't just victims of musket and cannonballs. Many had partially severed limbs.

She whispered to Mrs. Carberry, "What happened to those soldiers?"

The older woman covered the lad's ears. "Wolves were attracted to the bloodied bodies in the field during the night. They chewed on the men. Some were eaten alive." Mrs. Carberry's lips trembled. "No one could rescue the injured or they themselves were shot."

Abigail covered her mouth in horror. But what drew her intense compassion was the haunting look in the matron's eyes. It was as if this dear woman had seen one tragedy too many in her life. *Dear Lord, help her.*

Mrs. Carberry lifted the boy's head to face her. "What's your father's name, lad?"

"Colum, ma'am. Colum Abbot."

The older woman smiled bravely. "Well, Mr. Abbott, let's see if your father is here."

They walked the length of the patients as the matron called out. "Colum Abbott. Is Colum Abbott here?"

A voice rose above the cries of pain. "'E's over 'ere."

The lad raced toward the man but stopped short. The boy grimaced and rubbed his hand frantically through his hair. He turned away for a moment, then forced his gaze back to the patient. "Father?"

A barely discernible voice spoke, and a slow-moving hand reached upward.

Tears now flooded the boy's face as he walked toward his injured father. "What 'appened to ya?"

Abigail couldn't hear the reply, but she could no longer watch the heartbreaking scene. She busied herself, getting fresh water that was left outside. While struggling to bring the heavy bucket into the tent, she nearly bumped into Mr. Salyer.

He grinned. "Whoa, Mrs. Gillingham. Let me assist you with that burden."

Others paused in their duties and looked at them. It was expected that a nurse should carry the burden, no matter how heavy.

"Thank you, Mr. Salyer, but no matter. I am doing well enough." She curtsied awkwardly while holding the heavy water and hauled it toward the patients.

"Don't you have patients to attend, Mr. Salyer?" The surgeon's irritated voice splintered the atmosphere.

"Yes, sir." The redness in Mr. Salyer's cheek brought a chuckle from the other surgeon's mate.

Abigail was embarrassed for him and grateful for his efforts to help her. She looked at him and smiled.

He returned a sheepish grin and went about his tasks.

She headed for the young man with the injured leg that she'd nursed the day before. His skin was pale and moist, but he was awake. "Well now, how is the leg this morning?"

He gave her a defeated look. "Not well."

"May I look at it?"

"Of course."

Abigail lifted the blanket and narrowed her eyes. There was something not quite right. When she pressed around the edges of the wound, the soldier winced.

She smiled bravely. "I think 'twill be fine, but let's change the dressing, shall we?"

Removing the pledget of discolored lint, she tried not to show any alarm. Tears rolled down the soldier's face as she dug out the wadded lint as carefully as possible. "I'm so sorry this causes you such pain." The dressing change went as quickly as she could accomplish it—but it never seemed fast enough when a patient suffered from it. "I'll check it again later." She patted his arm and stood up.

Turning toward the door, she saw the slumped shoulders of Colum Abbott's young son. She approached him from behind. "Master Abbott?"

He turned to look at her and ran into her arms. "Father's dyin'! He asked me to look after Mother and the little ones." His whole body convulsed.

She held the boy for a long while, praying that God would bring the boy comfort. She knew what it was to lose a father. But she wasn't a young child when she lost her own. Tears escaped her eyes and dripped onto the boy's head.

Once again, she could feel someone staring at her. Glancing toward William Carpenter, she found the culprit. His own eyes were filled with moisture that reflected the anguish she felt, and she found comfort in his sympathy.

Chapter 7

Everyone working in hospital assumed British General Burgoyne would attack the Patriot army the next day. Much to Abigail's surprise, word spread that the general would wait until the following day—a Sunday.

Sabbath day. Abigail longed for the sermons of the reverend that she'd taken for granted before this week's events—before everyone's lives were turned upside down. She struggled to recall even bits and pieces of Bible passages that the minister had recited. Not one verse found its way into her memory.

When Sabbath day finally arrived, Abigail prayed for the strength to bear the expected sounds of battle and the onslaught of new patients. But they never materialized. Instead, a young messenger arrived early with news that Sir Henry Clinton was to arrive with British reinforcements.

While the wounded patients cheered with weak voices, Abigail's heart sank.

More troops. More wounded. More lives lost—on both sides.

Disheartened, she straightened her apron and took a deep breath. She must do her job. Stay the course, whether her choice or not.

Abigail strode toward the long row of patients and stopped at William Carpenter's side. "How do you fare, Corporal?"

He gave a questioning smile. "You do not seem reassured by the news of Clinton, Mrs. Gillingham."

Why did he seem to read her mind? She found it both curious and annoying.

"More troops means more wounded and dying, Corporal." She looked down at the floor then met his eyes. "I daresay, the sounds of pain are difficult to bear."

"You have a tender heart."

Mesmerized by his eyes, which reflected specks of silver highlighting the blue, she forced her gaze away. "I must examine your arm." Holding his right arm off the mound of straw, Abigail observed a greenish tinge on the bandage. She swallowed her concern and unwrapped the dressing. A sickening smell reached her nostrils, but she forced herself to remain stone-faced. "I fear I may need to try a stronger medicinal for your wound."

His eyebrows knit together, and she heard a discernible increase in his breathing. "Mrs. Gillingham, please do not let the surgeon take my arm. 'Tis my shooting arm." His left hand gripped her with force as his fingers trembled.

She kept her voice low. "I must caution you, sir. A green wound can take your life. Are you willing to risk it? Have you no family to await your return?"

William's eyes welled. "No, ma'am. Not anymore." He sniffed and scrubbed the tears away. "So you see, if your medicinals can cure it, at least I can still fight. If not ... 'twill not matter to anyone."

Abigail's chest tightened as she touched his good arm. "'Twould matter to me, sir." She looked away. "I shall prepare the balsam and oil forthwith."

She pushed herself up from the floor and sought Mrs. Carberry. When she did not see her, Abigail approached Elizabeth Pomeroy.

"She's still in the nurse's tent, Mrs. Gillingham."

Mrs. Pomeroy was not the kindest nurse in the group, but she was capable with the job. Although she'd never said an unkind word to Abigail, the newcomer always felt ill-at-ease in her presence. Perhaps it was Mrs. Pomeroy's unhappiness at losing her husband in the war. Somehow, it seemed to be more than grief, however. She couldn't put her finger on the discomfort but vowed to keep the nurse at a safe distance.

Abigail took the balsam from the cloth pouch and left the tent. During the battle, when most of the men were gone, there were few soldiers to be found between tents. Now the rows of marquees were lined with the king's soldiers squatting by open fires for warmth. They lifted their dirt-smeared faces when she walked by. Most looked back down, but a few held their eyes on her. Some elbowed their mates and grinned.

"She's not one of the trulls, you blaggart. She's a nurse—married."

A trull? Abigail sped up her feet to get to the nurse's tent. By the time she arrived, she was out of breath.

Mrs. Carberry was pinning up her hair before donning a mobcap. "Is everything well, Mrs. Gillingham?"

"Aye. I just …" She breathed heavy. "I just wanted to hurry by those men."

Mrs. Carberry's eyes narrowed. "Did they bother you?"

She flushed. "No, they just … What is a trull, Mrs. Carberry?"

"Is that what they called you?" Sarah Carberry was a force to behold when she placed her hands on her hips and raised her voice.

"No. I mean, one of them told his mate I was *not* a trull." Although she didn't know the meaning for certain, she guessed it wasn't complimentary.

Mrs. Carberry sighed and covered her mouth in an attempt to conceal a grin. "Lydia is a trull. Ladies who service our soldiers are also called doxies."

"Oh." Abigail looked at her shoes and wished she could clean off the mud without stepping in more on the way back to hospital. "I … I came to find some olive oil and wine to mix a medicinal for Corporal Carpenter."

Mrs. Carberry's eyes widened. "To ingest?"

"Nay, nay. To mix with balsam to make a pledget for his wound. My father says 'tis the only way to save an arm." She bit her lip, realizing she had said too much. She doubted the matron would agree to William's request to forgo seeing the surgeon.

The older woman's nod surprised her. "Yes. 'Tis likely the surgeon would remove his arm. With so much blood lost already, he would likely not survive amputation." She patted Abigail's arm. "We shall endeavor to work on this ourselves and keep Mr. Braithwaite away."

She beamed. "Thank you!"

Mrs. Carberry's face drew into a pained expression. "You look so much … never mind." Turning around rapidly, Mrs. Carberry went to a trunk, unlocked it, and pulled out the supplies Abigail needed. "I keep these under lock and key lest they disappear. How much do you need?"

"Just a small amount."

Mrs. Carberry picked up an empty vial and poured in the oil and wine until Abigail said it was enough.

"Thank you, Mrs. Carberry." She turned to go but spun back to face the matron. "I'm certain Corporal Carpenter thanks you as well."

"You are a capable nurse, Mrs. Gillingham. I'm grateful God has seen fit to send you here."

Abigail's mouth turned downward. She didn't know how to answer the unexpected comment. "Thank you, Mrs. Carberry." Turning back toward the tent flap, she went outside and stopped.

You saw fit to send me here? Rage coursed through her spirit. *Could You perhaps have devised a different plan for me, Lord?* Stomping her way past the ogling soldiers, she stopped at the tent's entry and took a deep breath. *Very well, then. If this is Your plan, Lord, perhaps You can tell me why?*

The rustling breeze in the trees was the only sound she heard. But her heart bore an inescapable thought: *Trust Me.*

She whipped the canvas door aside and returned to her patients.

* * *

Before removing the bandage from Corporal Carpenter's arm, Abigail found a bottle of rum.

"You shall need a quaff before I change your dressing." She knelt and handed it to the soldier, who painstakingly propped himself up on one arm. Realizing he had no way to drink and sit unassisted, she held up his shoulders while he swallowed a long drink.

When he'd had enough, she took the bottle back and helped him lie down before setting to work. Between removing the dirty bandage, dousing the wound, mixing the medicinal, and packing the injury, both Abigail and Corporal Carpenter were covered with sweat when the task was complete. After applying the clean bandage, Abigail apologized to the soldier. "Once again you were so brave, but I beg your forgiveness for causing such pain."

He smiled slightly and put a limp hand on her arm. "You did what you must. And I am grateful."

"Was this bandage from this man?" The surgeon's voice pierced the quiet as he held up the old linen Abigail had just removed.

She looked up with widened eyes as she gripped her bottle of balsam. "Aye, sir."

Mr. Braithwaite turned bright red. "And you did not call me?" The blood vessels in his neck throbbed.

"I … I …" Abigail's stomach roiled and her heart raced.

"I told Mrs. Gillingham to use her father's medicinal." Mrs. Carberry, who had arrived during the dressing change, placed herself between Abigail and the surgeon. "Her father had much success with this treatment. And removing a limb has its own dangers. Besides, Corporal Carpenter is well apprised of the situation and agrees to try this medicinal first. Do you not, Corporal?"

William looked straight at the surgeon. "If you take my arm, sir, I cannot shoot. I am worthless. If the medicine works, then I can shoot again. If not, then my life will rest in God's hands."

Mr. Braithwaite's jaw moved back and forth as he seemed to contemplate the situation. "Very well. But if this medicinal does not work, I will take you to the surgeon's tent myself. If it isn't too late." Without saying another word, he stomped off.

Abigail's knees weakened and she plopped into a sitting position onto the hay beside William.

Mrs. Carberry merely touched her shoulder then went to assist another patient.

Abigail stared into the distance. The surgeon could have dismissed her instantly. When she realized someone held her hand, she looked down to find William's fingers intertwined with hers.

"I am most grateful."

Chapter 8

While there was a respite from the sounds of war, the terrifying thunder of falling trees filled the entire British camp instead. Burgoyne was fortifying the area to protect against attack. Abigail stood in the tent doorway that Tuesday and stared at the demise of huge oak trees and proud-looking white pines, one after the other. She'd never seen so many logs felled by so many men. It seemed as if America was being torn asunder.

As the weight of the water bucket she held brought her out of her thoughts, she turned back to the hospital to tend the felled soldiers. Mr. Salyer greeted her with his usual warm smile, but Abigail was not of a mind to return it today.

"What troubles you, Mrs. Gillingham?" Mr. Salyer paused from carrying blood-covered tools.

"The forest. It seems a pity to lose the beauty of it." She attempted a weak smile.

"'Twould be more pity to lose the beauty within the camp if we were attacked." Mr. Salyer squeezed Abigail's arm. He dropped his hand to his side just as quickly and glanced around. "I must return to the surgeon's tent." His gait seemed faster than normal as he walked away.

Abigail carried the bucket toward her first patient—the young man she'd tended on the first day. His bed of straw was vacant. Abigail stopped and turned to the nurse nearby. "Mrs. Pomeroy, where is this lad?"

The nurse barely glanced at her. "Dead."

Abigail's throat dried instantly. "Dead? I thought he was doing well."

"I thought so too. Mr. Braithwaite came middle of the night, said the leg must go. He took him to surgery. Lad never came back."

Her mouth twisted. *He should not have died!* If she'd been there, perhaps she could have stopped the surgeon from taking his leg.

An enormous battle occurred between her will, which was determined she would not cry, and her eyes, which insisted on pouring out her grief. She nearly choked on the struggle as she walked outside and found a quiet spot behind the tent and facing the river.

"I'm sorry about the lad."

She whipped around to face Thomas Salyer. "Why? Why did the surgeon do this? 'Twas not necessary."

Thomas seemed lost for words before he finally spoke. "Yes, it was, Mrs. Gillingham. The lad developed a fever rather quickly. Amputation was his only hope but, alas, it was too late. He lost too much blood." He walked slowly toward Abigail and took her hand. "I am so sorry. I know the lad was important to you."

She pulled her hand away. "All my patients are important to me." She covered her face with her hands as she slumped her shoulders, grief and exhaustion stealing every ounce of her defenses.

She felt Thomas's arms wrap around her. After a moment, she realized she must gather her wits—and be released from Thomas's embrace before they were seen. Without saying a word, she pushed the man away and stumbled toward the tent. But not before catching Elizabeth Pomeroy staring at her. Had she seen Mr. Salyer holding her? By the look on the nurse's face, she had. And the accusation in Mrs. Pomeroy's eyes sent a cold chill through Abigail.

Chapter 9

Day after day, Abigail was never certain if this would be the time for the next battle. But there was one certainty she knew too well. The army's food supply was dwindling—and quickly.

To make the salt pork last longer, cook made a thin soup for the patients. But there were no vegetables to go into the mix and little flavor. It was all Abigail could do to encourage the ill to eat when she herself had little appetite for the tasteless gruel.

But a growling stomach and a pinching grip in her belly reminded Abigail that, tasteless or not, she must eat something to sustain her strength. Her gown was beginning to sag on her frame.

Besides herself, it was William Carpenter she was most concerned about. So far, the balsam medicinal appeared to be healing his arm's deep wound. But after witnessing the tragic turn of the young soldier with the leg wound, she wouldn't take a chance. She stayed all night in the hospital tent, lest she come in one morning to discover the corporal's bed empty. This possibility gripped her heart in a strange way.

Abigail also knew that good food was critical for William's recovery. There was a meager supply of flour for biscuits. Unbeknownst to William, she was feeding him most of her share.

Darkness had fallen, and a lamp was lit inside the tent for the night nurses. She yawned as she checked William's bandage for any signs of the infection returning. Had it been just seven days since she'd been torn from her home? It seemed a lifetime. The night air grew colder, and she shivered as she fell back onto the straw a few feet from William. She reached for a blanket and wrapped it around herself.

William reached out to touch her hand. "Mrs. Gillingham, I am doing well. You need not sleep on this cold ground."

"I am well." She rolled onto her side.

Hours later, Abigail's eyes slowly opened as the day nurses began their rounds. The surgeon barked orders with his booming voice while the surgeon's mates quietly conversed. With a start, she realized that she'd fallen asleep on the straw. As she sat up, a large, warm flow oozed from between her legs. *Oh no! Not here. Not now!*

She had suffered frequently from flooding of her courses. Being in the manner of a woman was an occurrence to be dreaded each month. Yet this was certainly not the time or place to be found with a hemorrhage. Where was the yarrow? Or willow bark? She must find the medicinal pouch.

Abigail tried to stand, but a severe cramp stopped her cold. She crouched down and held her stomach as spots flashed in front of her eyes and she broke into a sweat.

Help me.

* * *

Thomas Salyer was carrying tools for the surgeon, listening to the man's directions, when a loud shout from across the room drew his attention. "Help her! Someone! Please! Mrs. Gillingham is bleeding!" It was Corporal Carpenter.

Thomas dropped the tools and ran over. "Mrs. Gillingham. Mrs. Gillingham!" When she didn't respond, he picked her up. As he did so, warm moisture soaked his hands. She was indeed bleeding. Carrying her out the tent door, he realized the surgeon was close behind him.

"Someone get Mrs. Carberry!" Mr. Braithwaite panicked and stopped outside the tent.

Thomas carried Abigail into the surgeon's tent where, just a few days before, he'd shared tea with her. Laying her on the hard table, he felt helpless. He was not a physician, nor was the surgeon. Surely, Mrs. Carberry could help her. She was a midwife, after all.

He grabbed a cool, clean cloth and wiped her forehead with a gentle stroke. "Come 'round, Mrs. Gillingham. Please." He picked up her lifeless hand and kissed it gently. When he heard footsteps outside, he set it down quickly.

Mrs. Carberry ran into the tent, slightly unkempt, her brow drawn. "What has happened?" She checked the nurse's pulse.

Abigail moaned and stirred.

Mrs. Carberry shooed him with her hands. "You need to step outside a moment."

He exited at her command, although he looked back twice to make certain Abigail was still breathing. After securing the tent flap with two hands, Thomas leaned his forehead against the tent pole and stayed there a moment.

His emotions propelled him like a musket ball ricocheting out of control. He could not deny his strong feelings for Abigail

Gillingham, which seemingly bloomed overnight. And yet this could never be for so many reasons. She was married. And he was promised to another. And he could not let his father down by refusing an arranged marriage. It would be a disgrace. He'd already disappointed his father by refusing a commanding officer's position and instead settled for life as a surgeon. He had too much respect for his parent to disappoint him twice.

But this torment over seeing Abigail losing her lifeblood only reinforced his desire for her.

Mr. Braithwaite interrupted his misery. "This can never be, you know—you and her."

A long pause ensued. "I know."

It seemed an eternity before Mrs. Carberry exited the tent. She motioned to the two men to walk a distance away.

"Well?" Thomas tried to lick his dry lips, but his tongue stuck to the roof of his mouth.

"She will be fine. She's just resting now. I will find some yarrow in her pouch. It seems to help her excessive courses."

The surgeon inhaled deeply. "So that's what it is. I feared perhaps a miscarriage. That would be a frightful loss for a soldier during war."

"Aye, it would." Mrs. Carberry pressed her index fingers over the bridge of her nose then dropped her hands abruptly. She kept her voice low. "But that would have been quite impossible since Mrs. Gillingham is *Miss* Gillingham."

Thomas was dumbfounded and, by Mr. Braithwaite's wide eyes, he was as well.

"Miss? I don't understand." Thomas feared what the surgeon might do.

His superior inhaled as if to speak, but Mrs. Carberry cut him off. "Before you decide to drum her out of camp, Mr. Braithwaite, please hear me out." Mrs. Carberry stood her ground with arms crossed and feet firmly planted. "Miss Gillingham came here to be a nurse quite unwillingly. Her beast of an uncle brought her here after beating her into submission. The poor lass had no choice. At least the uncle had the decency to tell others she was married to protect her from the men."

The surgeon listened without interrupting.

"She has proven herself to be a capable nurse—one of our best. Did I tell you she stitched a blood vessel in Corporal Carpenter's arm? And how many other lives has she saved, all the time terrified we'd discover the truth? And she'd have hell to pay for it from her uncle."

Mr. Braithwaite nodded his head. "Yes, I see your point." He was quiet for a moment then looked back and forth between the two. "This must go no farther than the three of us. We will still call her Mrs. Gillingham. If anyone finds out the truth, I'll know it was one of you."

He started to walk away and turned back. "And if anyone else finds out the truth, I cannot be responsible for protecting her."

Thomas watched his supervisor walk away.

Then I will be responsible for protecting her.

Chapter 10

Abigail shut her eyes while being carried by stretcher to the nurse's tent. It wasn't the glare of the sun, but the concerned expressions on the soldier's faces, that made her want to hide from the world. At the moment, embarrassment overwhelmed any concern for her own health. *Dear Lord, make me invisible, please.*

"What's wrong with nurse?" said one voice.

"Mrs. Gillingham's face is deathly white," said another.

A third soldier wondered out loud, "Is she dead?"

"Stand back!" Mr. Salyer growled at the gawking men.

The swaying of the canvas stretcher added to Abigail's nausea. What seemed an eternally long transport to the nurse's tent—yet, in fact, was little more than fifty rods' distance—finally ended as Mr. Salyer and the other surgeon's mate carried her into the dimly lit marquee. It was still morning and the fog had not yet burned off.

"Bring her here." Mrs. Carberry's weary voice prompted Abigail to open her eyes once again.

At least no one will stare at me here.

Two men lifted her from the stretcher toward a cot, where she was quickly covered with the softest quilts she'd ever lain under.

She had found her cocoon of privacy and breathed a quiet sigh of relief.

"I'll take over from here, gentlemen." Mrs. Carberry tucked the blankets snugly around her.

"Will she recover?" Thomas asked.

"Mrs. Gillingham requires rest and sustenance. She has worked far too hard."

Abigail glanced at Thomas as he exited the tent. He turned back to stare at her a moment, and his face contorted as he pursed his lips. Then he exited the nurses' tent along with the other surgeon's mate.

Mrs. Carberry gave a slight smile. "All manner of gentlemen are concerned for your well-being, Miss Gillingham. I trust you will rest for a few days and partake of your allotted sustenance." She raised her eyebrows.

Abigail's eyes widened. "You knew?"

"I told you, I have eyes to see. I doubt those extra biscuits served to Corporal Carpenter were taken from the other patients' portion." Her eyes fixed on Abigail.

Abigail swallowed. "No. I just … couldn't bear the thought of him suffering with hunger whilst recovering from his wounds."

Mrs. Carberry walked over and sat on a chair next to her. "'Twas a noble thought. However, 'tis a necessity to keep the staff well, lest we risk the health of all who require our care. Whilst helping one, you put all at risk of losing a nurse who has saved many a life in the last week. Do you understand?"

Abigail turned away and covered her eyes. "I did not consider that. Please … forgive me."

"I did not mean to upset you, Miss Gillingham. I only wished to encourage you to tend to your needs as well." She touched Abigail's shoulder with a gentle hand. "I've sent for cook. Her daughter will feed you some broth if you are too weak to manage yourself."

"Thank you, Mrs. Carberry." She uncovered her eyes and focused on the matron. "You have been so kind."

Mrs. Carberry stood. "I must hasten back to hospital." Walking toward the door, she turned and pointed directly at Abigail. "You will rest." She smiled and exited.

Against her will, Abigail's eyes grew heavy and she drifted off to sleep.

She woke up when the cook's daughter tapped her forehead. "Mum says to feed you soup, Mrs. Gillingham."

She moved slowly. The weight of the quilt felt like a pallet of bricks as she pushed it aside and sat up. "No need to feed me, lass. I shall manage, thank you." As she took the cup of broth from the child, her hands trembled and her stomach growled.

The young girl covered her mouth and giggled. "'Tis well I brought you victuals, ma'am, before that bear escapes your tummy."

Laughing at the child's jest, Abigail grinned while the girl continued to giggle all the way to the door.

Though the soup was thin, its warmth soothed her and the flavor enticed her to finish every drop. Cook must have added something special.

She set the empty bowl on the ground and returned to her blanket cocoon. The little girl giggling at her growling stomach was the last thing she thought of as she fell asleep with a smile.

* * *

When Abigail awoke, darkness enveloped her. An unsettling presence set the hair on her neck upright. "Who's there?" Sleepiness garbled her voice.

Silence.

Fear needled its way through her. She slowly sat up, her heart pounding. "Who's there?" She heard a rustle at the door and then nothing more. When the flap of the tent opened, she screamed.

"Mrs. Gillingham? Are you having a nightmare?" Mrs. Carberry released the tent's door flap. "I'm just back from hospital."

It was difficult for Abigail to speak with her throat so dry. "I … I thought I heard someone at the door. Perhaps 'twas a nightmare. I know not."

Mrs. Carberry set a lamp on a stand and walked back toward her. "Perhaps excitability of your nerves, brought on by your courses, has stimulated your system. But I'll *not* inform Mr. Braithwaite, lest he try to bleed it out of you."

Abigail winced as she couldn't help but laugh. "I think my body is doing that well enough on its own."

Smiling, the matron poured Abigail a tankard of ale and brought it to her. "Take this. It should help. Cook left it here for you. Perhaps it was she you heard at the door."

"Yes, perhaps so. Thank you." She sipped on the brown ale while Mrs. Carberry gazed at her with a small grin. "Pray, why do you seem so amused?"

"You have made quite a favorable impression on your patients, Miss Gillingham. One in particular."

Abigail's heart took on a strange beat. She stared into her ale, avoiding the matron's gaze. "What do you mean, Mrs. Carberry?"

"Well, all day long I've been asked about you. 'When will Mrs. Gillingham be back?' 'Is she well?' One even declared he was praying for you." Mrs. Carberry poured herself some ale and sat in a chair near her.

"Praying for me?" She could not fathom such concern. "Who is praying for me?"

Mrs. Carberry gave a pensive smile and then spoke. "That is for you to find out."

Although grateful for Mrs. Carberry's presence in the next cot, Abigail's mind would not rest that night. She wondered where Mr. Carberry was. Turning her head, she listened for the gentle snores of the matron but didn't hear them. The other nurses had tossed and turned on their cots before finally dozing into rhythmic breathing. Yet she still couldn't hear Mrs. Carberry.

She hesitated before asking, "Mrs. Carberry? Are you still awake?"

"Yes?"

"Pray, forgive me for askin'. Where is Mr. Carberry?"

Silent seconds turned into several minutes. Finally, the matron answered. "Mr. Carberry was killed in the French War."

Her eyes stung. "I'm terribly sorry."

"Yes. 'Twas long ago. Yet I still miss the man."

Abigail wanted to comfort her, but words would not come. The young woman knew nothing about love, or the loss of it, even though her father had promised her hand to Samuel Garrick. She didn't love him. She barely knew the man.

"Did you … did you ever have children?"

A longer pause ensued. This time Mrs. Carberry's voice thickened in its resonance. "Yes." The matron shifted on her cot.

No further explanation was offered. And Abigail dared not ask.

Chapter 11

Although darkness had yet to lift, the day nurses stirred from their slumber. Work began early in Burgoyne's camp—and apparently in the enemy camp as well. The distance to the Patriots was so close that their drummer's tapping out the wake-up call coincided with the Regulars' drummer boy. At times, it seemed to be a competition as to who could beat their drum the loudest.

Abigail hugged the quilt tighter around her shoulders, as a damp chill still embraced the inside of the tent. It seemed colder than usual, and fatigue continued to plague her. She forced herself to sit up, and her unkempt hair fell in front of her eyes. She abhorred the sticky filth on her clothing, longing for water to bathe and a fresh gown.

As if reading her mind, Mrs. Carberry came through the doorway with a basin of hot water and linen cloths. "I'm certain you'll be wanting to wash up today, Mrs. Gillingham."

Abigail noticed that the matron always referred to her as "Mrs." when others were around. When the other nurses exited the tent, however, Mrs. Carberry became friendlier and less formal. "You likely have no other gowns to wear, do you, Miss Gillingham?"

Abigail averted her eyes from the head nurse. "My uncle didn't allow me time to pack any clothing."

Mrs. Carberry touched her arm. "Let us not dwell on that memory. I'll find something for you." The matron pulled out the trunk key and lifted the creaking wooden lid. She removed a few bottles and began searching through some clothing. When she recovered a dark-blue dress with a pattern of small flowers, she nodded as she held it up. "Here. This should fit you."

Her jaw dropped as her eyes widened. "'Tis lovely. Is it yours?"

The matron smiled. "No. It belonged to my daughter." She flicked out the linen dress as though shaking away memories. The woman's mouth firmed into a thin line.

Abigail's eyes widened even more. "I didn't know you had a daughter."

"Yes. She was a beautiful lass … not much older than you. Her hair was the flaming red of autumn leaves, much like yours." She paused and her lips trembled. "You favor her countenance as well." Mrs. Carberry inhaled with resolve, pulled her shoulders back, and walked toward her. "Here. You must use it. It would give me joy to see you wear it."

Abigail wanted to reply in meaningful sentiments, but she stared in shock instead. Taking the gown from the matron, she blurted out, "What happened to your daughter, Mrs. Carberry?"

The older woman plopped onto the chair near Abigail's cot, and her shoulders slumped. "It was summer last when she went to visit her aunt near Skenesborough. Mary—that was her name—hoped to see her intended, who was with the Loyalist militia up north. But she never made it to my sister's cabin." Tears rolled down Mrs. Carberry's face, and she swiped them away. Her brows furrowed. "One of Burgoyne's Indian allies showed up with a red-haired scalp hanging from his waistband." The woman sobbed. "It was my Mary's."

Abigail covered her mouth to keep from screaming. Nausea threatened to empty her meager stomach contents. *Scalped?* Abigail could neither fathom such brutality, nor the connection with the Regulars. "You ... you say these were allies of the general?"

Mrs. Carberry wiped her face dry with her apron. Her grief metamorphosed into anger as her eyes darkened into hatred. "Yes. Some of the Indian tribes have made themselves useful against the insurgents with their barbaric and frightening ways. But God help us that we have resorted to such an alliance. Our general has made a bargain with the Devil, and I fear our leader shall pay dearly." She stood and fixed her gaze on Abigail. "And perhaps he should," she spat. The matron turned on her heels and exited the tent.

The warm water from the basin was cooling rapidly in the chilly air, prompting Abigail to wash up with haste. Removing her stays and chemise, she kept the quilts close so she wouldn't freeze. She picked up the lavender bar soap and held it to her nose. *Heavenly scent!* Inhaling another whiff, she swished the soap in the water and stroked it across the linen cloth. She smoothed it across her arm and chest but nearly dropped the bar when a voice came from the doorway.

"And how does the lovely nurse fare this morning?"

Her breath caught in her throat, and she grabbed the nearest quilt and held it against her exposed bosom.

A uniformed soldier stood in the opening of the tent. The look in his eyes reminded her of her uncle's lustful gaze.

Her fingers gripped the edge of the quilt as she pulled it tight against her chin. She feared the intensity of this soldier's scrutiny and quivered. "Who are you? You should not be here."

The man walked slowly toward her. "Just came to check on the nurse. Heard she wasn't feeling so well. Thought perhaps there was something I could do."

Abigail wanted to scream, but her parched throat smothered her voice. "Get out." It sounded so weak. Although he hadn't even reached her yet, she felt as if all ten of his fingers had found their way to her skin. She retched at the thought. "I am ill. You should not be here."

"Lieutenant Baggley! What are you doin' here?" Nurse Sedgewick was back from night duty. She stomped across the ground and grabbed his arm.

He pulled it away.

"You ain't supposed-ta be here. I'm reportin' you." Folding her arms across her breast, she glared at the intruder, who obviously hadn't anticipated an interruption.

"I was merely checking on the patient. I heard she was ill, and I know the men were concerned." He shifted his stance and adjusted his breeches.

Nurse Sedgewick tilted her head and firmed her mouth. "Is that so, Lieutenant? Well, you can take your manly fever and go visit the trulls near the river. Nurses are for hospital." She turned to Mrs. Pomeroy. "Go get Mrs. Carberry."

Mrs. Pomeroy hurried out the door.

"Are ya well, Mrs. Gillingham? That blaggard did not touch ya, did he?" Mrs. Sedgewick covered Abigail's shoulders with another quilt.

"No." Abigail's voice thickened from tears. "It just felt like he did."

Mrs. Sedgewick rolled her eyes. "I know what ya mean. Some of these men have their brains in their breeches all the time. He's one of 'em." The nurse stroked the hair back from Abigail's face. "Doesn't help none that you're charming 'em with your sweet face." She grinned, revealing a missing front tooth.

"I'm not trying to encourage them." Abigail bit her lip.

"I know that, Mrs. Gillingham. You're a good nurse. Sometimes in a war camp, beauty can get ya into trouble—even when you're not lookin' for it."

A rustle at the door was followed by the appearance of Mrs. Carberry and Mrs. Pomeroy.

"Mrs. Gillingham, are you all right?" The matron nurse hurried toward the cot and searched Abigail's face.

"Aye, Mrs. Carberry. I'm so grateful the night nurses arrived. 'Twas terrifying." Her lip quivered.

The matron's eyes narrowed and darkened. "This will not happen again." She turned toward the other two nurses. "Ladies, go find an armed sentinel. I'll get orders myself from General Burgoyne to assign someone to guard this tent."

"Yes, Mrs. Carberry." The two nurses spoke in unison and exited through the flap.

The matron sat on the chair near her. Sticking her finger in the basin water, Mrs. Carberry inhaled. "That is cold water. I'll warm that up for you." She started to stand but sat down again and stared intensely at her. "Miss Gillingham, do you see why it is necessary to assure others you're married? Should the men discover you are not, we would have more Lieutenant Baggleys on our hands, I assure you. The longer this battle lingers and the men's discontent grows, the more we need to protect you. At least most of them will respect a husband—regardless of his existence." She picked up the basin and left in haste.

Lord, I never wanted to come here.

She lay down and rested her head for a moment while awaiting the warm water, allowing the thought of it to soothe her anxiety. But the moment that peace had settled her fearful spirit, a rustling in the grass outside the tent induced her to sit up ramrod straight. Had someone heard their conversation through the canvas?

Dear Lord, protect me!

Chapter 12

After three days of rest, Abigail begged to return to her duty with the wounded. She couldn't bear the thought of deserting them, nor could she tolerate her constant vigil. Despite the presence of an armed sentinel at the door, the terror of the encounter with Lieutenant Baggley lingered, and she worried he may come back.

She had nearly regained her strength thanks to the coddling of Mrs. Carberry, who now fretted over putting her back on duty. "Now remember, those with ginger tresses must guard against excessive flow. It seems unfair that lasses with the loveliest shade of hair must suffer such a curse. Should your courses return, come back and rest." The matron reached out briefly to pat Abigail's arm before folding her hands at her waist.

She found herself smiling. "I shall, Mrs. Carberry. And I will be cautious."

She wistfully stroked the soft linen of the dress that had belonged to Mrs. Carberry's daughter. Abigail didn't have a looking glass to observe her reflection, but just viewing the floral material was enough to brighten her spirits. *'Tis like a spring morn. I wish it truly were spring instead of winter's eve.*

"Mrs. Gillingham?"

"Yes, Mrs. Carberry?"

"Do stay away from the edge of camp. The Rebels have been kidnapping our sentinels in the night. These insurgents are a reckless bunch who seem to be without fear or conscience." A cloud darkened the matron's countenance.

"I shall take care, Mrs. Carberry. Thank you."

She wished they would kidnap her so she could escape. Yet even as that thought crossed her mind, a desire to return to hospital to tend patients interrupted her musing. She must be losing her senses. *Abigail, you are a Patriot! Do not forget yourself.*

She left the nurses' tent for the first time in days. Although it was morning, a heavy fog persisted in hiding the sun. Despite the lack of light, the young woman strode with enthusiasm toward the tent.

As she walked, she sensed a tension among the soldiers in camp. Their faces strained with worry as they shivered over small campfires. A few argued over whose turn it was to cook their meager rations. She didn't understand the ways of war or why there were so many days since the last battle. But she understood discontent and fear, and it screamed silently from every man who wore a scarlet coat.

As Abigail walked by the rows of Regulars, a few tipped their hats to her, but most acted as though she were an unseen spirit moving in the mist. She shivered and hugged herself, wishing she had her woolen cloak. She realized she'd never reclaimed it from Corporal Carpenter's hospital bed.

When she arrived at the hospital tent, her heart lurched in a strange rhythm. She paused. *What is the matter with me?* Shaking her head, she entered and began to attend patients. After a moment, everything seemed remarkably quiet. She looked around and noticed everyone had paused in their duties. Grins spread across faces throughout the marquee.

"Welcome back, Mrs. Gillingham." Mr. Braithwaite approached her, bowed from the waist without smiling, and resumed visiting patients.

Behind him, Thomas Salyer smiled broadly as he clicked his heels together, his arms behind his waist. "Welcome back. We are grateful for your return and good health."

She gave him a slight nod. "Thank you. I'm grateful to be well, indeed."

He followed the surgeon back on his rounds, but he kept his gaze on her as long as he was able.

Abigail felt heat flushing her cheeks as she resumed walking toward her row of patients. As she neared the straw beds, her heart nearly stopped. Corporal Carpenter sat upright while Mrs. Sedgewick fed him broth. Abigail had never seen him sitting up before, and his eyes captured her. She attempted to smile and move on, but his gaze fixed on her like a magnet. She was unable to break the connection. "Corporal Carpenter." She swallowed and forced herself to turn away. "You seem to fare well."

"As do you, Mrs. Gillingham."

Raising her eyes back to his, Abigail suddenly felt as if everyone in the tent observed her every move. Glancing toward Mr. Salyer, she imagined a flash of anger darken his countenance, yet he smiled when he noticed her looking at him. Shaking herself out of a motionless state, Abigail determined to focus on the needs of her awaiting patients.

Mrs. Sedgewick beckoned her. "Mrs. Gillingham, I've a dressing to change. Might you help the corporal here to finish his meal?"

Clearing her throat, Abigail reached for the spoon. "Of course, Mrs. Sedgewick."

While her new friend gathered a supply of bandages and moved toward a moaning patient, Abigail tried to settle on the straw next to Corporal Carpenter without touching his leg, but there was little room to maneuver.

The corporal seemed amused. "I'm comfortable, Mrs. Gillingham. I hope you are as well." His blue eyes shimmered with warmth.

"Aye. Quite comfortable." *How many lies will I speak today? Lord, do forgive my many sins.* She ladled out a spoonful of thin broth and carried it to his awaiting lips.

He carefully sucked it from the utensil and smiled with satisfaction. Then he whispered, "Don't tell Mrs. Sedgewick, but the soup is more delicious when you serve it." He winked at her.

Abigail nearly burst out laughing but covered her mouth. "Do not speak ill of my friend," she whispered, and then she giggled. "I am certain it tastes just the same."

He smiled weakly. Abigail continued ladling the soup into the corporal's mouth, and she grew increasingly enamored as his lips hungrily swept each drop of liquid from the spoon. She realized she had paused in her task too long when he asked, "May I have more, please?"

Flustered, she nearly spilled the bowl but caught it just in time. "I am quite the fumbling fingers today. Please forgive me."

"And just when I thought to ask for a shave." There was that warm grin again.

She startled. "A shave? Pray, do not fret, Corporal. I am quite adept at shaving a man."

Corporal Carpenter swallowed quite forcefully. "Of course you are. You've likely shaved your husband many a time."

She glanced downward. "No. 'Twas my father's face I shaved—until he died."

William Carpenter sat quietly for a moment. "How blessed he was to have such a daughter."

"I was the blessed daughter to have such a father." She sniffed and turned away. *I must stop these tears. If I am ever to find my way home, I must be strong.* Abigail stood. "I'll fetch the basin and razor."

After fumbling through the knapsack embroidered with the initials "WC," she pulled out the folded wooden handle, opened it to reveal a razor, refolded it, and set it aside. As she closed the leather pouch, she noticed a lace kerchief with his belongings. She fingered the fine weaving for a moment. Abigail silently berated herself as she stuffed the woman's personal item to the bottom of the sack. *'Tis not your concern, Abigail.*

She went to the fire outside and poured a basin of hot water before she hurried back to her patient. When she nearly tripped over a soiled rag, she realized she wasn't heeding the advice of the matron. *Pace yourself, Abigail.* She walked in measured steps back to the corporal and attempted a friendly yet impersonal smile.

"There now—fresh water, soap, and razor. And I promise, no 'fumbling fingers.'"

"That's a relief."

The more Abigail set up for the shave, the faster her heart thrummed. The application of soap and the stroking of the razor were far more intimate in this moment, with this man, than shaving her dying father. That was done out of parental love and concern. This was … this was what? Abigail couldn't sort through her feelings.

Her fingers shook while she concentrated on not dropping the razor. She couldn't bear the thought of possibly nicking his neck when he'd already bled enough. "Perhaps if you lie down, 'twould be easier to shave you."

The soldier lay back on the hay while she stuffed the folded material behind his head, allowing his neck to stretch out.

Lord, don't let me cut him with this blade.

"I can help to apply the soap with one hand." He reached for the bar, sloshed it in the water, and attempted to lather it across his neck and cheeks. More water seemed to trickle down his neck than soap remained on his skin.

"Here, let me help." Abigail rubbed the bar between her hands, creating thick foam. She took both palms and stroked his face and neck, covering every inch of his skin with the suds. She concentrated so much on her task that it took her a moment to notice William's eyes fixed on her, his face contorted in an expression she couldn't read. She sat back for a minute. "Are you well, Corporal?"

He swallowed with force. "Yes. Quite well."

His deep voice left an imprint of desire in her heart that she hadn't experienced before.

Had she lost her senses? He must have a woman back home. Besides, he didn't know who she was. He was her enemy.

But her attraction to the corporal was the singular moment of pleasure in an otherwise horrible situation. No wonder she had responded with these unexpected feelings, she reasoned. Surely that was all there was to this unfamiliar yet extremely agreeable sensation. *Surely.*

Expertly unfolding the steel blade again, she focused on the task of removing several days' growth of stubble on Corporal Carpenter's face and neck. As needed, she readjusted the blanket roll behind his neck, all the while being careful of his wounded arm. She swept the glimmering blade across his skin while sweat dripped down her own neck. The heat was stifling in the tent.

She swished the razor through the basin water and continued to remove each row of stubble with the sharp instrument. The scraping of the blade made a scratchy sound as she swiped it from the base of his neck to his chin, and she pulled his skin tighter to avoid nicks. As she moved his head around to reach different places with the razor, the feel of his freshly shaved neck sparked more desire for this man she'd only known for several days. Every encounter drew her closer to this man, evoking feelings she couldn't explain. None of it made sense.

Why now, Lord? Why do You fill me with flames of desire when this cannot even be a possibility? Lord, take this from me. I am so vulnerable—help me.

She completed the shave and used linen to dab his face dry. "There." She cleared her throat. "Handsome enough for your lady love."

Did she just say that? She concentrated on cleaning the razor.

William reached out and touched her arm. "There is no lady love."

She squinted her eyes and tilted her head, far too quickly. "'Twould not be so difficult to believe, sir, yet the presence of her lace with your razor would indicate otherwise." Abigail faced him with a determined set to her jaw.

He reached for her hand. "There was a lady love. But she died in passage—on the boat."

She sat stock still as remorse flooded her. "I … I don't know what to say. Pray, forgive my impertinence."

He shook his head. "You could not have known."

So there is no one. Lord, this does not help my prayer.

"But there is someone awaiting you." He released her hand. "He is … a most fortunate man."

Abigail turned aside. "Aye." Standing so quickly she nearly lost her balance, she hurried to her next patient.

Chapter 13

Thomas Salyer seethed at the sight—the woman who had filled his thoughts night and day, tenderly shaving the face of that corporal. How dare she perform such a familiar act on that man?

Yet even in the midst of his anger, Thomas knew his fury was irrational. Of course a nurse should help a patient in this manner.

But it was the look on their faces that distorted sound reason into jealous insanity. If he'd not known any better, he would have expected a passionate embrace to occur next, right in front of God and man.

What is wrong with me? I must control myself.

Thomas exited the hospital tent and stood outside, inhaling deeply.

Calm yourself.

The fresh air cleansed the filth of anger that muddied his thoughts. He was a surgeon's mate, after all. He'd chosen this course, much to the chagrin of his father, who desired his only son become a prominent officer during the war. The disappointment had been obvious on his father's face when Thomas announced he preferred healing arts to battle cries. All his father's dreams seemed to die at that moment, except for one. He wanted Thomas to marry Miss Jane Etheridge, daughter of his best friend. In this, Thomas could and would comply.

The intent to marry had seemed so easy—until Miss Abigail Gillingham had arrived in camp.

Thomas had become enraptured without reason or sense. From the lush red hair that crowned Abigail's beautiful face to the luscious curves of her form, Thomas had awakened to feelings and desires that were never part of his commitment to the gaunt and austere Miss Etheridge. He loved Abigail more than any other.

When he thought she was married, it forced him to adjust his attraction within reasonable constraints. Now that he knew she had no consort, a burning desire had filled every part of his being. He was determined to have her.

"Are you ill, Mr. Salyer?" Mr. Braithwaite interrupted his musings.

Thomas recovered his thoughts in time to prevent reprisal from the irritated surgeon. "I just needed some air for a moment, Mr. Braithwaite. I am well now."

"Very well. Carry on then—inside hospital." The surgeon trudged off.

Thomas exhaled with relief. The last thing he needed now was to be on unpleasant terms with his superior.

The surgeon's mate re-entered the hospital marquee and sought out the object of his affections. He found Abigail changing a dressing on a young boy and, once again, fought his compulsion to sweep her into his arms.

But he had a plan. And he hoped that Abigail would be amenable, lest his heart despair. "Mrs. Gillingham, Mrs. Carberry said to remind you to work a portion of this day—no more."

Abigail looked up at him with green eyes that reminded him of a rich jewel he'd once seen. But not even the gem he'd viewed as a child had incited such excitement in him. Nothing could compare with the passion he saw in her eyes. And Thomas wanted to be the recipient of such ardor.

"Very well, Mr. Salyer." Abigail leaned over the boy. "I must beg your leave, young man, but I shall attend to you later." She patted his arm in a motherly manner and stood up.

Thomas thought he saw her sway a bit and grabbed her arm. "There now, Mrs. Gillingham. Steady."

He made sure that he held Abigail's arm securely as they walked by Corporal Carpenter. Thomas imagined the fury on the man's face. As he turned to look at the corporal, Thomas wasn't disappointed.

Imbecile. Did he really think he could draw the likes of her?

Thomas maintained a smile and allowed Abigail to lean on his arm. They walked toward the woods, and Abigail paused. "Mrs. Carberry said to stay away from the woods. Sentinels have been kidnapped."

"Not to fear, Mrs. Gillingham. The sentinels are sent farther out in daytime. You'll be quite safe with me."

As they drew farther away from the camp, the relaxing sounds of the woods replaced the tense chatter of the army. Wind whispered through the maples and oaks, occasionally abducting leaves from their former attachment.

Nearby, the river rippled over rocks and surged along the banks with quiet, forceful strength. Thomas watched Abigail stare into the distance, a look of longing in her eyes as she seemed to search the horizon. Who, or what, was she longing for? He inhaled sharply. Could it be him?

Curling tresses of her hair had escaped her cap and rippled invitingly over her shoulders. He reached out with a finger to touch them, eliciting a surprised exclamation from Abigail.

"Mr. Salyer?" Her look questioned his advance.

"Miss Gillingham." He shifted his feet. "Abigail." Before he could think what to say, he grasped her shoulders and drew her to himself. The desire that had built up in him drew him to clutch her with searching fingers. His mouth covered hers as he sought her moist and exhilarating kisses. He drew her downward and moved to lie on top of her.

She gasped, pushed him away, and then sat up. "Mr. Salyer." Her flushed face was wet with tears.

"Abigail ..." He reached a hand toward her and she scooted back on the dry grass.

"How ... how dare you touch me in such a manner?" She folded her arms across her breasts. "Who do you think I am that I should stoop to such affections when we are not man and wife?" Her lips quivered. "I thought I could trust you."

"Abigail, you can trust me. I would never force you to do anything against your will. I thought ... I thought you felt the same affection toward me. The same desire that has burned in my heart for you since we met."

Abigail tilted her head and sniffed. "Have I led you to believe so?" She rose to her feet with difficulty and faced him squarely. "If I have, I must apologize. But I had no knowledge that you entertained the idea of being my consort."

Consort? Thomas shook his head to clear his thoughts and forced himself to stand. "Abigail." He struggled to find the right words. "Why, pray tell, did you imagine I was offering you my hand in marriage?"

Her mouth opened wide. She shook her head before answering, her voice needled with ice. "You would lay with me with no thought of marriage?"

Bewilderment clouded Thomas's thinking. "Well, yes. It's the custom of most of our officers to have a camp wife. Even our general lies with another man's wife. Abigail, you have enflamed me with a passion I've not held for another woman before. I … I barely know what to do with my ardent love for you. Abigail, please …"

She narrowed her eyes at him. "*Camp wife?* To be tossed aside when you return home to England, perhaps leaving me behind with your sons and daughters?"

"I have thought that through, Abigail." He licked his dry lips and shifted his glance to the side. "I would send you a subsidy, sufficient to support you and any children we might have. I would see to your needs. Please." He faced her again. "I beg of you, do not leave me unsatisfied."

The cold look on Abigail's face stopped him from reaching out to her.

"Any passion that might have kindled in my breast for you was just smothered in the cruelty of your expectations." She turned and walked back to the camp alone.

As Thomas watched her leave, every sinew of his being longed to pursue her and beg her to change her mind. But the memory of her words sliced through his heart, paralyzing his dreams. This was a nightmare he had not expected.

Chapter 14

Days had ensued since the battle at Freeman's Farm, yet the army still encamped on the ridge without moving. They would also soon be without food. Some of Burgoyne's Regulars had given up hope, deserting the cause of the king and joining with the Rebels, it was assumed.

"No wonder they despair. With little food here to spare for man or beast, the soldiers at least imagine a full belly with the insurgents." Mrs. Carberry sat on her cot after a long day in hospital, her weariness evident in her drawn expression and slump of shoulders. "Now these wounded are expected to recover for another battle. They've barely got the strength to walk."

Abigail plopped onto her own cot, utterly exhausted. Mrs. Carberry's words concerning the recovering soldiers disturbed her. "They must prepare for battle again? They've barely healed from the first one."

Mrs. Carberry lifted her eyes and glanced toward Abigail. "We need to get some of the men up and walking tomorrow. They will never survive a march, as weak as they are now. Walking and fresh air should strengthen them. And they need to get out of these plague-infested tents."

"Aye." Abigail had been concerned with the increase in fevers. Men were being carried out to the burial ground daily—not just from wound infections, but from the outbreak of illness as well.

Lord, protect us from this fever.

A disturbing thought crossed her mind. She sat up. "Mrs. Carberry, some of these men are terribly weak. Will they be expected to fight again, even if their shooting arms are crippled?"

There was a long pause before the matron answered. "You must help Corporal Carpenter to regain use of his arm. Otherwise, you will cripple his chances of survival." Mrs. Carberry fixed her gaze on Abigail. "This is what it means to nurse soldiers during war, Mrs. Gillingham. You cannot cosset their health. Nor your sentiments." The matron stretched out on her cot and was sleeping soundly in a matter of moments.

Abigail lay on her side as hot tears pooled onto her pillow. She gritted her teeth at the thought of sending so many soldiers, who'd barely survived, back onto the battlefield. Didn't their injuries exempt them from such an obligation? Abigail clenched her pillow so tightly she heard the material tear.

Despite her anger, she knew the numbers of troops had dwindled and, from all accounts rumored in camp, the Patriot soldiers increased in number. Burgoyne's army was quickly being outnumbered and, as far as anyone knew, Sir Henry Clinton had yet to send advance word of his imminent arrival.

While inwardly Abigail rejoiced at the possibility that the American Continentals may win, an unfamiliar heartache consumed her. William Carpenter may lose his life in battle.

The pool of tears on her pillow soon resembled a river.

* * *

The incessant morning mist seemed to grow thicker each day. Abigail clutched her cloak around her shoulders, yet she still shivered. Hoarfrost covered the meager stubble of grass underfoot, and she tried to ignore her freezing toes inside her leather shoes as she made her way to hospital.

It would be hours before the sun broke through. She longed to see a glimmer of light, yet there were times when she wondered if it would ever appear. The thick blanket of cloud that lingered overhead each morning challenged her belief in the unseen. Would she forever remain a prisoner in this cold dark? Would the light of her liberty be smothered in hopelessness?

Abigail longed for the comfort of home and her father's embrace. It seemed impossible it had only been a month since he'd died.

Lord, where are You?

Approaching the marquee, Abigail entered and closed the flap behind her. The warmth inside was inviting, but the stench was overwhelming. Sweat-covered patients and dirty bandages infused the scent of contagion throughout. Mrs. Carberry was right. These patients needed fresh air.

Mrs. Pomeroy was already tending some of the fever-ridden, and she glanced up at Abigail. "Those soldiers need lookin' after." She pointed toward some new men who'd been admitted since last night.

Taking a deep breath, Abigail began her tasks, offering sips of boiled water, washing sweat off their moist faces, helping men outside to relieve themselves while she averted her eyes from their nakedness. It was exhausting and laborious.

Yet, arriving near the hay-covered bed assigned to Corporal Carpenter, Abigail could not withhold a smile. "Good morning, Corporal. Fare you well?"

"Yes." He pushed himself up to a sitting position with his good arm. "Mrs. Gillingham, I need your assistance."

Abigail squatted so she was face to face with him. "How can I help you, Corporal Carpenter?" It was a mistake looking into those sky-blue eyes. They provided the only source of illumination in her darkened world, and she longed to dwell in the warmth they radiated.

"I need to walk. Frequently. I need to regain my strength." His voice held the strength of a soldier, yet it was edged with fear. "I must be able to fight again, and I'm certain it will be soon."

Abigail looked down. "But you have only barely healed." She met his eyes again. "Must you fight again so soon?"

"Yes. Will you help me?"

His resolve was admirable, yet the heaviness in her chest increased her breathing.

She swallowed back all the words that rose in protest—words she knew would go unheeded. Mrs. Carberry had made it clear. This was the way of war. But the ache in Abigail's heart lurched in a painful rhythm, and she clutched her breast to soothe its wound. She was learning the unseen lesions of war could be as painful as the damage inflicted by weapons.

"Aye. I will help you."

His grateful smile only made her feel like a traitor. Was she assisting him to his death? And if he died in battle, could she ever forgive herself?

With shaking legs, Abigail pushed herself up from the ground and reached down to help him stand. He started to sway a bit, and she caught him by the waist before he fell.

"Corporal …"

"I'll be fine, Mrs. Gillingham." He inhaled slowly and closed his eyes for a moment. "Very well then." He opened his eyes again. "Shall we carry on?" He attempted a smile but Abigail held onto him with a firm grip and watched his face carefully, lest he overexert and need to rest.

He slowly walked next to Abigail with his good arm draped over her shoulder. Despite his obvious weakness, his arm around her felt comforting and warm. His left hand gripped her shoulder and, for a moment, she imagined he caressed it. *I must be mistaken.*

As she held the canvas aside so they could leave the tent, she noticed Thomas Salyer standing nearby holding surgeon's tools. She ignored his longing gaze that seemed to beg forgiveness of her, as well as the dark coldness he extended toward William.

"Let us walk now, Corporal." She spoke it loud enough so Mr. Salyer would take note. She wanted nothing to do with the surgeon's mate—a man she knew she could no longer trust.

The soldier's steps seemed stronger than she imagined they would be after so much blood loss. He took his arm off her shoulder and attempted to stand taller and straighter.

As she watched him for signs of weakness, she found herself focusing on the handsome features accentuated in his profile—nose strong and straight, chin firm and steady, and always, those eyes filled with warmth.

He interrupted her musings. "Perhaps upon returning to the tent, you can assist me in pulling my hair back into a club. I tried last night to no avail. My arm needs to be stronger."

She looked down at her feet and smothered a giddy smile. "I would be pleased to help you." She glanced at the man walking beside her. "Is there anything else I can do?"

"I need you to work my arm—help me get the robustness back." He walked slower now and breathed with some effort. "Even if it pains me to do so, you must assist me. Please."

"I will help you, Corporal." She attempted to swallow, but her throat was so dry. "I know you need strength to hold your firelock."

"Yes." He smiled as they strode slowly toward a hill. With great effort, he walked the small incline.

Abigail bit her lip. How would this soldier be ready to fight?

At the top of the slope, the mist enveloped their view.

"One more thing, Mrs. Gillingham." He hesitated. "Would you pray for me?"

Abigail stared, eyes wide. "Pray for you?"

He looked at the ground. "Never mind. It was only a thought."

Without thinking, she reached toward his uninjured arm and gently squeezed it. "Of course I shall pray for you. It's just …"

He still didn't look up. "If you do not wish to, Mrs. Gillingham, please do not trouble yourself." His face reddened.

She wished she had water to drink. Her mouth felt like dry linen.

"It's just … I do not feel I am in favor with our Creator at the moment. My prayers don't seem to get heard." She concentrated on her dirty shoes. "Perhaps He does not care for me anymore or … perhaps I have displeased Him." She looked up and stared into the mist, hoping to see the landscape.

"I understand your feelings, Mrs. Gillingham." He stood closer to her. "I have often thought in these last months—years—that God had deserted me when my life seemed filled with woe. Yet, in the last week, I have felt His presence in a remarkable way. Even with all this pain. And …" He paused as if embarrassed. "… I have seen your tender care and concern for all the men, even when you yourself have been through your own pain." He touched her cheek where the bruise from her uncle's slap was nearly gone.

Her eyes welled with moisture, and Abigail tried to speak. No words would come.

"Was it your husband who abused you?"

"Nay." She wiped her face dry with her apron and shook her head. "Nay. 'Twas my Uncle Richard. He is"—she sniffed—"a most cruel man. He forced me to come here to tend the wounded even though he knows I …" She stopped herself before revealing too much.

"Even though your heart is aligned with the Rebels?"

Abigail gasped and covered her mouth with trembling fingers. "How did you know?"

"Do not fear, Mrs. Gillingham. I have watched you nigh a fortnight. Your response to our army's predicament rarely brought sympathy." His eyes softened. "Yet you have shown great sympathy for your patients."

"Please don't tell anyone." She melted into tears, and William held her close.

"Mrs. Gillingham, I'll not reveal your loyalties. You have been most loyal to the wounded men, and I am grateful. Perhaps that's why you have been so vague about your husband's regiment."

These incessant lies wore on Abigail's spirit. How much longer could she falsely represent who she was? She grew weary with this duplicity. "I have prayed for God to deliver me from this place, yet He has not answered me. Why must I endure this?" She clung to his red coat and watched her tears roll down the scarlet wool.

He drew back from her but kept his hands on her shoulders. "Perhaps because He has another plan." He dropped his hands and turned aside. "I have often wondered about His ways. The terrible crossing on the Atlantic. The illness that took my Priscilla. It all seemed so unfair. 'Why God?' I asked Him over and over."

"And what answer did you receive?" Abigail's voice was thick as she wiped the rest of her tears on her apron.

William shook his head. "No answer. Just the admonition to trust Him. I remembered the Proverb that said, 'If thou faint in the day of adversity, thy strength is small.'"

Abigail stared at him. "That is all?"

He gave a sheepish grin. "That is all. I had not prayed for a long time. Until that day the drummer boy died." A large tear rolled down his cheek. "I saw the tender care you gave him. It reminded me of the care I'd received from my own mother when

I was a child. Without thinking, I prayed for you. It just happened." He paused for a moment. "I've been praying ever since."

Her jaw opened. "So 'twas you? You were the one praying for me whilst I was ill?"

William's face turned as red as his coat. "Yes. It was me." He forced his shoulders back and stared at nothing in particular that she could see.

She spontaneously reached out to squeeze his arm. "I am grateful. And I shall pray for you when you go to battle."

The sun broke through the thick mist, shedding light on his long brown hair. "Look." He pointed into the distance. "There's nothing like this in England."

Forests of red maples, beech, and elm were woven in the scenery with the startling scarlet sumac leaves that stood more brightly than the rest. Abigail held her own breath at the sight. "This is my favorite time of year." She could feel his eyes upon her as she beheld the now-revealed landscape.

"It's like the autumn leaves were dyed to match your glorious hair." He looked downward. "Forgive me, Mrs. Gillingham."

How she longed to tell him she wasn't married. But he knew too much already. If he were aware she had no husband, he might feel compelled to betray her.

"There is nothing to forgive, Corporal. Thank you." He seemed a bit unsteady on his feet. "Perhaps 'twould be best to end this walk while you rebuild your strength."

William swallowed with difficulty. "Yes. But there may not be time to spare." He looked at her with moist eyes. "Perhaps I'll walk again later today."

"Aye."

As they walked back toward hospital, Abigail found herself praying with more earnestness than she had done in weeks. She prayed boldly and fervently. But it was not for herself. It was for William.

Chapter 15

What is the matter with you? You nearly kissed her. William berated the passion that overrode all reason in this latest encounter with Abigail Gillingham. The woman was married, and he had no claim on her affections. Why was it so difficult to reconcile his heart with his head?

He rolled over onto his side on the hard bed of straw. It hadn't been changed in days. Supplies had dwindled, and even fresh straw was a luxury. He'd even heard that many of the horses in camp were near death.

When one of his officers had come for a visit to rally him before the next battle, William's curiosities had been confirmed.

"I went to visit Mrs. Riedesel," the sergeant informed him. "I heard she had some extra food she might share. She is most kind. She gave me what she could spare, though was little enough." The sergeant continued, his gaunt cheeks working over a twig between his teeth. "I saw her eyes ablaze as sounds of carousing could be heard from the general's quarters. She looked none too pleased."

So it was true. Burgoyne had plenty with which to imbibe when the wounded had little rum to ease their pain. He wrestled with his conflicted feelings of loyalty.

Ever since his older brother had died in the war, he'd determined to carry on the cause "For King and Country." He'd left his job as a potter and enlisted as a soldier before meeting Priscilla. After they'd fallen in love, he didn't want to marry her before heading out of port months later. She told him he must marry her and take her with him. His heart won the battle and, much to his horror, she didn't survive the journey onboard ship.

My heart turns me into a fool with regrets.

He would not be so foolish when it came to Mrs. Gillingham.

Perhaps he would die in the next battle and spare everyone the pain.

But even he knew life was God's to give—as well as take away. Not ours to pray for the ending before He was finished with us on earth.

"Ready for your exercise, Corporal Carpenter?"

William rolled over and pushed himself up. "Yes, Mr. Salyer. At your service." His voice dripped with sarcasm as he was loathe to show the surgeon's mate any pleasantness. He'd seen Mrs. Gillingham come back upset and flustered that day Salyer took her from the tent. Ever since then, he could tell she had avoided Salyer's company. He didn't wait for the mate to offer a hand, as he wasn't about to rely on him—for anything.

Anger surging through his blood strengthened William's stride as he followed Salyer out of the tent.

"I hear you need readied for the next battle. I hear it will be soon." Salyer sounded as though he held no regret over the possibility of more bodies. Perhaps even William's.

"Yes. Time to use those manly arts of war again." He glanced sideways at Salyer.

"I believe there are manly arts in many a profession. Including being a surgeon. And where would the injured be without our capabilities?" Salyer spit the words under his breath at William.

"I dare say some might still be alive."

Salyer gripped William's wounded arm. He winced but wouldn't give the surgeon's mate the pleasure of knowing how deeply it hurt.

Was it guilt that prompted Salyer to release his grip? Or the realization he was being scrutinized by a few men who stopped in their tracks to observe them? The subsequent smile seemed forced.

"Well now, shall we find a splint to prop your arm on? Mr. Braithwaite has said it will help support your aim with each shot as you fire your musket."

William rubbed his arm. "Of course." His eyes narrowed as he resisted the urge to use his manly arts on the surgeon's mate.

"Very well, then." Salyer threw a sly smile at William and headed for the trees.

Although he didn't trust the man, William knew Mr. Braithwaite had directed him to prepare William's arm for war. To ignore this order would be a form of sedition. So William followed him toward a grove of trees hidden from the campsite.

Salyer searched the branches for the right width and length to use as a splint. "Here. This one should do." He took out a knife from his sheath, cut off the small branch, took a seat on a nearby rock, and started whittling the branch into the proper shape.

He watched the surgeon mate's hands as he worked, imagining how Salyer might have used those fingers to molest Mrs. Gillingham. "What did you do to her?"

Salyer looked up from his task. "To whom?"

The soldier pulled him to his feet by his shirt. "You know exactly who I mean. What did you do to Mrs. Gillingham that day?"

Salyer's face reddened and the veins stood out in his neck. "I did nothing. Not that I didn't want to." He shrugged. "But she wouldn't have me."

"She is a married woman!" William felt his own blood boiling in his neck.

"That is none of your concern!"

"Perhaps your supervisor would like it to be his concern. You cannot molest the married women in camp."

Salyer placed his hands on his hips. "That doesn't seem to stop our leaders, now does it? Besides, I offered to send her a stipend after the war."

Without thinking, he thrust his right fist into Salyer's face. He immediately knew it was a mistake. Moaning, he gripped his injured arm.

Salyer rubbed his cheek while he grinned at William's discomfort.

William glared at him. "It must invigorate your spirit to treat the wounded. No thought of facing a line of firing muskets. No trembling at the sharp bayonets. No blasts of cannon nearby deafening you. You just wait in your tent for the wounded, picking up the mess afterwards. It must put you at ease, Mr. Salyer, does it not?"

The surgeon's mate drew closer to William. His face contorted with rage and reddened in the sunlight. "Are you calling me a coward?"

"I never said that, now, did I?"

A forceful blow to his left jaw knocked William off his feet. He winced and tasted blood. As he sat up, he spit out the red liquid pooling in his cheek. "Feel more manly now?" William smirked at him.

The two men glared at each other for a moment. William's heart pounded with fury.

Without speaking another word, the surgeon's mate threw the wood he'd been whittling at William's face and stalked back to camp.

William held his face and moaned in pain.

Chapter 16

A single cannon shot jolted Abigail from her slumber.

Heart racing, she threw off her blanket and grabbed her cloak. Shivering and barefoot, she couldn't find her shoes. All the nurses were now awake and out of their cots.

"Heavens, has the enemy attacked our camp?" Mrs. Carberry still appeared half asleep in the lamplight, but her voice rang clear and firm. "All nurses prepare for the wounded."

The whistle of three rockets, followed by a burst of light in the sky, sent even more terror through Abigail. The flares lit the entire night sky and illuminated the canvas roof of the tent, revealing the faces of the women in their quarters in its temporary brilliance. They looked as frightened as she. Just as quickly, the rockets fizzled out. The only glow remaining in the tent was from the burning lamp.

A flurry of male voices drew Abigail outside to beg for explanation. "What has occurred? Has battle begun? In the middle of the night?"

One of the officers turned to her. "No, Mrs. Gillingham. We're not certain, but perhaps our general is sending signals to Sir Henry. Perhaps he is close enough to see." A glimmer of hope grew in his exhausted eyes.

"Oh. I see." Perhaps if more troops come, William need not go to battle. She smiled at the officer but then frowned when she saw Lieutenant Baggley staring at her from just a few feet away. Although she was dressed in a chemise and covered in her cloak, she suddenly felt naked and exposed. Pulling her cloak more tightly around her neck, she went back toward the nurses' tent.

"Mrs. Gillingham."

Turning toward the familiar voice, she scowled. "I must return to my tent, Mr. Salyer."

He reached toward her arm and she stopped.

"Please. I must apologize for my rude behavior the other day. I pray you can forgive me."

In the moonlit sky, he appeared truly dashing. A handsome figure in his linen shirt with ruffles at the neck. The crown of dark-blond hair pulled back with a black ribbon only added to his appealing presence. But Abigail knew she could not trust him again. He had already exposed his true character. "I forgive you, Mr. Salyer. But I will ne'er be found walking with you again."

"Mrs. Gillingham." His voice thickened. "Truly, I regret my behavior."

She heard him swallow and looked up at his distraught face. "Good night, Mr. Salyer."

Mrs. Pomeroy stared at Thomas Salyer. As Abigail passed, the nurse glanced at her with disdain and then strode toward the surgeon's mate in a huff.

Walking past Mrs. Carberry, who was in earnest conversation with one of the officers, Abigail returned to the tent.

* * *

Thomas watched Miss Gillingham return to the nurses' tent. He was such a fool. Even if he offered to marry her now, she would never believe him. And why should she?

He hadn't noticed one of the other nurses approaching him until she stood directly in front of him.

"It's a cold night to be alone, is it not, Mr. Salyer?" She fixed her eyes on him.

Taken by surprise, he barely knew what to say. "It's … it's Mrs. Pomeroy, is it not?"

She smiled flirtatiously. "Yes, Mr. Salyer." She stepped closer to him and cocked her head to the side. "You do know my husband is no longer with us." She wove her fingers beneath his crossed arms and began stroking his chest.

Utterly shocked by her advances, Thomas stepped away from her. "I must return to my quarters, Mrs. Pomeroy. I beg your leave." He whipped around and stumbled through the night toward the surgeon's tent.

While he regretted distressing Mrs. Pomeroy, the thought of being with any woman besides Abigail repulsed him. Even imagining Miss Jane Etheridge, who awaited his return in Cornwall, triggered waves of remorse. What a fool he had been to make such a promise to her.

He stretched out on his canvas cot and threw the thin blanket over himself. A chill crept over him, but it wasn't from the cold. It was the realization that there would never be warmth in his bed with Miss Etheridge. Unexpected tears trickled down his cheeks. *God, what have I done?*

Chapter 17

No explanation was ever provided for the unsettling explosion in the night. If its purpose was to distress Abigail and the other nurses even more, then the plan had succeeded. Nerves were so raw these days, the slightest sound elicited panic in Abigail. Her heart frequently pounded like a drum. She could see similar distress on the faces of her fellow caregivers.

It wasn't just the cannon shot at midnight. The frequent skirmishes on the edge of camp created frenzied feelings of imminent doom. Then a band of Indians from Canada—friendly to the Regulars—appeared. These native tribesmen seemed far too fascinated with Abigail's long, red hair. She avoided them as though they carried a deadly contagion.

She also tried to avoid William as much as possible, although her heart longed to tell him the truth. That she was not married. And she yearned to feel his comforting arms around her and hear his soothing voice as he assured her all would be well.

But that was a dream. How could all be well when the threat of the next battle hung over their heads like a fruit-laden orchard ready to release its entire crop? They were sitting under those frightful trees, just waiting for the assault. And the fruit would be bitter indeed.

The impending winter, so evident in the coating of thick frost each morning, only added to the trepidation and sadness. It brought a sense of foreboding to Abigail, and she could read it in each soldier's eyes. Even Mrs. Carberry appeared overwhelmed with the tension.

"Mrs. Gillingham, have you walked the wounded yet today?" The edge in the matron's voice snapped Abigail's attention away from rolling a linen bandage.

"Aye, Mrs. Carberry. Is there anything else you'd like me to do?" Despite their differing loyalties, Abigail had the greatest respect for the matron. Her dedication and kindness were truly inspiring. Abigail's affection grew for her—even on the days when the older woman seemed irritable. Abigail certainly understood her temper and often struggled with the dreadfulness of the situation herself.

"Yes." Mrs. Carberry looked at her chapped hands for a moment. "Do you know how to style the men's hair?"

Abigail's eyes narrowed and she frowned. "Do you mean for battle?"

"Yes. Have you done this before?"

She stuttered. "Nay ... I've never worked with the army before." Unwanted tears welled in her eyes. She wiped them away as fast as she could. But not before Mrs. Carberry noticed.

The older woman touched her arm. "I shall show you how." She led Abigail to one of the patients who had suffered a leg wound. "Private Banner, may I show Mrs. Gillingham how to club your hair?"

The young man looked up and smiled. "Yes, Mrs. Carberry. Pleased to have two ladies stroking my head." He laughed.

Surely he must have known what this meant. How could he be so jovial?

As Mrs. Carberry showed Abigail the proper technique, the young woman carefully observed each step. While the top and sides of the men's hair were kept short, it was long in the back, nearly covering their shoulder blades. By gathering the lengthy strands together, folding it over itself twice and tying it with a ribbon, the club kept loose hair away from the musket. It was practical and kept a uniform appearance in the ranks of soldiers.

Abigail stayed focused on the task and tried out the technique on the private's hair. It was simple and easily accomplished—far easier than taming her waist-length hair with pins under a mobcap.

Private Banner spoke as Abigail finished tying the ribbon around his hair. "It's about time we're attacking them Rebels. Blaggards killed my best friend on that farm. I want to fire at them devils as much as possible. Kill 'em all."

A chill wove its way through her. She released the completed club and swallowed. "There now, Private. 'Tis finished." Nausea filled her empty stomach and rose in her throat, but she swallowed it back down. She could not afford to lose what little she had eaten.

"Mrs. Gillingham? Mrs. Gillingham?"

She wondered how long the head nurse had been calling her name. "I'm sorry, Mrs. Carberry. Pray, what can I do for you?"

"Corporal Carpenter. Can you do his club for him?" The older woman put a gentle hand on her shoulder.

Does she know my heart longs for him? Can her "eyes that see" delve into my soul?

Abigail struggled to control the quiver in her voice. "Aye, Mrs. Carberry. I shall help him."

Her leaden legs lifted her frail frame with difficulty. Without speaking, she went outside to procure warm water from a kettle heating over the fire. She carefully ladled the liquid into a basin, much as she had done to clean wounds and ill bodies these last weeks. But this was the first time she had drawn water to brush through a soldier's hair as he prepared for battle. She felt like a betrayer to the art of healing. Warm tears mixed with the water as she carried it to William.

Looking at him sitting there, so dedicated and committed to a cause, inspired her to do her part to prepare him to face whatever lay ahead. It broke her heart, yet she could not let him see such pain in her countenance. She would be strong for him, even if her fortitude was false. *Lord, do not let him see the fear I bear for him.*

"Corporal Carpenter, may I assist you with your hair?" She forced a smile with closed lips.

His look threatened to melt all her resolve. He grinned and said, "I'd like no one else to help me."

She sat down on the flattened straw with weakened legs and heart. She cleared her throat as she knelt behind him. "Mrs. Carberry instructed me how to do this."

Obviously anticipating her appearance, he handed her his brush and a black ribbon.

She laid the ribbon on her lap, dipped the bristles of the brush into the water, and gently stroked them through William's long hair. As she came across tangles, she paused and held the hairs upward while she undid the collection of unkempt strands. She swished the brush in the basin and small, dried flecks dissolved into red liquid—blood left from his first battle. She continued to remove any particles until the brush washed clean.

Tenderly smoothing William's clean hair, Abigail's fingers trembled as she wove them through, preparing the strands to be gathered and folded.

She knew she caressed his hair far too long, but he didn't seem to notice—or maybe he didn't mind. She reveled in the feel of him and wished she could indulge herself longer. After tying the ribbon around the folded hair, she released the club with regret. "There. I believe that should hold."

He turned to her with seductive eyes that threatened to make her reveal her feelings for him. "Are you done so soon?" He visibly swallowed.

"Aye. I fear 'tis so." She pushed herself to her feet.

William reached out and took her hand. "I am grateful for your tender care, Mrs. Gillingham. I shall never forget you."

Abigail knew she could never withhold her tears now. "Nor I you, Corporal Carpenter."

She nearly spilled the basin of water as she hurried to leave. When she got outside, she went several feet from the tent and poured the contents onto the ground. She observed the puddle of water as it slowly soaked into the sparse grass, then watched her tears spill silently into the fading pool of moisture.

Chapter 18

Abigail barely slept that night. Rumors had been rampant about the impending battle, especially since General Burgoyne had called together his main advisers for a meeting two days ago. Earlier today, rum had been distributed to the troops, a luxury during a time of paltry rations.

Although not privy to war planning or strategies, Abigail knew that the time was near. As she repeatedly tossed on her cot in the nurses' tent, concern for William clouded any other issue—even her own safety.

She must tell him. She could not bear the thought that he didn't know how she felt. What if he got killed and she lost all opportunity to tell him? She must tell him she was not Mrs. Gillingham … but Miss. She must tell him of her great affection for him.

This was a great risk, especially since William already knew her Patriot leanings. But Abigail was willing to take the chance, even if it meant being sent away from camp—or worse.

Could they hang her as a spy?

She shivered. Taking in a deep breath of courage, she resolved to tell him. She would rather die with the truth on her lips than live a lie.

* * *

The mist still surrounded the camp the next morning when Abigail strode with purpose toward the hospital tent. To her surprise, many of the soldiers were gone, including William.

She clutched her cloak tightly around her torso. "Mrs. Carberry." She barely could hear her own voice as she hurried toward the matron, who was changing a bandage. "Where have the men gone?"

The experienced nurse met Abigail's eyes with a look of sympathy. "They are fitted for battle. Just awaiting the tattoo of drums."

Her lips trembled. "But where are they?" Her heart pounded so hard she grew dizzy.

"Corporal Carpenter is with his regiment on the way to headquarters. Follow the surge of troops." Mrs. Carberry turned her head away so quickly, Abigail wondered if it had not caused her pain.

"Thank you," she whispered and ran outdoors. She glanced about in the mist-filled darkness for soldiers dressed for battle. They were everywhere, but she couldn't discern one particular direction they were heading.

She stopped one private. "Sir, which way to headquarters?"

"Nurse, what are you doing out here? You need to seek shelter soon."

His concerned voice touched her. "Thank you, Private, but I must find Corporal Carpenter." She bit down on her lower lip, attempting to stop the trembling.

He must have seen her desperation. "He's with the 62nd, Mrs. Gillingham. I'll take ya there." He put his arm out for her to take it.

She could barely see the hem of her blue linen dress, but she could hear it swishing against the ground and against the private's gaiter-trousers.

Soldiers dressed in full regimentals scurried everywhere, occasionally bumping into her. "Sorry, ma'am." They kept going.

Despite the cold air, the hustle of hurrying troops warmed the atmosphere, the smell of their sweat filling the air with their own worry. Abigail struggled to keep up with the private. It seemed they would never find William in the fray.

"There's the 62nd, Mrs. Gillingham. They'll know where the corporal is."

"Thank you, sir. I am indebted to you."

He tipped his hat and hurried off to his own regiment.

Abigail squinted her eyes at the dozens of men standing in a group, apparently awaiting orders.

"Excuse me." She approached one man. "Might I inquire where Corporal Carpenter is?"

He stared at her with confusion in his eyes then opened his mouth in recognition. "Oh, you're his nurse. Come to check on your patient once more?" He winked and gave a leering grin, which exposed his stained teeth.

Abigail's cheeks flushed with warmth. A nearby soldier intervened.

"Knock it off, Fleming." He spoke to Abigail. "Corporal's over there, Mrs. Gillingham. I'll show you."

He led her a short distance to a man standing sideways. In the thick fog, she likely would not have seen him on her own. But even when confronted with her friend, she barely recognized him in full regimentals.

William appeared much taller in a tall felt cap emblazoned with the number "62" and topped with a crest made from strands of animal hair. Over his red coat, he carried a bulging haversack, a canteen, and a leather pouch that was attached to his belt. Most alarming of all was the long, sharp bayonet carried in what looked like another belt slung over his shoulder. And, of course, he held his musket firmly in two hands.

When he saw her, his mouth opened in surprise. "Mrs. Gillingham. What are you doing here?" His voice dropped to a whisper. "You're not safe." He glanced around.

The tears she'd withheld for so long could no longer be prevented. "I … I must speak with you. Alone."

He gently took her arm and hurried her away from the throng of nervous soldiers. He brought her through the mist toward a grove of trees where she could speak without being heard.

"Mrs. Gillingham, I fear for your safety. Once the troops are called to arms, they could run you down." His questioning eyes searched hers. "Why—"

"I must tell you." She inhaled deeply, mustering her courage. "I must tell you before you leave. I am not Mrs. Gillingham."

His eyes narrowed. "What? Well then, who are you?"

Abigail couldn't tell if he was confused or distrustful. Or angry.

She began to sob. "I am Miss Gillingham. Miss Abigail Gillingham. My uncle made me tell everyone I was married so I would be allowed to tend the patients. I never wanted to lie. But he threatened to harm me if I did not." She'd been living a lie for so long, the truth rapidly escaped from its prison of guilt. "I couldn't let you go to battle without telling you how … how … fond I am of you. What deep regard I have for you. I could not let that happen." She covered her face and wept.

His arms encircled her and drew her close. "Abigail?"

She looked up at him, standing so close she could count the beats of his heart through her breast.

"Abigail." He removed his cap and held it with his fingers while caressing her back with his other hand. His mouth found hers, and he hungrily pressed his lips over and through hers.

Abigail had never experienced such a kiss before, and she reveled in the warmth and passion that sprung within her. She placed both hands over his cheeks and drew him closer.

He complied without resistance, breath quickening as the kisses continued.

Unable to breathe, she pulled back and locked her gaze on his while holding his cheeks and caressing his skin.

"Abigail, I love you. Why did you not confide in me before?"

He closed his eyes as she stood on tiptoe and kissed his cheek. "I feared you would feel compelled to turn me in. I did not wish to make you compromise your duty." She was delirious when he kissed her neck. She steadied herself and looked him in the eyes. "William, I couldn't condone lying to you anymore. My heart would not allow it."

"I've struggled with my duty to God and country. I have resisted my attraction to you, thinking you belonged to another. I couldn't understand why …"

The tattoo of drums shattered the stillness.

His brows furrowed as he held her at arms' length. "Do not reveal your true situation to any other. It would endanger you. I've heard rumors."

"Rumors?" Her breath came in quick spurts as the drumbeats increased in intensity.

He held her closely again. "I must go. But look sharp. Stay with the other nurses, and they will watch out for you until I get back." He kissed her tenderly. "When I return, I will watch out for you. But go back to camp. Go that way." He pointed.

She regretted when he released her and donned his regimental cap. Even in the mist, Abigail could see the longing in his eyes.

"I love you, Abigail. And I will come back."

"I love you, William. I will pray for you."

He smiled and hurried back to his regiment.

An owl hooted nearby. Feeling faint with both love and fear, she forced her feet to quicken their pace and returned to camp.

Chapter 19

Despite bearing the weight of his armaments and the pain in his arm, William's spirits soared. Abigail Gillingham loved him.

He hadn't allowed himself to acknowledge his affection for her until now. Knowing she was free of obligation to another changed everything. For the first time in years, he wanted to sing and dance. He could think of nothing but the sweetness of her lips. Yet he was about to face an enemy he needed to kill. The contrast in his emotions tore at his spirit as despair shrouded his thinking. Especially when he realized he would be killing Abigail's fellow Colonists. The thought sickened him. *Dear God, help me.*

The call to arms sounded and William gathered with his fellow soldiers. Indian allies, bedecked in war paint, headed toward the woods.

Without moving his head, he scanned the soldiers who surrounded him. They were a sad lot with torn and filthy uniforms, once known for their scarlet brilliance that attracted everyone's attention. Today, the uniforms hung on thin torsos, smeared with dirt and blood. Their condition spoke of months of pain and sweat as they struggled to smother the defiant ones who inhabited the colonies and dared challenge their king. England's army had shriveled, not only in size but in spirit. An outsider observing these troops might wonder who was on the winning side. Everyone believed the King's Army was unstoppable. But William wondered if that was true.

The October sunshine broke through the fog earlier than usual, and the sudden warmth was a welcome relief. But as the troops stood at attention and awaited the appearance of General Burgoyne from his headquarters, the glaring light ceased bringing comfort. It became an annoyance. The group murmured as their empty stomachs growled. A few of the discontented men mused that Burgoyne might be delayed due to one more dalliance with his mistress. Exasperation and fatigue were palpable, even with the well-disciplined troops, who waited three hours before they were finally underway.

William tried to ignore the pain in his arm. He wasn't sure if the splint added to his discomfort, but he told himself it would provide support when it came time to fire his weapon. He hoped this was so.

The march became a struggle with unfriendly terrain. They made frequent stops to throw makeshift bridges across streams so the artillery could continue onward. It was early afternoon when they were ordered to halt in a wheat field. William and his comrades collapsed to the ground, awaiting further orders.

A nearby officer complained about their "miserable position." The same officer seemed upset as he pointed to the woods on either side of them. "Knowing the Colonists' style of warfare, those woods could conceal an entire Rebel army."

Despite the intense heat, William shivered. The quiet was unnerving, but it did not last long.

"Over there!" One of the majors spotted a large number of insurgents slipping through the trees on the left. The British cannon opened up but made little impact in the dense forest. The armed Rebels moved forward, ever closer.

William and his unit positioned themselves to fire. Sweat poured from his brow as he faced the Americans once again. But this time, he saw not the enemy.

He saw Abigail's people.

* * *

Abigail could still feel the comfort of William's arms and the passion with which he had kissed her. Hugging herself with her cloak, she hurried toward the hospital tent to find Mrs. Carberry. She must share the news with her friend. William loved her.

Every time she thought of him, shivers traveled up her spine. But when she thought of him in battle, the shivers of joy turned to tremors of fear.

Dear Lord, protect him.

The camp seemed empty compared to just an hour earlier. Abigail hadn't heard any musket fire yet. She prayed that perhaps a battle might not occur.

Her thoughts still consumed with William, she threw open the tent flap to the hospital and screamed at the sight she had long feared and dreaded. "Uncle Richard!"

"So there you are, my sweet niece." His disingenuous tone of affection sickened her.

Abigail glanced around for Mrs. Carberry, but she was nowhere in sight. The young woman's throat instantly dried and, despite wanting to be brave, she trembled uncontrollably. As her uncle approached her, she stumbled backward, shrinking away from his false civility and familial tenderness. "Stay away from me." She gulped back the acid in her throat.

From the corner of her eye, she noticed one of the wounded patients struggled to sit up. "Get away from Nurse," he uttered weakly.

She was grateful for his bravado but knew the soldier was too frail to help her if Uncle Richard became abusive.

"So, you've got the allegiance of the king's soldiers." He gave a leering grin. "I'm certain they appreciate your skills."

She backed into a table and felt for something—anything—she could use to defend herself. But there was nothing.

As her uncle drew closer, she could smell rum on his breath and the stench of sweat that revealed many weeks without bathing. If he came any nearer, Abigail feared she would lose her meager breakfast.

"I said I'd be back. As soon as this battle is over, I'll take you home." His laugh revealed filthy teeth. He drew ever closer, and the smell of corruption from his purulent mouth forced Abigail to turn her head aside.

"I do not think so, sir."

Thomas! Abigail had never been more relieved to hear his voice. She pushed her uncle away and ran behind the surgeon's mate, who wielded a surgical saw and stared down her uncle.

Uncle Richard's face dissolved into ugly hatred. "And who are you? This woman belongs to me."

Thomas stood erect. "I think not, sir. She belongs to her husband, does she not?" He held the saw a bit higher in one hand and placed the other hand on his hip.

Richard snorted. "Husband."

Abigail watched as her uncle contemplated the lie he'd birthed. His shoulders slumped in defeat. He'd rather stand down than reveal his deception to the army. Uncle Richard recovered himself and faced the surgeon's mate with defiance. "We'll just see if her husband returns—or gets his bloody head blasted off."

"Such concern from her loving uncle. It nearly brings tears of endearment from all." Thomas stood his ground.

Uncle Richard harrumphed and stalked outdoors.

Thomas watched Uncle Richard leave and then turned toward Abigail. "He is a blaggard. You must stay away from him." Rubbing his chin, Thomas added, "I'll report him to the sentries, to keep him away from camp."

Abigail searched for an empty spot on the floor and sank onto it. "He'll always know where to find me." Hot tears poured down her face.

Thomas squatted in front of her. "Then you must stay close to camp. We will protect you." He searched her face.

Was he hoping she would change her mind about him?

"I'll stay close," she assured him.

Thomas reached out to put his hand on her shoulder.

She pulled away. "I'm well now, thank you." She forced herself to stand and wiped her tears away with her apron. "I'm grateful for your help. Truly."

She could feel his gaze follow her as she assisted the patients. There was much to be done. Out of the corner of her eye, she saw Thomas turn his attention to the wounded. The number of illnesses had increased by dozens in the last few days. Fevered bodies filled every hay-strewn bed vacated by the recovered soldiers who had left for war.

Where will William go when he returns? If he returns ... Abigail couldn't contemplate such a thought. He must return. *Please, God, bring him back to me.*

Grabbing an empty basin, she approached the tent flaps with trepidation, wondering if her uncle was nearby. She crept to the nearby fire and glanced around like a deer at a watering hole, ever vigilant. After ladling the warm water from the large outdoor kettle, she scurried back inside the tent. It was her refuge, albeit one filled with contagion and stench. She far preferred it to the fetor of her uncle.

The heat of the day increased to unbearable warmth. Abigail only escaped the hospital for brief moments, breathing in the outside air as deeply as she could. She listened intently for the sounds of battle but, so far, no musket fire greeted her ears with an unfriendly assault. She prayed it would not begin.

But by mid-afternoon, a barrage of bullets and cannon fire could be heard in the distance. She tensed and waited for the newly wounded and wondered where they would put them. Two privates from William's regiment entered the tent with a load of straw to add to the flattened, filthy bedding. It had been weeks since they'd had fresh replenishments. Did this mean more injured were on their way?

It wasn't long before that answer arrived in the form of crying men with bullet holes oozing red. Abigail thought by now she'd be used to this human slaughter. But she would never get used to this misery. It made her ill—and angry.

She set to work. The nurses were once again orchestrated by their conductor, Mrs. Carberry. She knew exactly where they could lay each new arrival and swiftly assessed who needed what. "Abigail, check this one's chest."

Abigail had long ceased being shy about tearing off clothing that hid the damage. She looked for the source of assault and determined if the surgeon was needed.

Mr. Braithwaite busily poked and prodded the wounds, trying to determine if lead balls remained in the gaping flesh holes.

Abigail tried to shut out the screams of pain, but they became louder as the day turned into evening. A chill enveloped the tent, and the soldiers shivered in the night air, so she covered them with blankets. As she moved among them, she came across the soldier who had helped her find William before the unit left for battle that morning. He was one in a long row of new patients.

After dressing his injuries, she quietly addressed him. "Sir."

He moaned and opened his eyes.

"You were with Corporal Carpenter, were you not?"

He attempted a slight smile. "Yes. I remember you."

She swallowed and returned the smile. "Have you seen him?" She tried to keep the desperation from instilling her voice.

"No. Not after the firing started. There was so much smoke, I couldna' see a thing." He shivered.

She touched his arm with trembling fingers and covered him with a blanket. "Rest now."

Abigail stood on shaking legs and walked unsteadily toward the door. Under the stars, with the horrifying music of artillery in the distance, she looked toward the sky and mumbled a Psalm she'd memorized as a child. "I will lift up mine eyes unto the hills, from whence cometh my help. My help cometh from the Lord, which made heaven and earth."

As the sounds of war continued in the distance and the wails of the wounded stung her ears, she covered her face with her hands and wept.

Chapter 20

Abigail didn't bother returning to the nurses' tent that night. There was too much work to be done. None of the caregivers took time for rest. Neither would she.

Bleary-eyed surgeons and women bumped into each other as they tended the wounded and ill. Someone brought ale for the staff, but Abigail wasn't certain who it was. She merely guzzled the offering and returned to her tasks. She forced herself to keep working and ignore the thought that repeatedly knocked on her heart—there was no sign of William.

No one seemed to know where he was. Whenever she saw a soldier she recognized, she inquired of William's whereabouts. Corporal Carpenter was not among the wounded, and no one had found his body.

Dear Lord, You know where he is. Please ... bring him back to me.

The battle continued to go poorly and rumors filtered through the hospital tent.

"We're outnumbered. Our mates kept shootin', but they were shootin' more." Abigail's patient gasped for air as she stitched the wound in his chest.

"Try to rest, Private. You are safe here in hospital." Abigail gave the distraught soldier another drink of rum—just a sip with supplies so low.

More arrivals to the marquee carried similar tales of one defeat after another. Abigail overheard Mr. Braithwaite pause long enough in his duties to declare, "How can an undisciplined group of farmers defeat His Majesty's finest? I never thought this possible." He wiped his face with angry hands and returned to his tasks.

Everyone in the tent appeared stunned as this news spread rapidly.

Abigail's mind was a battlefield of emotions, relieved at the American victory yet terrified about the outcome for William. Was he lost to her forever?

Another group of soldiers arrived carrying comrades downed in the assault. One sergeant declared news that caused the whole staff to stop in their tracks. "Fraser's dead."

Nurse Carberry whimpered unashamedly, and the surgeon's mates covered their eyes. The news even startled Abigail as Brigadier General Simon Fraser was frequently spoken of with great admiration. He was an obvious favorite of the troops.

"There's more." The sergeant paused and his voice thickened. "There's talk of a retreat. Burgoyne's planning to withdraw by nightfall—after Fraser's buried."

The sound of cannons in the distance continued to assault the atmosphere.

Everyone appeared benumbed by the news of retreat. Mr. Braithwaite stood erect and attempted a firm tone of voice.

"It's either retreat or surrender. Undoubtedly, the patients and hospital staff will remain behind." He paused and his voice lowered. "I'm certain the American General Gates will treat us with consideration."

Nurse Sedgewick covered her mouth as she moaned. "May the Lord have mercy on us."

Shock reverberated through Abigail's thoughts at this news. Would the Americans understand who she was? Would she be in danger of her fellow Patriots? Her mind swirled with distress and fatigue.

And then the man who sent tentacles of fear and disgust through her appeared in the doorway. Lieutenant Baggley had returned, and, if it were possible, his face reflected even more lust than his first encounter with her in the nurses' tent.

Right behind the lieutenant, Nurse Pomeroy slipped into the hospital tent. She and Baggley exchanged meaningful glances, sending a sickening horror through Abigail. She had seen them together once before. What were they plotting?

Abigail drew in a deep breath and turned away. She glanced around the room, looking for Thomas Salyer, but he was busy tending a wailing soldier.

Mr. Braithwaite had seen the lieutenant enter the hospital and intercepted him. "What's your business here?"

Abigail watched as they conversed.

Baggley's tone of voice was dutiful and sincere. "I was just escorting Nurse Pomeroy to work."

Braithwaite harrumphed and returned to his patient.

As Baggley turned to go, Abigail shivered when he looked her way and grinned.

Nausea gripped her, and she turned away. Someone grasped her arm. She jumped.

"Easy there, Abigail." Mrs. Carberry spoke low. "I see our unwanted visitor is back. Stay close to the staff. If he comes near you, inform Mr. Braithwaite or one of the sentinels." She smiled reassuringly, but that didn't hide the worry lines around Mrs. Carberry's mouth.

"I shall." Abigail attempted a smile, but it was weakly carried out.

Dear Lord, be my strength.

She dared not leave the tent, although she longed to search for William. She knew that were he able, he would return to her. This could mean only one thing. Despair and sadness filled every pore until it seemed her entire person would ooze with the grief of one abandoned.

She was so alone.

Blinded by tears, she rubbed them dry with angry fingers.

Stop coddling your heart, Abigail. There is work to be done.

She went to a newly arrived patient and removed his jacket. Numb to the cries of pain, she worked as though in a trance, washing away the blood, assessing the depth of destruction in the skin, determining whether or not the surgeon needed to attend. Her arms became rigid as she moved from one injured soldier to the next, avoiding their eyes at all cost. She could not be swept away by their torment, lest she become paralyzed by their misery.

Nightfall approached and the sentinel outside the door opened the tent flap. "General Burgoyne has ordered His Majesty's troops to begin retreat at eight o'clock. Long live the King!"

"Long live the King." Mr. Braithwaite and the staff muttered their reply with disheartened voices.

Few patients had come into hospital in the last hour. Abigail assumed that the influx of wounded would slowly ebb then eventually cease.

When she heard shouting outside the tent, she thought it was orders to march. But a rustling at the tent flap drew her attention. William's superior officer, who had visited him a week ago, sought her eyes. He motioned for her to come.

Setting down a filthy basin, she walked stiffly toward the opening. After looking at the sergeant's face, she hurried her pace and followed his lead toward the edge of the woods. She inhaled sharply and covered her open mouth. "William!"

Bending over the gasping figure propped up by a comrade, Abigail could not withhold her relief as she covered his gunpowder-smeared face with kisses.

He smiled weakly as he slowly reached up with his hand. Too weak to hold it up, he dropped it onto his lap.

The officer looked at Abigail. "We found him dragging one of his mates to safety. I guess the other man died on the way."

William's face contorted. "He was alive. I tried to bring him back."

"Of course you did." Abigail stroked his cheek. "You would do everything you could to save a friend. You did all that you were able and more." She tenderly kissed him again.

"I hear we have another casualty."

Abigail met Thomas Salyer's eyes. In the darkness, she couldn't read his expression, but his voice carried the tenor of sadness and resignation.

"Aye." Abigail stood up. "I'll tend any wounds he has."

Thomas stared at her in the moonlight. "I'm certain you will." He placed the stretcher down next to William, and the officer helped lift the patient onto the canvas.

Abigail winced when William moaned. *Dear Lord, let him recover.*

Chapter 21

Abigail watched her exhausted soldier sleep. She wanted to hold his hand but knew the others would wonder at her impertinence. Most of the observers in hospital still thought she was Mrs. Gillingham, and it was dangerous to reveal otherwise.

William occasionally jerked then winced with the motion, grabbing at his side.

Thomas Salyer had sewn William's laceration with intricate stitches worthy of a fine tailor. The surgeon's mate was well suited to his profession. And despite his obvious pain at Abigail's refusal of his affections, Thomas had shown kindness and care in tending William's wounds. It improved her estimation of his character, at least a little.

Abigail struggled to keep her eyes open but startled when she felt a hand on her shoulder.

"Why do you not rest, Mrs. Gillingham? You need your strength. There is an empty spot nearby, and I have a blanket for you."

She met Mrs. Carberry's kind gaze and accepted the woolen piece from her. "I am so grateful to you." The two women hugged, and Abigail staggered toward the empty straw. It was stained with blood, but she didn't care. Nor did she remember falling asleep.

* * *

Abigail awoke with a start. She wasn't certain what woke her, but an icy fear prickled up her neck. She heard voices nearby through the canvas wall of the marquee. They were hushed, yet their earnest tone made them more audible.

"I'm not leavin' on retreat 'til I have my way with her. You promised you'd find a way to get her on her own so I can have her."

A woman's voice answered. "Do ya think I've not been trying? We've been a bit preoccupied with the wounded, you may have noticed. Every time I try to get her alone to go outside, she's back with another patient. Besides, there's others who seem to be on her guard. This is not so easy as you might think, Lieutenant."

Abigail sucked in her breath and held it. *Mrs. Pomeroy!*

She heard her fellow nurse moan. "Let go my arm!"

"See that you do it, trull, unless you want some of what's coming to 'er."

Footsteps echoed on the hoarfrost-covered weeds outside and diminished until she heard them no more.

She shuddered and exhaled. Her throat still tight, she had difficulty catching her breath. She must be calm. She must tell William.

She crawled as quietly as she could toward William's straw bed. She longed to cling to him for comfort. Drawing close to his ear, she whispered, "William. William, you must awaken."

His eyes opened and he looked confused, then he turned toward her and smiled. "Abigail." He reached for her face and drew her closer, stopping when he saw her expression. "What's wrong?"

She nearly choked as she tried to swallow.

He sat up and winced.

"William, one of the nurses conspires against me. She's leading me to a trap with an officer who … who terrifies me. His name is Lieutenant Baggley."

William leaned forward, wide awake. "Baggley? He's notorious for his cruelty and …" William firmed his mouth and lowered his voice. "And other things." He stroked the hair that had fallen from her mobcap and inhaled deeply. "How do you know this?"

"I heard them outside. He means to have me before he retreats with the army. William, I'm terrified!"

He held her close and whispered in her ear. "Shh. Do not fear. I'll take care of you."

She clung to him and shook with greater trepidation than she could recall.

"Abigail, help me up."

She stood on unsteady legs and pulled with all her might to help him stand.

Most of the patients and staff were asleep. Exhaustion and rum had brought stillness to the usually frantic atmosphere.

The couple crept toward the opening of the marquee and carefully stepped outdoors. Holding their breath, they tiptoed toward the woods. She had expected a sentinel to be outside the door, but every soldier who was able to march had already left.

All, that is, except for Lieutenant Baggley, who had stayed behind, prowling like a wolf.

William stopped short. "Wait. I need my firelock and cartridge box."

"Where are they?" Abigail tried not to panic. She just wanted to get away but knew he needed his armaments. They both needed them.

"Take me where they found me."

She looked around until she saw the stand of trees where the officer had brought him. "Over there," she whispered. Stepping around each piece of firewood and every rock she could see in the moonlight, she stumbled once or twice until she located the spot. "Here."

She heard his breath intake sharply as he bent over and felt around the rocks. "I remember removing my equipment so I had the strength to call for help. I laid it right here." He held up his musket and gathered the strap of his cartridge box, which he carefully slung over his shoulder.

Shaking uncontrollably, Abigail waited for him to approach her. "Where will we go?"

William put his arms on hers and met her eyes with his. "I'm taking you home. I'm taking you where you will be safe."

"Is that so?" A terrifying voice broke through the darkness.

William drew her down to the ground and readied his weapon. "Stay still." He whispered the command to her, but his voice trembled.

"I've already got my pistol pointed at your head, Carpenter. Move away from the lady, so she don't get hurt."

William's jaw moved. He abruptly stood. "I don't care what you do to me. But let the lady go."

A deep laugh burst from Baggley. "How about I get rid of you *and* have the lady. Suits me well enough."

The click of the gun hammer elicited a scream from Abigail.

Another shadow ran into the darkness just as the pistol fired. A scream. A body hit the ground. But it wasn't William, as he still stood before her.

Abigail strained her eyes to peer through the darkness.

It was Thomas Salyer. He grabbed his side and aimed a gun at Baggley, who ran toward a figure standing outside the tent. The two raced toward the woods in the opposite direction.

The sound of gunfire and cries of alarm awoke the tent.

"Thomas!" Abigail screamed.

"Get out. Take her away from here," Thomas shouted.

William grabbed Abigail's arm and started to run but turned back toward the surgeon's mate.

The two men stared at each other. "Take care of her." Thomas gasped and rolled back on the ground.

A crowd emerged from the tent, and William drew Abigail with him into the woods. They didn't stop running for an hour or more, tripping on branches, slipping on the frost. Racing until they could race no farther, the couple slumped into a large hollow in an ancient oak tree.

Gasping for air, William wrapped his arm around Abigail and held her close. Soon their breathing slowed in unison. Abigail didn't have the energy to speak but nestled closer into the comfort of William's embrace.

The last thing she recalled before falling asleep was William telling her he loved her.

Chapter 22

It took Abigail a moment to realize where she was. When she felt William's hand move to touch hers, she smiled.

"So 'twas not a dream." Her eyes were still closed, but she felt William kiss her hair.

"No. If it was a dream, may I never awaken." William kissed her again, this time on her lips.

She reveled in the warmth of his kiss but soon pushed him away. "William."

"I know." He stopped nuzzling her neck. "We need to find our way to your home."

Abigail uncurled her stiffened limbs from the tree hollow and kept her head low as she stepped out and perused the terrain. "I wonder where we are." She drew her cloak tighter around her shoulders in an effort to keep the cold wind from reaching her already chilled skin.

William moved with difficulty, and she helped him to an upright stance. He looked around then stared at her. "I was hoping you would know where we are since it's your home."

She searched the terrain in the distance. "Aye, yet I feel like a foreigner. I am turned about and not certain …"

He looked at the sky with a scowl. "And there is no sun to guide us." He secured the top button on his scarlet coat. "We must find shelter. And soon."

The sky was full of clouds. An ominous dark cluster moved slowly toward them, sending tentacles of threatening rain.

Abigail tried not to panic. She craved water and her stomach growled. "Perhaps there is a stream nearby. 'Twould be a pleasure to quench our thirst."

"If nothing else, we could lick the frost from the leaves."

She laughed for the first time in weeks. "You are a clever one." She held onto his arm as they stepped across a downed tree branch in the thick forest. "The closer we get toward the river, the more likely we'll find a stream."

She tried not to think about the dryness of her mouth or the weakness in her limbs. The last several weeks had taken their toll on them both. But she knew that William suffered the most. Yet he didn't complain.

A gurgling sound reached Abigail's ears. "Is that what I pray it is?"

His eyes widened. "Water."

Their steps hurried as they followed the sound of liquid rushing over rocks. At the moment, it was the sweetest sound she could imagine.

Abigail cringed as she watched William lean over. He winced with every movement. A cold wind whipped the tails of his coat as he cupped his hand and drank from the stream.

"William, we must get to my cabin. You're still injured."

He plopped onto the hard ground and let out a low moan. After a moment, he met her gaze. "So, tell me where your home is in relation to the battlefield. North? South?"

She squeezed her hands together. "That's just it. I've no idea. I feel so confused and foolish. Even when I've tried to imagine my cabin, the path there seems all twisted and turned in my mind. Nothing is familiar to me."

"It doesn't help that the battles have left their mark. I imagine the farmers who own the land might have difficulty discerning where their fields are. Or were." William stared at the ground.

Abigail placed her hand on his shoulder. "When I was a young girl, I would play near my home. But Mother died when I was ten, and I stayed even closer to home, taking care of father and doing the chores."

"You never wandered about? Not even with a suitor?" he teased her with a half-smile.

Despite the wind chill, her face warmed, and she glanced down.

"So who was he, Abigail? You can tell me."

She raised her head. "Timothy Cochran."

"I knew it." His laugh was a delightful respite from their situation. "So, did you ever wander the woods with Timothy?"

Her eyes widened. "Yes!"

His smile faded. "Well, you seem quite engaged with his memory. Should I be jealous?" He scratched his head.

She put her hands on her cheeks. "Jealous? No! But we used to play a game of putting our initials on our favorite trees, then an arrow to point toward home. Timothy knew I was terrible at directions, and he said he never wanted me to get lost."

William rose from the ground with difficulty and stood next to Abigail. "He must have cared deeply for you. Did he ever kiss you?"

"Well …" She giggled.

"Did he ever kiss you like this?" He pulled her into his arms and covered her mouth with his until she couldn't breathe.

Pulling away, she inhaled deeply. "Nay. No one has ever kissed me as you do."

He leaned his forehead onto hers. "I pray I am the only one to ever share that pleasure with you, Miss Abigail Gillingham."

Her heart melted at the passion on his face. "I pray 'tis so." Pulling back, she looked around for trees that seemed a little familiar. It had been years since she'd walked in the woods with Timothy.

Lord, help us find the path. You've taken us this far. Don't let us wander like the Israelites of old in the desert.

Their wandering didn't last forty years, but it seemed like at least an hour before a tree, standing out on the edge of a cliff, caught her eye. She pointed. "There. Let's try that one."

The wind had picked up, and freezing droplets of rain made their marks here and there on the ground. Hurrying toward the thick tree trunk, Abigail drew in a deep breath. "Here! Right here."

William walked more slowly toward the oak tree and touched the initials that would be their map: AG and TC. Right next to the letters was an arrow, slightly mottled with time, yet pointing clearly in one direction.

It pointed toward home.

Chapter 23

As they approached Abigail's home, the heavy rain poured relentlessly, and the wind drove it over and under their clothes. There seemed no part of their bodies the wetness and mud hadn't reached. It was like hell without the fire—just unending rain and cold that bogged their trek and weighted their clothing and their spirits.

By the time the drenched couple reached the cabin door, it took their combined strength to open the swollen portal. Had another human been inside, they surely would have wondered what species of animal had entered.

Abigail collapsed onto a chair and bent over, breathing heavily.

William looked around the room and noted sparse furnishings. But his eyes set upon several wooden hooks on the far wall, holding dry clothes. His freezing hand quivered as he touched Abigail's shoulder. "We must get out of these clothes—and quickly."

She didn't move. He lifted her with a reserve of strength he didn't know still existed. "Abigail, please." He started to undo the clasp on her woolen cloak, which was heavy with water. When he pulled it off her shoulders, she shivered uncontrollably. "Abigail, open your eyes."

She obeyed his instructions then whimpered. "I'm … so … cold."

When he started to undo her gown, she suddenly found her strength. She removed his hands and said, "I can do it." Still shivering, she walked stiffly toward the hook that held a dry chemise. Abigail pointed to a wooden chest. "My father's clothes lie therein. Take whatever you need."

"Thank you." He struggled to unbutton his scarlet coat with fingers that refused to manipulate as usual. When he finally managed to get his coat open, he threw it on the chair. Removing his gaiters and boots, he now struggled with the buttons on his breeches. Losing patience, he tore off the garment, made all the easier by his thinner frame. His waistcoat buttons were the most frustrating. Because he had grown so thin, he pulled the coat over his head, not caring if a button or two were lost in the effort. Last was the long shirt that stuck to his torso like a second skin. He peeled it off over his head, wincing as it rubbed against his bandage.

He wasn't particular as he grabbed clothes from the wooden chest. Anything dry would do.

When he finally donned the colonial clothing—unfamiliar and uncomfortable—he glanced at Abigail, who was now lacing up stays over a dry gown. She appeared to be shivering less. "Fare you well?"

"Aye. Better. We must make a fire." She grabbed a woolen shawl from another hook and wrapped it snugly around herself.

After gathering some wood from a corner, Abigail searched the bottom of a nearby box, coming up with a small handful of twigs and leaves. "This will have to do for kindling." She placed it on the empty hearth and looked at William. "Can you light the fire? My hands feel so weak."

"Of course." William reached for his cartridge box and pulled out the steel and flint he stored there. "Do you have some cloth? Perhaps some twine?"

Abigail scurried toward the chest of drawers and located a small wedge of linen cloth. Another drawer held some jute twine that she pulled out, trimmed off a thick strand, and separated the fibers into a nest of sorts. "Here."

He leaned into the hearth over the kindling and wood. Taking the cloth, he held it next to his flint and struck it on the curved steel bar. Within a moment, a wisp of smoke told him the linen had sparked. He quickly set it inside the nest of jute and laid it on the leaves. A flame erupted and soon blazed into the warmth they longed for.

Abigail closed her eyes and spread her hands near the flames. "Thank you."

Even with her strands of hair damp and disheveled, she drew his admiration. She was beautiful in both form and spirit.

Abigail opened her eyes and met his gaze. "I could feel you staring at me."

William stroked her hair with one finger. "Do you mind?"

She smiled shyly and stared at the wooden floor. "Only if you think me worthy to be seen."

He reached for her hand. "I wish to see you wet or dry, unkempt or adorned. You are perfect to me anytime."

She grinned. "I pray we have victuals. Perhaps even cider. 'Twas the last hogshead of cider my father ever made." She stood and checked the barrel. A wide smile spread across her face. "It's still here! No one stole it. I feared the troops might take all"—she glanced around her—"yet the room is strangely untouched."

Reaching for a pewter tankard, Abigail filled the cup with a hefty portion of cider and handed it to William.

"You drink first."

"No, I—"

"I insist."

Grasping the large mug, she took a long drink, closed her eyes, and sighed. "Father's best." She handed it to William. "Now you drink. 'Tis my turn to insist."

He took a long draft of the sweet beverage and swallowed. His eyebrows raised as a smile formed on his lips at the taste. He finished the offering and handed it back to her. "Thank you. It's perfect."

She poured another tankard full and shared it with him again. As the soothing brew filled the vacancy in their stomachs, Abigail settled snugly next to him before the warm fire. William drew her closer and stroked the length of her drying hair, occasionally brushing against her supple form. His longing for Abigail grew. He drew her chin upward to look at him. "Abigail, please kiss me."

She smiled but lowered her chin. When she looked back at him, she said, "William, I want nothing more than to feel your embrace. But we're here alone. I don't think we can begin to feel the pleasure of a kiss without it turning into more."

This wasn't news he wanted to hear. "Abigail, I wish to marry you."

"Yes, but there is no one here to do this. I want you as well, but you still need to recover." She gasped and leaned back to fully face him. "Your dressing! I must change it! We cannot risk infection setting in."

She pushed herself up and hurried toward another cabinet, then stopped abruptly. "Father's medicinals. They're all gone." She slumped into a chair, rested her face in her hands, and shook her head slowly.

William forced himself to stand and walked toward the cupboard. "I once knew an apothecary. He was always concerned someone might take his medicinals, so he always kept a stash hidden somewhere. Is there a secret place your father may have hidden them?"

Abigail lifted her head and seemed to contemplate the question, then rose from the chair. Reaching her father's bed, she removed the mattress and inspected the boards underneath with her hands. Her eyes widened. "I think this board is loose."

William approached and helped her lift the edges of the concealed compartment. Popping it off, they beamed at the sight.

"More medicinals!" Abigail's joy was contagious as they pulled out several small jars of labeled herbs, most of her father's favorites.

She sank to the floor and exhaled with relief. Looking upward she closed her eyes. "Thank you, Father." Opening them again, she gave William a grateful look. "And thank you, William. For so many things."

"No. I have you to thank for so many things." He leaned toward her and pecked her cheek. He would have preferred kissing her lips, but she'd already expressed her fears. And he knew she was right. Between the cider, the warm fire, and her embrace, he doubted he would stop at a mere kiss.

Dear God, please send someone to marry us. And soon.

"Let me change that dressing."

He stood and removed her father's waistcoat and shirt then sat on a chair so Abigail could remove the bandage wrapped around his torso. He tried not to moan, but the rain had sealed the linen against the laceration.

"Dear William, please forgive me." She cringed as she pulled the linen free.

He reached for her hand even as he gasped from the pain. "There's nothing to forgive. You're doing what you must."

She covered the wound with her medicinals and quickly applied a dry dressing. "There. All done."

He was suddenly overcome by weakness. "I need to rest, Abigail."

"Aye, please lay on Father's bed."

She guided him to the mattress, and he collapsed into the softness. He couldn't remember the last time he'd slept on a feather-filled bed. It was a comfort he remembered from his dwelling in England. As he closed his eyes, he prayed that—at last—he had truly found his way home with the woman he loved.

Chapter 24

"William. William."

He felt a tender kiss on his cheek. Opening his eyes, William found Abigail standing over him, smiling.

"I'm going out to the garden to look for vegetables. There might be a few left that we can use."

He pushed up on one arm and looked toward the window, where early morning light streaked through the panes. "It stopped raining." His voice sounded groggy, and his throat was parched.

"Aye. The downpour finally ceased. 'Tis cold enough, but no storm to make us miserable." Abigail threw another log on the fire and stirred it with a long stick.

She had wound her long hair into a knot and covered it with a mobcap. Her clothing was simple, but when she smiled at him, she looked as beautiful as any royalty. Perhaps more so. He couldn't imagine being more in love.

"Take a weapon with you, Abigail."

"Nay, I shall be just a moment." She closed the wooden door with difficulty as she exited. It must have still been swollen.

He lay there for a moment, contemplating these last weeks. His entire life had changed so much, he could barely fathom it. Had he thought a few months past that he would fall in love and then desert the King's Army, he would have questioned his own sanity. Now, his choices seemed clear—and so very right.

There was so much about the military campaign that had troubled him. Every time he had pondered outrage over a situation, he had swallowed back his disdain and said nothing. He was always the obedient soldier.

Yet the situation with Baggley had undone his complacency. The man should have been disciplined for his cruel ways long ago, yet others had sought to appease those who didn't wish to offend his highly influential family.

And then there was the adulterous atmosphere condoned by those in charge. William could never understand why an officer would allow General Burgoyne to dally with his wife. William would rather be drawn and quartered than allow Abigail to be touched by another. Should not a man have a right to protect the one he loved?

William tried to shake away these thoughts and dwell on the peace he had just now found. He prayed it would remain so.

As he sat up in bed, every sinew and bone in his body ached, reminding him how much it had endured these last months. He craved time to heal nearly as much as he craved time with Abigail, who seemed to bring health to his spirit. He smiled at the thought.

He stood and walked toward the hogshead of cider to drink a long, steady draft. While lifting the tankard high and draining the liquid, his eye caught movement in a field nearby.

"Abigail!" William hurried toward his firelock and put the strap of his cartridge box over his shoulder. He checked to make sure the weapon was loaded with one shot, then threw the door open and ran as fast as his legs could carry him. As he got closer, the hair on the back of his neck stood.

Abigail's uncle had returned and struck her to the ground. She was pleading with him to leave her alone.

As William's heart pounded, his neck throbbed. He aimed his weapon at her uncle and yelled, "Abigail, move away!"

Uncle Richard turned to look and pulled Abigail from the ground. He held her in front of himself.

William lowered his firelock, gripping the barrel with whitened knuckles. With gritted teeth, he said, "Always the brave man, hiding behind a woman."

He continued walking slowly toward the man, keeping his eyes fixed on Richard's face. A glint of steel shone in the early morning sun as her uncle pulled a knife with one hand while holding Abigail with the other. William couldn't look at her for fear of being distracted from his goal—to kill Richard Cawthorne once and for all.

"You cannot have my niece. I'll not allow it."

"And I'll not allow you to hurt her. Ever again."

Abigail pushed away from her uncle, but he grabbed the hem of her gown just as William held up his weapon and fired. The man dropped while still holding onto the lower rim of her dress.

She screamed and tore her garment out of his weakening grasp.

William ran to Abigail and wrapped his arm around her, all the while keeping an eye on the man on the ground. Richard Cawthorne stared at the sky and drew his last breath before William turned his full attention to Abigail. His heart raced as he held her closely. She'd buried her face in his chest and continued sobbing.

"He's gone now. He'll never hurt you again."

William guided her as she stumbled toward the cabin. He took her around to the front door, where she could no longer view her uncle's body.

She continued to wail and would have collapsed onto the ground had he not held her up.

He lifted her chin with his finger until she looked into his eyes. Tears streamed down her pale cheeks. "Abigail, listen. He's gone. It's over."

She shook her head. "When will they stop? When will the evil stop?" Deep sobs escaped from her throat.

"God has seen us this far. He's spared us from so much. And now He's spared us from this evil. Please, Abigail." William drew her closer, and she rested her head on his chest. "Please, be strong. I cannot do this without you. I need you. I need your love. I want to start a new life with you and make little ones with you. I want all our little ones to look just like you. I want to love you 'til I die."

As he held her, the trembling subsided as the sobs faded. After what seemed an eternity to him, she lifted her tear-stained face. "No."

William looked down into her eyes while his soul sank in despair. "No?"

Abigail reached up and tenderly stroked his cheek. "I want all our little ones to look like you."

A laugh erupted through William's anguish. He kissed her tenderly at first, then deeply and with a passion he'd never felt before. Not even with Priscilla. He had loved his first wife, but his heart beat as one with Abigail.

In the midst of fervor that threatened to draw them to their knees, a voice in the distance interrupted their ardor.

"Ho! Miss Gillingham! Ye have returned. Praise our Father in heaven!"

William turned toward an older gentleman, followed by a man perhaps forty years old.

Abigail's face turned red. "Reverend Worth! I am so grateful to see you."

The parson eyed William. "Well, I can see ye were not expectin' me. Is all well with ye?"

Abigail's eyes narrowed and her mouth firmed. "Reverend, my uncle lies in the south field, dead."

"Richard Cawthorne?"

"Aye, Reverend. He sought to beat me again after I left the enemy camp. He forced me to go there some weeks ago."

"I wondered where ye'd gone, Miss, and I feared for thy safety. Praise be, ye have returned to us. We prayed for thee every day."

"Thank you, Reverend."

He looked at William. "And who be this?"

"This is William Carpenter. He rescued me from my uncle—and so much more."

The reverend's eyes smiled, although he refrained from grinning. "And Mr. Carpenter, where be your kin from?"

William swallowed but stood resolutely. "They hail from England, sir." He took a deep breath. "I'm a deserter from King

George's army. I've no intent to return, and I'll remain loyal to the American cause."

Silence ensued. After what seemed a lengthy pause, the reverend answered with a nod. "Good." He looked at Abigail. "From what I viewed from a distance, it seems ye may have intentions to become man and wife. Is this so?"

"Aye!" Abigail had answered so enthusiastically, her face turned red and she looked at the ground.

The reverend smothered another grin as he turned his attention to William. "And do ye, Mr. Carpenter, plan on being faithful and true to Miss Gillingham, daughter of my dearest friend? Because, although I am a reverend, I'm quite accurate with a firelock myself. Should ye endanger her in any way or not see to her needs, I will personally visit this cabin and have a discussion with thee about Matthew 19:12."

William narrowed his eyebrows. "Matthew 19:12?"

The reverend grinned. "Look it up, young man."

Abigail placed her arm on the reverend's. "How did you know to come, Reverend Worth?"

"My friend and I were hunting. We heard the gunfire then saw the smoke from thy chimney." He placed his hand over hers and patted it in a paternal manner. "Praise be. Ye have come home."

He turned to walk toward the cabin door. "We have hunting to do. But first, let's get inside where it's warm so I can declare ye husband and wife."

The man who'd arrived with the reverend said, "Whilst you do that, I'm dragging that Tory body to the river. No sense stinking up the farm with 'im." The man never removed his pipe as he walked around the cabin to find the corpse.

* * *

Abigail had been so distraught earlier that William insisted on going back to the field with her to gather root vegetables. They located a few onions, turnips, and sweet potatoes.

Now she squatted near the hearth, stirring the kettle and adding some salt pork she'd found in the barrel in the barn. Foragers had taken all of the animals, but Reverend Worth promised to send over some chickens and, come spring, new piglets.

William double-checked the lock on the door, and she sensed his eyes upon her. "Are you not tired, Abigail?"

"Aye, I'll go to bed as soon as we've had some soup."

She ladled out a generous portion for each of them, yet she wondered if she could eat. She was strangely nervous, especially when her new husband kept staring at her.

"Why do you not look at your food instead of me?" Sweat rolled down her neck, though why she was so warm, she couldn't fathom. She wiped it with her apron.

He grinned at her. "Because I would much rather stare at my wife."

She focused on her bowl and wouldn't meet his eye. He ate with a ravenous appetite while she picked at her food. After what seemed to be the longest meal of her life, Abigail rose from her chair and nearly tripped on a nearby stool.

"Careful." His look of concern warmed her heart but made her more nervous yet. He stood and carried the empty bowls to the basin.

"I'll wash them, William. You can rest. You still need to heal."

He didn't say anything as he lay on the bed that had belonged to her father.

After cleaning everything more than once, she undid her hair and brushed it out. She combed through the strands far more times than necessary before turning her back to her new husband and removing her outer gown. Untying her stays with nervous fingers, she slowly removed the corset and inhaled deeply. She grabbed her shawl and wrapped it around her shoulders, covering her sheer shift, and stood still for a moment. *Surely he is not well enough for me to share our marriage bed? Of course he isn't.*

She blew out her candle and started to climb into her own bed when he asked, "Will you not lie with me?" His voice was so filled with love and passion that she paused before pulling the quilt over her.

"Are you well enough?"

He grinned in the moonlight. "I shall be far better if you lie with me."

She got up from her bed and let her shawl drop to the floor, knowing her thin chemise revealed her form in the firelight.

William opened up the blankets on his bed.

When she crawled in beside him, all anxiety melted away in the comfort and exhilaration of his embrace.

Chapter 25

One Year Later

Abigail carried a basketful of vegetables from the garden toward the front door of their cabin. A figure carrying a musket headed up the path toward their door. She stopped on the porch and watched him approach. He didn't seem menacing, just purposeful in his stride. "Ho there. Who goes?" Abigail shielded her eyes from the late afternoon sun.

A man grinned with white teeth amidst a sunburned face. "Abigail! 'Tis I, your Samuel!"

Abigail scowled. Putting the basket on the ground, she put her hands on both hips. "And why are you calling yourself 'my' Samuel, Mr. Garrick? You've no claim on me, nor my home."

He slowed his pace and frowned at her. "You must be mistaken, Abigail. Remember? Your father promised me your hand …" He looked around, seemingly more taken with the cabin and land than with the woman who stood in front of him. "… and this home."

"Well, perhaps you did not hear that my father died over a year ago. This home belongs to me. Now it belongs to my husband."

Eyes narrowing with anger, Samuel stood his ground. "I've been a loyal Patriot, escorting Johnny Burgoyne's pathetic soldiers to prison camp and nursemaidin' 'em for a year. I didn't go through all that expecting you to go back on yer father's word. This farm, by rights, belongs to me."

She twisted her closed mouth in disgust. "'Twould be a far more gracious thing if you'd said that I'd been the one you missed instead of my land."

He sputtered, "Well, of course I missed you, Abigail. Who wouldn't miss such a lovely lass as yerself?" He approached her far too close as William came round the corner.

"I'll caution you to stand clear of my wife."

Samuel scrunched his face in disgust. "Your wife? She was promised to me." Redness even brighter than his sunburn radiated from the man's face as his fists gripped his firelock.

William held up a pistol and cocked the hammer. "I said, stand clear."

An infant's cry broke the silence.

Samuel moved back a step.

"Excuse me, Mr. Garrick. I must attend our child." Abigail turned and ran into the cabin.

* * *

The men stared at each other for what seemed an eternity before Samuel lowered his firelock. "I wouldn't want a tainted consort." He spat on the ground and spun on his heels.

William watched him leave. When he was certain Samuel wasn't returning, he picked up the basket of vegetables and carried it inside, closing the door with his foot. He set the overflowing basket on the table board and walked over to Abigail, who sat in a rocking chair and nursed their son. He leaned over and kissed his wife. "And how is Joshua doing?"

She grinned. "He eats almost as much as his father." Abigail's face sobered. "I only wish his namesake were here to meet his grandson."

"You've been a faithful daughter."

She looked up. "Thank you, William, for agreeing to use his name."

He walked over to the table board. "I see you've been writing letters to our son again."

"Aye. You're welcome to read them. I want him to know how we met—and how much I love his father."

Joshua had fallen asleep again.

William hurried over and, with the gentleness of a nursery maid, took his son from Abigail and laid him in the cradle. Although the infant rested, his lips suckled the air as though they remained attached to his source of nourishment. William smiled at his son and then watched his wife cover herself. "You needn't get fully dressed, you know."

She looked at him curiously, then smirked. "I know that look. But 'tis still daylight, and I've work to do."

He grinned at her like a naughty schoolboy. "Ah, but I have work to do as well."

"Is that so?" She shivered when he kissed her neck.

"That is so." He kept his voice low while undoing her stays. "You see, Joshua has brown hair like me. And I told you I wanted a child who looks like you. If we are to do that, we must work at it." He laughed as he drew her to their bed.

"William, you are fevered as if it were spring."

He caressed her and thrilled that she didn't resist him. He kissed her neck again. "When you are in my bed, it's always spring."

Part 2

Saratoga Letters 1977

Chapter 1

Redlands, California, September 1977

Abby Carpenter rolled over in bed. The early autumn sun, dimmed by thick smog, made a brave attempt to filter through her yellow sheers.

Another beautiful day in the neighborhood.

Her wry humor melded into sadness as her eyes rested on the framed photo on her dresser. "I still miss you, Daddy."

She squelched the deep-seated grief as she flung off the top sheet. Sitting on the edge of her too-soft mattress, Abby sank into its ancient fibers. *How old is this thing, anyway?* She was too tired to consider whether or not the bed qualified for antique status.

Tripping over her sandals, she headed for the bathroom but was interrupted by her ringing phone. She moved a few items on her bedside table and reached for the receiver.

"Hello?"

A laugh. "You sound great. Did I wake you?"

"Thanks." She rolled her eyes. "How do you sound first thing in the morning, Scott? And no, you didn't wake me."

"Good. Have you decided if you're going to Saratoga with me? You need to make your reservation if you are."

Abby was silent for a moment. "I don't know. I know it's a big deal and all, but I'd have to use all my vacation time at work."

This would be a difficult journey for both of them, as they'd planned to go with their father. Before a land mine got him in the jungle, that is.

"Abby, it's for Dad." Scott's voice sounded a bit garbled with emotion.

"I know." She bit her lower lip.

"You know how much he was looking forward to the anniversary reenactment." She heard a sharp sniff on the other end of the line. Then he inhaled deeply. "I remember making fun of Dad's obsession with family history. I thought he was such a geek." He chuckled. "I guess I'm carrying on the geekiness in his place."

She smiled as she tried to straighten her bedcovers with one hand. "Yeah. But it's a good geekiness."

"So, whaddya say? Are you in?"

Did she really have an excuse? It was for Daddy, after all. She spun the twisted phone cord around her fingers a few times and sighed.

"Okay, Scott. I'm in."

What was she doing?

"Great! Let me give you my flight info. Hopefully, there are still seats on the same jet." He paused. "Abby, you won't regret this. And if Dad can see us from heaven, he'll be smiling down on us."

Her eyes welled. "Yeah. I guess we geeks need to stick together. For the family's sake."

After fumbling through envelopes on her desk, she found a phone bill and scribbled her older brother's flight information on the back.

Hearing the excitement in Scott's voice almost made her enthusiastic about the trip. Almost. The truth was, she feared the trip would make her miss her dad even more—as if that were possible.

Although it had been eight years, she would never forget the knock on the door that day. When she opened it, two men dressed in formal United States Army uniforms stared at her with grim faces. Abby couldn't even remember what they said. She just covered her mouth as her mom came to the door and bravely stood there, listening to the soldiers, nodding her head in apparent understanding.

The men offered to sit with them for a few minutes, but Mom said, "Oh no, we'll be fine." She closed the door and stared at fifteen-year-old Abby and seventeen-year-old Scott. Her mother clasped and unclasped her hands as she calmly explained to her teenagers that their dad had been caught in an ambush in Vietnam. He was killed. His body would come back to them for burial. After stating these facts, their mom had swung around and marched toward her bedroom that she used to share with her husband.

It wasn't until the door was closed that Abby heard her cries of bereavement.

Even today, she shuddered whenever there was a sharp knock at the door.

Pushing the memory to the back of her thoughts, she forced her legs toward the bathroom. A shower would wash the tears from her face. Besides, she needed to get to work. And she had an airplane reservation to make.

* * *

"So you're going? I'm so proud of you!" Abby's friend, Maureen, had recently moved to Southern California from Massachusetts. Giving Abby a quick hug, the unit clerk at Redlands Community Hospital squeezed her friend's arms. "You won't regret this!"

Abby couldn't squelch a smile—not just because of Maureen's enthusiasm, but because of her thick Boston accent too. "You're" became "Yaw." "Not" morphed into "Nawwt." Abby always smiled when Maureen told folks she was from "Summaville, Mass."

"I hope you're right." Abby adjusted her white nurse's cap. "Is this thing on straight? I hate this. It makes me feel like Florence Nightingale."

Maureen stepped on her tiptoes to see the cap's situation on Abby's red hair, which was pulled back into a braid. "Perfect. And Florence should have been so beautiful."

"Right." She rolled her eyes. "Maybe someday we won't have to wear white. It's not exactly practical for nurses who drink gallons of coffee." She grabbed her Styrofoam cup full of the steaming brew. She took a sip while reading her list of assigned patients and balked at the coffee's heat—promptly spilling some on her clean, white uniform.

Groaning, she grabbed a paper towel from a dispenser on the wall. "See." She dabbed the stain with the towel, hoping it would get rid of the evidence. Nothing would hide the fact that she could be a bit klutzy. At least with her pediatric patients, her hands were steady and sure.

She placed her stethoscope around her neck and prepared to visit her first patient, who had his tonsils out the day before.

When she entered the room, five-year-old Chad looked at her with sad eyes. His voice trembled. "When can I go home? I miss Scooter."

"Scooter? Who's Scooter, Chad?" She squeezed the boy's arm then loosened it as she felt the pulse in his wrist. She would count his heart rate through the stethoscope, but she always liked to feel a strong radial pulse, as well.

"Scooter's his dog." The boy's mom threw off the blanket that the staff had given her last night. "He's Chad's best buddy."

"Wow, I wish I could have a dog in my apartment." Abby flashed a grin that brought a matching smile from the young patient.

"You need to get a dog," Chad said. His voice was a bit hoarse from yesterday's surgery. "They are your friend, even when kids don't wanna play with you."

She set her expression to neutral, but her heart ached for the boy. "Some kids just don't know what they're missing. I bet most kids would love to play with you."

Chad looked at his intertwined fingers in his lap. "Not really. They make fun of me 'cause I can't keep up."

Abby squeezed his hands, trying not to stare at the boy's lifeless legs. Spina bifida was a cruel condition for a boy wanting to be just like everyone else. "Well, I think you can outrace them with your wheelchair. And when you're older, I'll bet a boy as smart as you could out-spell anyone in the school spelling bee."

Chad grinned. "Do you think so?"

She nodded sharply and put her hands on her hips. "I know so." She smiled. "Now, I need to listen to that drum beat in your chest, okay?"

"Okay."

The boy's mom put her finger to her lips while Abby listened to the steady thump and counted his heartbeats. At an unexpected tug on her arm, she turned to find Maureen standing behind her, her pale face etched with worry.

"Abby, it's the ER. Your brother is down there."

She whipped the stethoscope from her ears and gripped it tightly. "Chad, I'll be back in a minute."

Maureen led the way.

Abby grabbed her arm. "What's wrong with him?"

"Not sure. The nurse in the ER said something about his appendix."

She stopped short on the linoleum. "Oh no." She ran to the nurses' station and searched for the head nurse. "Mrs. Moyer, my brother's in the ER. Can someone cover for me, at least for a few minutes?"

Mrs. Moyer's eyes softened and she looked up at the list of patients on the wallboard. "Peggy and I will divide your four until you can get back. Go see what's up with your brother."

"Thank you!" Abby ran for the stairwell.

Keep calm. Don't fall! She sounded just like Mom ...

Reaching the first floor, she ran toward the swinging doors leading to the ER. They were mercifully not busy this morning, so finding Scott took less than a minute.

She had to wait a moment while the doctor examined him behind a curtain. Abby winced as her strong brother groaned in pain when the doctor apparently pressed on his abdomen. When Scott asked for an emesis basin, she moved away a few feet. Although she was used to hearing vomiting in her profession, Scott's retching made her cringe.

Why, Lord? Why now?

Abby knew how much Scott looked forward to the trip to Saratoga. This wasn't fair!

As she swiped away angry tears, the ER doctor stepped out of the curtained area while a nurse tended her brother.

Dr. Talbot recognized Abby. "It's a classic case of appendicitis. We'll do labs to confirm, but the writing seems to be on the wall."

Her shoulders slumped. "Dr. Talbot, Scott and I planned a trip to New York State for a family—thing—for our dad. It's in less than two weeks. Do you think he'll be able to make it?"

She knew the answer before he spoke.

"Not likely. I know that you're aware of the recovery time for abdominal surgery. And your brother's one sick camper." He patted her arm. "I'm really sorry."

If it were possible, her shoulders slumped even farther. Forcing herself to stand tall and take a deep breath, she strode toward the curtained area.

"Knock, knock. Can I come in?" She plastered a practiced smile on her nurse face.

Scott could only groan as the ER nurse handed him a tissue to blot his mouth. She smiled with sympathy at her as she left them alone.

"Abby, I'm so sorry." Scott hugged the right side of his stomach and groaned. "I wasn't feeling so great when I called you and, real quickly, it got bad."

Pity encompassed her. "Scott, the only thing that's important right now is that you get well."

"I'm so sorry about the trip." He flinched.

"It's not important. We can go another time. I'll call the airline back and explain. I'm sure they'll give me a refund."

Scott looked at his sister with an earnest plea. "You've got to go."

She shook her head and stared at him. "No. I can't go alone. The only reason I agreed to go was because I'd be with you. I've never been to Saratoga before. No, I can't …"

"You were born there." He gave her a half-teasing, half-pained grin. "You've got to go—for Dad."

"I know I was born there." She sighed. "You know what I mean. It was fine knowing I could count on you for help. Now I'll be all alone. I can't do it—"

"You can't? Or you won't?" He pointed toward the ceiling. "You know He'll be with you. Just like He was when we got the news about Dad."

Hot tears burned Abby's eyelids. Her mouth trembled as she turned toward the oxygen equipment on the wall. She didn't want to look at Scott's face, just like she avoided his glance when the army officers came eight years before.

"Abby, I'm so sorry. But I just know this trip is important. Would you do it for Dad? And me?" He groaned again and twisted on the hard gurney. The sheet laying over him contorted into tight folds.

Gathering her strength, she grabbed his hand and squeezed. "All right. I must be crazy, but I'll do it."

He squeezed back. "Thanks so much."

An orderly came in and pulled the curtains back. "They're ready for you. They'll draw labs in the surgery area when they start your IV. Mr. Carpenter, you didn't have anything to eat today, did you?"

"No." Scott's voice sounded so weak. "I took one look at breakfast and changed my mind."

"Good." The orderly whisked her brother away as Abby yelled after him. "I'll pray for you, Scott." Then both men disappeared through the swinging doors.

As silence enveloped the ER, the enormity of her promise to her brother suddenly hit Abby. She'd be bearing this difficult journey all on her own.

What had she agreed to?

Chapter 2

Crowds of angry men swarmed at the line of police officers. Voices screamed in anger, and at first, only fists flew. Then broken bottles were flung, and someone drew a knife that glistened in the daylight.

"No!" Ian Thacker jerked upward but was held fast by a seatbelt. "What …?"

"Mr. Thacker? Mr. Thacker." A flight attendant with a soothing voice was tapping his shoulder. "Are you all right? You seem to be having an unsettling dream."

Realization slowly materialized. After an overseas flight to New York City from London, he was now onboard a jet headed for Albany, New York. His face grew warm with embarrassment. "Sorry." He looked around.

A little girl in the seat two rows ahead watched him with furrowed brows. She turned to her mum and asked, "What's wrong with that man?"

He gripped the armrests with trembling fingers.

What's wrong with me, indeed? When would the dreams stop?

He practiced the steady breathing he'd been taught at the hospital in London. Breathe in slowly through your nose. Exhale through your mouth.

He sounded like Anne during labor.

His sister, Anne, had called him at the police station where he worked. "I can't find Simon, and my water's broke, Ian. Can you drive me to the birthing center in your car—maybe use your siren?"

Good—a diversion in his thoughts. That's what would help stop the memories of the riot. The doctor said so.

Ian focused on the memory of his sister's labor. It was a good thing he took her in his police car that day. She was no sooner in the hospital door then ready to deliver his nephew. He'd never seen an infant birthed before. For the first time on this long journey to Saratoga, Ian smiled as he thought of the look on his sister's face when they handed her the boy. It was pure beauty in a world of such ugliness.

Ian felt inside his tweed jacket. He breathed a sigh of relief—the letter was still there.

Have to read it later. At least he'd remembered to bring it.

An announcement overhead told the passengers they would soon be landing in Albany. Ian gazed out the window from his aisle seat. As the plane veered at an angle, his breath caught at the sight of forests of crimson and gold leaves that carpeted the view. It was unlike any scenery he'd ever beheld—and it was splendid.

* * *

Walking toward the sign that said "rental cars," Ian stopped at a trash can long enough to drop in the paper on which the stewardess had written her phone number. He'd thought she'd been quite attentive to him on that flight. He'd never asked her for it and was surprised at her boldness.

Colonists. Ian smirked, thinking how often his father used to say that when referencing Americans. It was a bittersweet memory.

Dad should have been here for this ceremony.

Shaking off the thought, Ian focused on the car rental desk and then noticed a more-than-attractive redhead in animated conversation with the receptionist. It was impossible to ignore her distress.

"Please. I promise the card is good. I need to rent a car to get to Saratoga. Your ads say you'll put me in the driver's seat!"

"Miss Carpenter, I know your card is good, but the credit limit will not accommodate such a long rental. I'm sorry." The desk clerk tilted her head and patted the customer's arm.

Auburn hair covered the woman's face as she slumped onto her outstretched arms atop the counter.

Ian stepped forward and pulled out his wallet. "Excuse me. I could not help but overhear. May I be of assistance?"

The brunette at the counter grinned with obvious delight. "Well, you're not from around here. What is that accent?" She batted her eyes.

The red-haired woman turned sideways to look at him through strands of messy hair then stood up. She tipped her head as she stared at the brunette. "Don't you watch *Masterpiece Theater*? He's from England." She exhaled loudly.

Ian smothered a smile. "Correct, Miss …?"

"Carpenter." She gave no first name. Her bottom lip quivered. "If Scott had come, I wouldn't be having this trouble. I forgot to ask him for his credit card." Tears rolled unhindered.

171

Ian cleared his throat. "Your husband couldn't come?"

"My husband? No, Scott's my brother. He was supposed to come but he got appendicitis." Miss Carpenter fumbled through her purse and pulled out a tissue. She blew her reddened nose, then pulled out a mirror to check her makeup, which streaked in black rivers down her cheeks.

She groaned and threw her hand up in the air. "I knew I shouldn't have come. I might as well walk home—all 3,000 miles—to California."

Ian put his hand on her shoulder. "Miss Carpenter, I think I have a more practical solution. Perhaps it would help us both."

She stared at him through eyes smudged with makeup. "Help us both?" She paused. "I'm going to Saratoga."

He grinned. "Excellent. That's my destination, as well."

A woman's voice from behind them startled Ian. "That's where we're going too! We're going for the two-hundredth anniversary of the battle!"

"Me too." Miss Carpenter had stopped crying and seemed calmer.

Ian continued. "Well, here is my offer. You see, I've been somewhat concerned about driving in America, since you Colonists seem to prefer the wrong side of the road."

Miss Carpenter narrowed her eyes. "Colonists? Wrong side of the road? Perhaps you redcoats do not recall who won that war?"

Ian stiffened. "We 'Redcoats' recall it quite well." He smothered his irritation. "Miss Carpenter, I'm willing to put a rental car on my credit card if you would agree to drive. What do you say?"

Miss Carpenter squinted. "How do I know you're not some psycho maniac?"

Ian whipped out his warrant card. "I'm a constable from London, Miss. And I assure you, I am not a maniac of any sort."

She took his identification and scrutinized it. "Ian Thacker."

She stared for such a long time that Ian grew impatient. "Are you satisfied, Miss Carpenter? You are not a psycho maniac yourself, are you?"

Her mouth opened and she glared at him. "I should say not. I'm a pediatric registered nurse, for your information." She stared at his ID again.

The woman behind them spoke again. "Oh, go ahead, honey. He's a good guy. I know these things." She winked at Miss Carpenter. "Besides, my husband and I will drive right behind you to make sure he doesn't try any funny stuff. A girl with your looks needs to be careful."

The woman turned toward her middle-aged husband, who was studying a New York State map. "Harry, we're going to follow this young couple all the way to Saratoga. Won't it be exciting? It'll be like a convoy. We'll be like Burt and Sally in *Smokey and the Bandit*."

Miss Carpenter covered her mouth and laughed. Even with the smudged makeup, her smile stole Ian's breath. Recovering, Ian stood taller.

"Very well then. Is this agreement satisfactory to you, Miss Carpenter?"

There was that smile again, shrouded in hair the color of the autumn leaves he'd seen as his flight landed. "Yes, Mr. Thacker. It's quite satisfactory to me." She held out her hand.

Without thinking, Ian took it and kissed her sweetly scented fingers. His face flushed with warmth as she laughed. Clearly, he had misunderstood her intent.

"I'm sorry. I suppose you meant to shake in agreement." He grabbed her hand and shook it hard.

"Well, yes. But the kiss was quite gallant."

Embarrassed, he quickly placed his ID in his wallet and handed the credit card to the receptionist.

The woman behind the counter giggled. "Quite gallant, indeed."

The red-haired beauty spoke up. "My name is Abby, by the way. You don't need to keep calling me Miss Carpenter."

Ian dared glance her way once again, despite his discomfort. "Please, call me Ian."

"I will. Before we get into the rental, I need to visit the ladies' room."

"Certainly."

Grinning, she spun on her heels and walked down the terminal. He watched her stride gracefully in the high wedge sandals that made her seem taller than she likely was. Her blue dress was not as short as some he'd seen, but it showed enough of her slender legs to keep him watching until she slipped into the door of the women's room.

The receptionist's voice brought his attention back to the matter at hand.

"Good thing she's driving." The receptionist smirked.

"Why's that?" He scribbled his signature on the rental agreement.

"The way you looked at her just now, you might get in an accident if you were behind that wheel." She dangled the car keys in front of him.

Ian tried to respond but words escaped him. He never was one to hide his feelings. He grasped the keys and slid them free from her fingers. "Thanks for the car."

Turning to the woman in line, he said, "I'll wait for you."

She giggled and whispered loudly, "That redhead is prettier than Sally Field, don'tcha think?" She snickered again.

Ian's cheeks warmed. "Yes."

She was prettier than anyone he'd met before. Perhaps it's a good thing they'd be in that convoy.

Chapter 3

Was she crazy? Getting into a car with a stranger? Abby attempted to insert the key in the ignition, but her fumbling fingers kept missing the right spot.

"Do you need some help?" The constable's gaze was annoying right now. Why did he have to be so disarmingly attractive?

I must look a mess.

Abby would have redone her makeup completely, but her cosmetic bag was buried too far in her suitcase. She glanced at herself in the rearview mirror and silently groaned at the lack of mascara and the haphazard eye shadow. What was left of it, anyway.

She jammed the key even harder. It still didn't find the keyhole.

"Let me help." Ian's hand covered hers and adjusted the position of her fingers to a slight angle. The key slid in, and the engine turned over.

Abby gave a sheepish grin. "Thanks. I'm not usually this inept with cars." She glanced at the map he held. "I'm glad you're navigating. Not exactly my strength." She looked in the rearview mirror as Harry and his wife, Beatrice, pulled up and parked behind them. She smiled and waved at them. Turning toward her passenger, she inhaled sharply. "Okay, navigator. Give me directions." She drew her aviator sunglasses out of her purse and perched them on her nose.

The British police officer studied the map given them by the rental car receptionist. She'd drawn a line from the airport terminal to the freeway entrance. He looked up and pointed. "It says to go left up here and then right. I'll get us there. With your capable driving, of course."

"Of course." She batted her lashes a few times then turned her focus back to the road. Abby checked her rearview mirror again, swallowed back her nervousness, and pulled out when it was clear.

Keep your eyes on the road, Abby. Don't let his smile get to you.

Driving an unfamiliar car always made her uncomfortable. Sharing it with a complete stranger made her antiperspirant work overtime.

If only Scott had come.

Once they were on the main highway toward Saratoga, Abby relaxed slightly. It was so different from the freeways in Southern California. She was used to multiple lanes of traffic and cars so close they made you clutch the steering wheel to keep away from them. This two-lane highway was like a drive in the country by comparison.

Once they were north of Albany, the scenery improved even more. Tree-covered rolling hills cradled the road with an astonishing view of autumn colors. She struggled to keep her eyes on the road.

Glancing at Ian, she noticed he took in the same view.

"This is incredible." There was a wistful tone in his voice.

"I couldn't agree more. There's nothing like this where I live."

"Nor I."

They drove in silence for several more minutes before Ian turned toward her. "Sorry for being so uncivil."

She shook her head. "You're not uncivil."

He turned to look out the passenger window again. "I'm so amazed at the forests here."

"They are remarkable." She glanced at the scenery for a brief moment then concentrated on the road. "Almost makes me wish we'd stayed and I'd grown up here."

He turned to look at her again. "Grown up here?"

"Yeah. I was actually born in Saratoga. My mom often tells the story of when she went into labor. My parents almost made it to the hospital, but I guess I was in too much of a hurry. My dad had to pull over and deliver me in the car."

Ian chuckled. "That must have been terrifying for your poor father."

"It was, but fortunately, he'd learned some medical skills in the Army. Besides, my mom told me every year—on my birthday—that Dad was so excited I had red hair, he almost forgot to hurry Mom to the hospital afterward."

"Why was a child with red hair so important to your father?"

"Well, there was an old family story that each generation waited for the return of the red hair. Apparently my great-great-great-great-grandmother had 'hair the color of autumn leaves,' and he wanted to have a child with the same. For generations, there were brunettes and blondes. But no redheads. Until I came along."

Ian was quiet until she looked at him. His smile seemed wistful. "That's a charming story. It almost sounds like a fairy tale."

Abby grew sober. "I suppose it might be, except it didn't have a happily ever after. The prince was killed some years later, in the war."

Silence.

"Your father? Where was he killed?"

"Vietnam. Eight years ago." She readjusted her grip on the steering wheel.

"I'm terribly sorry."

For a while, the only sounds she heard were the wheels churning on the highway. She clicked on the radio in an effort to replace the sorrow spinning in her thoughts. James Taylor's "Handy Man" filtered through the car.

Ian spoke. "So what brings you to Saratoga?"

Abby shifted beneath her seatbelt. "The two-hundredth anniversary of the battle during the American Revolution. And you?"

"Same." He paused. "Forgive me saying this, but you don't seem like your typical historian bent on reliving a 200-year-old war."

"Oh? I'm not certain what a 'typical' history buff is supposed to be. But you're right. I'm here to honor my dad. He was so into family history that every September he'd do the countdown toward the upcoming anniversary. Scott and I used to make fun of him. But now, I'd give anything to hear him talk about our great-great-great-great-grandparents again. I'd give anything to have him here, sharing this with me."

Her eyes filled with tears that threatened to remove the remainder of her makeup. She swiped them away and turned the radio louder. By now, they were so far from the city that all they got was static.

Ian turned off the annoying sound. "I'm so sorry, Abby. I'm certain this is difficult for you."

She readjusted her sunglasses. She had to think of something else—and fast. "So, why is this reenactment important to you? You flew across the ocean for it."

He frowned. "I'm here for my father as well. He was also into genealogy. Our family sets great store by our ancestor, who was wounded in the War for Independence. He is our family hero."

Abby glanced at him. "But … your dad couldn't come either?"

"No. He was in the Army as well. He was killed in '71."

"In Vietnam?"

"No. Belfast."

Abby could tell the conversation was over. She knew there were moments when reliving the past was just too painful.

This was obviously one of them.

*　*　*

Ian hadn't spoken for several moments when he realized his silence might be taken as rudeness. He turned away from the side window and glanced toward his chauffeur. He cleared his throat. "So, where are you staying in Saratoga?"

"It's actually Saratoga Springs. That's where most of the motels are. There's a small one called The Gates. That's where I made my reservation."

Ian knew he'd forgotten something. He fidgeted. "I forgot to make reservations. I hope they have room at the inn."

Abby flashed a grin. "The Christmas story. Well, at least you're not arriving with your pregnant wife." Her cheeks turned quite red.

He threw her a teasing glance. "You're not pregnant, are you?"

"No!" She huffed. "First, you ask if I'm a psycho maniac, then you inquire as to whether or not I'm pregnant?"

"Well, you were the first to ask me if *I* was a psycho maniac, if you recall." He folded his arms across his chest.

She looked chagrined. "You're right. But Scott told me to be careful. I was just checking."

"A word to the wise. Such a person would not likely confess to being such. In my profession, I'm acquainted with those who have homicidal tendencies. They can be a smooth-talking lot. Quite charming. You can tell by my rudeness, I'm not qualified."

She laughed. "Well, I'm relieved that you're rude. But just a little. You're really more … forthright."

He huffed. "That's one word for it."

He stole a glance at his driver, daring to linger a moment on her lips that pouted when serious, then blossomed into a rosebud when smiling. As he noted the vacillating moods of Abby Carpenter, he also noticed she enthralled him. Mostly, he was enamored with her overall beauty. And he agreed with her ancestor. Her hair was the same color as the autumn leaves. She was stunning.

Abby looked at him. "Am I still on the right highway?"

He held up the map and followed the route with his finger. "Just a few more kilometers on this I-87, then we exit onto Route 9. I'll watch for the sign."

"Good. Remember, I'm not a great navigator. I might take us all the way to Canada before realizing it."

He couldn't help but laugh. Ian hadn't found it easy to smile these last weeks. Not since the riot, anyway. But it was easy to relax around her.

"So, your distant grandfather fought against my distant grandfather. I suppose that makes us enemies." She grinned. "Or we could let bygones be bygones."

"I don't know." He forced a stern voice. "My father continued calling you 'those Colonists' as long as I could remember." He leaned slightly toward her. "I suppose if he had met you, though, he might have relented his lack of forgiveness toward 'those Rebels.'" He glanced at the map. "Take the next exit."

Suddenly aware of his own heartbeat, he watched her long hair swish across her shoulders while she looked for traffic. "I … I very much appreciate you doing the driving. I truly was concerned about driving in your country."

"Well, I'm the one indebted to you, Constable Thacker." She put on the car blinker to exit the highway. "If you hadn't come along, I'd be walking this entire way, lugging my suitcase." Her voice lowered. "Really. Thank you."

"It was providential for us both." He paused. "Perhaps we're close enough to get a radio channel here. Do you want me to try?"

"Sure! Thanks."

He turned the knob and began searching for a clear station.

"Oh, stop there. I like that song."

The soothing and romantic melody of Elton John's "Your Song" played throughout the car. As the sun began to set, Abby removed her sunglasses.

Once again, Ian attempted not to stare at his driver. But, as the song said, she had the sweetest eyes he'd ever seen.

But as charming as Abby Carpenter was, he wasn't ready for any relationship right now—certainly not one with someone who lived 6,000 miles from London.

Chapter 4

The town of Saratoga Springs was as charming as its name. Ancient homes both grand and cozy lined the streets, and a plethora of inviting storefronts and restaurants beckoned Abby to stop. The warm colors of the buildings were still visible at dusk. As if to celebrate her arrival, strings of illumination glistened, adorning each piece of architecture as if Christmas was just declared. Saratoga Springs was a piece of artwork in and of itself, and Abby found herself enamored with her birthplace.

It was just after dark when she saw the sign for the Gates Motel. Quite a few autos already filled the parking lot. Long rows of motel doors lined the building.

"I hope they have a room for you." She bit her lower lip.

"I was just thinking the same thing." Ian fidgeted in his seat.

Abby pulled into an empty spot on the end and turned off the engine. "Welcome to my birthplace."

"The town suits you." He grinned and exited.

She met his glance on the other side of the car. "I'll take that as a compliment. I think."

"It was." He grabbed their bags out of the trunk. She started to protest, but he dismissed her. "I've got them. Just lead the way to the office."

She walked ahead of him, her feet aching with every step in her wedge sandals. She couldn't wait to get out of these new shoes. "It's a lot colder here than Southern California. Glad I brought some sweaters." Opening the door to the small motel office, she greeted the proprietor. "Hi, I'm Abby … Abigail Carpenter. I have a reservation."

"Welcome, Mrs. Carpenter. I've got a room for you and your husband. Number 20, plenty of fresh towels."

Abby's jaw dropped. "Wait. I'm Miss Carpenter, and the room is just for me. Do you have an extra one for this gentleman?" As she pointed toward Ian, she noticed his hair was a bit disheveled after his long day of travel.

The man behind the counter looked at the reservation book. "No, we're booked solid. Wait … aren't you here with a Scott Carpenter?" He looked at Abby with a confused expression.

Her eyes brightened. "Scott! No, he's my brother. I forgot he had a reservation. He can't come because he had emergency surgery. Can you give his room to Mr. Thacker?" She motioned toward Ian.

"Well, as long as he pays, the room is his." Holding up two keys, the desk clerk declared, "Rooms 20 and 21. One for each."

"Thanks, Mr. …?"

"Cardwell. Jake Cardwell. Happy to have you folks here. Looks like you're both staying 'til October 10? Must be here for the big goins-on."

"That's right." Ian held out his hand to Jake. "Thanks for working me in."

"You got lucky. Now"—he held up the book—"if you'll each sign for your room, I'll be a happy motel owner."

Ian, holding the pen, paused and arched his eyebrows before signing. "So you don't just work here. This is yours?"

"Yep. It's the American way. Even named the place after General Gates." He saluted a picture on the wall of the Revolutionary War victor at Saratoga.

Abby felt a bit self-conscious in front of Ian. "Let … bygones be bygones?" She covered her emerging grin.

"Maybe I'll just call the motel The Burgoyne." He chuckled.

Abby almost burst out laughing at the look of shock on Jake's face. "Perhaps we'd best check into our rooms."

She spun on her wedge heels and waited until she was outside before covering her mouth to squelch the mirth rising in her throat.

Ian grinned so wide she thought his face would break. "That was quite hilarious."

"Don't. If I start laughing now, I won't stop. I'm way too tired to control my amusement."

Dragging their suitcases to the motel room, they each inserted keys into their respective side-by-side rooms.

Abby reached around the corner and flipped on the light switch. The room had two large beds, a dresser with drawers, and a modest desk with two glasses and a plastic bucket for ice. The table between the beds had a black phone and a notepad with a Gates Motel emblem declaring the allegiance of the owner in red, white, and blue print. The furnishings were simple and the room clean. It suited her just fine. All she cared about right now was resting her head on that pillow.

She pulled her luggage onto the bed closest to the door, unlatched it, and pulled out her pajamas. A tentative knock caught her attention.

"I assume you'll be closing this door? And locking it? A woman alone cannot be too careful."

Abby blinked. "You assumed correctly, Constable Thacker."

He rolled his eyes. "I'm quite serious, Abby. You shouldn't leave this door ajar after dark."

Hiding her pajamas back in her suitcase, she strode toward the door. "I know, and I'm grateful for your concern. I mean it, Ian. Thanks again. For everything."

He nodded. "My pleasure. See you in the morning." He shut the door tight, and she heard his voice outside. "Bolt the door, Abby."

She hurried toward the door again and bolted the extra lock. "Got it."

"Good. Goodnight."

"Night, Ian."

She heard his footsteps enter the next room and his own door close. A sharp click told her he'd locked his as well.

She was so exhausted after unpacking her pajamas, she didn't even bother hanging up her clothes in the closet. Instead, she collapsed onto the hard mattress and threw the covers over herself. Relaxation enveloped Abby as she thought of the police officer next door, and she quickly drifted off to sleep.

Chapter 5

The next morning, the motel office swarmed with history buffs, according to their apparel. Abby had never been in the presence of so many people wearing tricorne hats. As she walked toward the office, one fellow shouted "Huzzah" and waved a motel key in the air.

"I lost the first key, my lady." He tipped his hat and bowed in front of Abby.

She stumbled for a reply. "Well then, it's fortunate there is a second one." The man winked as she squeezed past him to enter the overcrowded office. All Abby wanted was to get directions to an eating establishment. Preferably a cheap one.

Mr. Cardwell, the owner, threw his hands into the air. "I'm sure our forefathers never took so many showers!" He directed the cleaning lady on where to take the towels. Then he noticed Abby and rubbed his head slowly. "I'm sorry, Miss Carpenter. What can I do for you?"

"I'm looking for a restaurant. Hopefully one that … doesn't charge too much." She'd been saving for this trip for years, but her income as a nurse was limited.

Another male voice caught her attention. "I can help you there."

She hadn't noticed another gentleman behind the counter. In sharp contrast to the historically dressed group surrounding her, this younger man wore a snugly fitting, zippered, blue jumpsuit. It might have been velveteen. Or velour. Abby never understood the difference. She couldn't help but be transfixed by the way the owner of the trendy one-piece outfit seemed to enjoy the soft feel. He stroked his own arm and thrust out his chest, emphasizing that the zipper was a bit too low.

She cringed at the bed of chest hair encompassing glittery chains. She supposed he wanted to show off that gold medallion. Swallowing back her distaste, she attempted a weak smile.

"Thank you," she said. "What do you suggest—for a restaurant, that is?"

Before answering, Mr. Chest Hair reached out a huge, tanned hand—also coated with dark fur.

"Ambrose Cardwell. Happy to show you around Saratoga Springs."

"Well, at present, I would just like to find a place to have a small breakfast. Nothing fancy."

The motel owner interrupted. "This is my nephew, Miss Carpenter. He's helping out while we're so busy." The older man eyed his nephew. "It'd be nice if he could wield a hammer now and then."

"Well, I'm not too handy with the tools. But I can help register folks. And give them personal tours." Ambrose winked at Abby again.

She drew in a deep breath. "Just a recommendation for breakfast would be nice. I'm quite hungry since I missed dinner last night."

The owner answered before Ambrose could. "There's a nice diner just down Broadway a bit. They'll take good care of you, Miss Carpenter."

Another motel guest approached the owner with what seemed to be a pressing need and engaged him in a lengthy conversation.

Ambrose stared at the registration book. "Abigail Carpenter. You don't have a Gillingham in your ancestry do you?"

"Gillingham?" Abby furrowed her brows. "Not that I know of. But I'd have to ask my brother. He's the family history geek. I mean, historian."

Ambrose laughed with far too much enthusiasm. He pointed a finger at her and gave a pretentious smile. "This event will require a bit of respect for the history lovers, Miss Carpenter. Now, you probably don't want to use that particular word in the next couple of weeks. Not here, anyway." He handed her a flyer. "By the way, they're looking for more reenactors for the festivities. If you go to the lobby of the Frederika Inn up Broadway, they'll set you up with a costume."

Abby glanced at the flyer and tucked it in her purse. "I'll remember that. Thanks for the tip."

He reached for her arm, squeezed it, and lowered his voice. "Are you sure you don't know if your ancestor was Abigail Gillingham? We might have something in common, you and I."

His eyes transformed from friendly to dark. The edge in his voice needled up her back.

She tore her arm away from his grasp. Glaring at his attempt to intimidate her, Abby huffed. "I've no idea." She squeezed past a woman in a long colonial costume and nearly tripped on the stoop as she headed back to her room.

"Watch yourself, Abby." Ian Thacker must have noticed her less-than-graceful descent down the office step.

Warmth flooded her cheeks, especially at the sight of Ian, freshly showered with his hair still damp, smelling deliciously of some unfamiliar men's cologne. His tweed jacket covered a polyester shirt that was unbuttoned slightly at the top.

Thank goodness—no gorilla chest.

"Good morning, Ian." She felt much shorter next to him today, now that she wore comfy flat shoes with her bell-bottomed blue jeans. He must have been at least six feet. He was as tall as Scott. And Dad. "I … I was just asking for a recommendation for a breakfast place. Mr. Cardwell said there's a nice diner down the street."

"I think I'd trust his judgment. May I go with you?"

"Sure." Her heart moved in an erratic rhythm. *Calm down, Abby.*

Ian tucked his hands into his pants pockets. "Show the way. I'm half starved. I missed supper last night, and I imagine you did as well."

They walked toward the diner, following Mr. Cardwell's directions.

When they entered the obviously popular restaurant, Abby inhaled the scent of bacon, pancakes, and coffee. "Oh, wow. I could eat the menu, I'm so hungry."

They sat in a booth, facing each other. When the waitress came and took their order, Abby ordered pancakes, bacon, and eggs.

"Good appetite." Ian seemed amused.

"Breakfast is my favorite meal." She looked around the diner and smiled self-consciously. "So, the motel owner's nephew gave me a flyer." Pulling it out of her denim bag, she handed it to Ian.

His eyes narrowed as he read. "They need reenactors? I guess I just thought I'd watch."

"Me too." She took the paper back from him. "But it might be kinda fun. The flyer says a seamstress from Hollywood will be doing the fittings and creating period clothing for the big event in two weeks."

Ian stared at her. "It might be fun to see you in colonial garb." His serious face broke into a grin.

Abby's jaw dropped. "Me? What about you? You could dress up like your ancestor and be an officer in the militia."

"Regiment. You need to get your terminology correct."

"Oh. Sorry."

"I was just teasing you." He reached across the table, took her hand for just a second, and squeezed it.

She swallowed and withdrew her hand from his, laying it in her lap. "I'm really not the historian in the family. My brother is. Maybe I need to call him and get ... umm ... educated."

The waitress appeared with small carafes of hot water, two cups, and two tea bags.

Ian scowled as he looked at the tea he'd ordered but placed it in the cup without saying a word. He poured the hot water over the bag.

Abby did the same. "Maybe we can go to the Frederika Inn after breakfast and get fitted. Of course, being measured after a huge breakfast might not be the wisest." She chuckled then noticed Ian staring at her hand while she dunked the tea bag up and down in the hot water. "What?"

"You're bruising your tea."

"Excuse me?"

"You're bruising it. You need to let it brew gently. Let the tea leaves open slowly to allow it to bloom into flavor."

Abby narrowed her eyes. "Really? Bruising it? People bruise. Even dogs bruise. But I didn't realize you could injure a cup of black tea. Perhaps I should have brought a first aid kit." Her glare turned into a witty smirk.

"Go ahead. Make fun of our British ways. But mark my words, a true tea connoisseur would never have dumped an entire cargo of tea into a harbor like you Colonials did." His lips curled as he shook his head.

Abby sat up straight. "Well, the Boston Tea Party certainly made its point, didn't it, Constable Thacker?" She nodded with self-satisfaction.

He sipped from his teacup and scrunched his face. "Well, this certainly tastes like it was thrown into a harbor."

Abby covered her mouth to keep from laughing. "I'm sure it's not up to your British standards. Sorry." She looked around. "Maybe someone here knows of a tea shop close by where you can get some 'real' tea."

"That would be appreciated." Ian sipped his tea with a wary look in his eyes.

"Hey, did you know that the site where the Boston Tea Party took place is now land? They filled it in and built on it. My dad took us there when we were little. It was great fun walking on the dirt and imagining we were really squishing tea leaves."

"You must have many fond memories of your dad."

"I do." The food arrived, and Abby was spared from bittersweet memories by the sight of a plate filled with three huge pancakes, bacon, and eggs. "Now this is a breakfast."

Ian stared at the English muffin the waitress had set in front of him. "This is not anything like the muffins in England." He picked up his fork and took a bite of the soft-cooked eggs. "But these are quite delicious."

It wasn't long before they'd devoured their breakfast. Abby sat back, satiated and ready to start her day.

Until Ambrose Cardwell showed up and ruined the moment.

Before Abby or Ian could object, he sat next to her in the booth—far too close—and she slid toward the wall as far as she could. She could still feel his velvet-covered pants warming the denim of her jeans.

Ian placed his elbows on the table, folded his hands in front of his face, and glared at the obnoxious intruder who seemed bent on sharing his business successes with out-of-town guests.

What felt like an hour later, Ambrose noticed a song by the Bee Gees playing overhead, and he got excited. "Hey, Abby, did you see *Saturday Night Fever*? There's a dance club in town I could take you to. We could do a few moves together." There was that annoying wink again.

"I went on a date to see that movie but I left early. I heard the 'F' word a few too many times and walked out." She glanced at Ian, who appeared to be smothering a grin at her reply.

Ambrose frowned. "So you missed the scene in the car? John Travolta and this girl—"

"Excuse me, I need to use the ladies' room." She pushed against Ambrose's legs, forcing him to let her out of the booth. Abby could feel his eyes follow her to the ladies' room.

* * *

Ambrose half-covered his mouth with his hand and spoke in a low tone. "Do you 'spose she's a virgin?" He rubbed his mouth with his hand. "I wouldn't mind jumpin' her."

Ian reached across the table so fast he nearly knocked his teacup over. He grabbed Ambrose by the front of his jumpsuit and twisted the material with all his might. Metal chain dug into his fingers. "Don't mess with her."

Ambrose's nostrils flared as his face flushed. "Who are you to tell me who I can mess with? You probably have your own plans for her. A bit jealous?"

Ian released his vice-like grip. "I said, leave her alone. I'm not dating her, but I'm watching out for her. And you *don't* want to touch her. Understand?"

Ambrose readjusted his collar and straightened his gold medallion. "Well, we'll just have to see who ends up with the lady. I have friends in this town. So don't mess with *me*."

Ian watched the lout saunter out the door while waving at the man behind the diner counter. The constable from London had met far too many predators like that one. But here, in an unfamiliar country, he had no jurisdiction. And the man had friends.

This unexpected situation portended a whole new Battle of Saratoga for Ian. And he felt as inadequate as the British Army, following their surrender to the American rabble in 1777. He suddenly had a whole new appreciation for his great-great-great-great-grandfather who had been wounded 200 years before.

I hope I don't end up on the losing side this time.

Chapter 6

Abby accompanied Ian into the Frederika Inn and gasped as her eyes were drawn upward to the glittering chandelier in the center of the lobby ceiling. "Wow, this is a bit fancier than our motel." She took in the warm golds and browns of the lobby furnishings and tried not to be envious of these more elite accommodations.

Be content, Abby. In all things.

As she continued looking around, she found herself drawn to a painting of a beautiful woman in an exquisite colonial blue dress. Abby immediately noticed the stately looking woman's red hair. Beneath the portrait was inscribed the name "Frederika Charlotte Von Riedesel."

Ian approached and stood close to Abby. "The Baroness has ginger hair, like you."

"Ginger hair?"

"Yes." Ian stared at the painting for several minutes. "She was well-loved by all. She was kind and charming. Shared food with the starving troops when there was little to be had. She was a great lady."

His voice sounded so wistful, jealousy swept through her thoughts. *Quit being ridiculous, Abby. It's a painting.* "She is quite lovely." Though she focused on the portrait again, she could feel Ian staring at her.

Turning toward him, she inhaled deeply. "What are you staring at?"

"More art." He smiled and looked around the lobby. "I see a sign over there for the fittings."

As they approached the open doorways—one marked "Gents" and one designated for "Ladies"—Ian seemed to have a change of heart when a tall, thin man waved him toward the room.

"I don't know, Abby. Maybe I shouldn't …"

"Ian, if I have to go through this, so do you." She reassured him with a pat on his left arm.

He winced.

"I'm sorry. Did I hurt you?"

"No, I'm fine." He hurried toward the tailor awaiting him.

As she watched him go into the fitting room, Abby wondered about his reaction. She didn't think she'd touched him *that* hard.

Her thoughts were interrupted by a familiar voice. "Miss Carpenter! So good to see you again!"

"Hi, Beatrice. Please, call me Abby." She shook the middle-aged woman's hand, which was covered with rings of every sort. Some looked authentic, while some resembled costume jewelry. Abby could always recognize costume jewelry, since that was the bulk of her own collection. The one stone that stood out was the large diamond on Beatrice's ring finger.

Good choice, Harry.

"Are you having a wonderful time so far? Harry and I are so excited to be in this lovely town! I had no idea it was so beautiful." Beatrice had that fun accent reminiscent of New York City folks: "Be-YOU-tea-ful!"

"It is lovely."

Looking around like a spy, Beatrice lowered her voice. "I saw that guy with you. You know, that cute one who picked you up in Albany? That one who talks like that actor, what's-his-name?"

"You mean Constable Thacker." Abby lowered her voice to match Beatrice's conspiratorial tone. "Yes, he's here. He's currently getting fitted for a British uniform. You know, one of the *bad guys*."

Beatrice burst out giggling. "His costume may be villainous, but I wouldn't mind being taken hostage by *that* guy's army."

"Beatrice! I am quite shocked at your admission." She chuckled. "Would that make you a turn-coat?"

"That would make me one happy prisoner, let me tell you." She glanced at Harry, who was deeply involved in reading some tourist guide as he sat down. Beatrice stared at her husband with obvious delight. "Of course, my Harry would rescue me and sweep me into his arms." She raised her voice a few notches. "Wouldn't you, Harry?" When he didn't reply, she stepped nearer and nudged him with her pointed black pump.

"Huh?" Harry stirred from his reading. "Yes. Yes, dear."

Beatrice smiled so widely, Abby thought her thick makeup would crack and fall onto the plush carpet. "See? My Harry. He's my hero." She leaned down and kissed his cheek, leaving red lipstick on his wrinkled skin. "I'd better go to the powder room and refresh my lipstick."

Abby watched Beatrice scurry off, then she sat in the avocado-green chair opposite the small table where Harry sat.

After a moment of silence, she felt someone staring at her. Meeting Harry's eye, Abby smiled politely.

The silent man spoke. "So, youse like that guy in there?" He pointed to the fitting room.

Abby stuttered. "Like him? Uh … I suppose so. What exactly do you mean, 'like?'"

Harry kicked his head back and laughed. "Little lady, that guy's got the hots for you. I'm a guy. I know these things." Beatrice's husband repeated the same shifty-eye maneuver that his wife had earlier. He lowered his voice. "So you wanna know the secret to our happy marriage?"

Abby didn't know whether to laugh or listen closely. She leaned in and whispered, "What's the secret?"

"Cotton."

"Cotton?"

"Cotton." Harry proceeded to remove wads of the fluffy material from both of his ears. "Get cotton for your husband. He'll be happy the rest of your married life." He inserted the wads back into his ears, sat back in his chair, and resumed reading.

Abby was now in severe danger of choking to death from swallowing back her laughter and was grateful at that moment to hear the seamstress call out, "Next?"

She walked toward the large open door and past a woman with a dress straight out of a fine boutique. It well displayed the figure of the brunette wearing it. The woman with model-type looks flaunted her designer dress by sashaying across the lobby floor. Her exhibition triggered whistles of admiration throughout the large room. The woman's face appeared unperturbed by the echoing whistles, as if they were the expected announcement of her presence.

So much for the liberated woman.

Abby raised her eyebrows and stumbled across the threshold of the fitting room.

"Come in, come in. Welcome to my dressing room. I'm Miss Swanson. If you like, we can close the door for privacy." She held up a measuring tape.

"Yes, I'd like that. And my name is Abby. Abby Carpenter."

Abby looked around at mannequins modeling various styles of colonial dress. Some were simple, humble gowns while others displayed dreamlike folds of gorgeous silk, enticing her to touch its smooth texture.

"They are beautiful, aren't they? Those are the ball gowns. Are you going to the ball at the Casino in October?"

She released the silk material of the gown. "I don't think so." Abby knew she could never afford such an expenditure. The most she could swing with her tight budget would be one of those linen dresses. Even with purchasing that, she'd be eating sparsely this vacation.

"So tell me, Abby, what keeps a pretty girl like you busy? Do you work?"

Touching the muslin fabric on one display, she smiled at Miss Swanson. "Yes. I'm a nurse. I work with kids at the hospital near where I live in California."

Miss Swanson looked pensive. "My mother was a nurse. Worked extra shifts to put food on our table."

"Oh?"

"My dad disappeared with his booze on a regular basis. One day, he took his bottle with him and never came back. My mom … she was a trooper. She did all she could to provide for us kids." The seamstress stared out the window for a moment. "We couldn't afford new clothes, so, early on, I learned how to sew. I made outfits for all of us. Even Mom." She turned toward Abby. "I guess even good things can come out of bad. Look at me now. Creating gowns for folks in Hollywood and special events."

There was no bitterness in Miss Swanson's tone. Just gratitude for her mother's provision and for the opportunity to become a well-known costumer.

"You have a remarkable attitude, Miss Swanson."

The woman with the professional-looking makeup laughed, revealing a row of perfect, pearly teeth. "Not really. I just saw my mom model a gracious demeanor and not feel sorry for herself. I guess it's all in a person's perspective. Let it hurt you or allow it to grow you. I chose the latter."

"You're quite wise."

Miss Swanson paused for a moment with one finger resting against her cheek then walked toward the mannequin attired in the ball gown.

"You know, I think this gown might fit you. I made these ahead of time as displays. Once all the dresses are made, I'll no longer need it. What do you say? Would you like to use it for the ball?"

Abby inhaled sharply. "Are you sure?" Her breathing quickened with thoughts of being a real-life Cinderella. But much like the fairy tale, she feared it too good to be true.

"Oh, I'm quite certain." Miss Swanson offered her beautiful grin. "I've no use for it after the costume ball. You would be helping out the county commissioners, who want as many attendees as possible to wear period dress."

Abby wanted to dance for joy but tried to smother her enthusiasm. "I'd love to."

"Very well. Let's get you measured. Show me which color linen you'd like for your everyday colonial dress. I think this blue might look lovely with your hair." She held it next to Abby in front of the mirror.

"Yes, it's perfect. How ... how much will it cost?"

Miss Swanson paused. "Will thirty dollars be acceptable?"

Abby knew it had to be worth far more than that. She exhaled with relief. "Yes. That's certainly acceptable."

Miss Swanson smiled. "Good. We'll get you looking like you've stepped into a time machine in 1977 and emerged in Saratoga 1777."

As Abby held out her arms and submitted to the efficient fingers of the dressmaker, she closed her eyes and imagined wearing the gorgeous green silk gown that was on the mannequin. She'd landed in a fairy tale.

The prick of a straight pin forced her out of her dream as Miss Swanson adjusted a swatch of material around her bodice. *That figures.* She should have expected a stab of reality.

Miss Swanson must have noticed her cringe. "I'm so sorry, Abby. These fingers are aging a bit."

"It's all right."

The straight pin was merely a reminder that life was often hurtful. And for Abby Carpenter, it never ended in happily ever after.

Chapter 7

Abby called Scott that night so he wouldn't worry about his little sister. To her surprise, her friend from work answered the phone. "Maureen? Did I call the right number?"

Her Massachusetts buddy laughed. "Yeah, I'm just bringing dinner over for Scott, and it was faster for me to get to the phone. He's still a little slow with his steps."

"Yeah, but … I didn't even know you knew Scott." She rubbed her brow.

"I visited him in the hospital, remember? I gave him my phone number for while you'd be gone, in case he needed anything."

Abby could hear Scott laughing in the background. "So … what are you two doing?"

Maureen laughed. "We're just watching TV together. I made him some popcorn, and we made a movie night out of it." There was also a tone in Maureen's voice she hadn't heard before.

Scott. With Maureen. Abby was still trying to wrap her head around this unexpected friendship. If that's all it was.

"Abby? You still there?"

"Yeah. I'm sorry. Just got distracted. Um, can I speak with Scott for a sec?" She scratched her head and plopped onto the motel bed.

"Sure. Hey, here's Abby."

She heard the phone being transferred to someone else. "Abby! How's it going, baby sister?"

"I'm not a baby, Scott." She sighed with exasperation. "I just called to tell you I got here and I'm okay. And Scott? I feel like a complete idiot around these historical people. I don't know the difference between a militia and a regiment. I don't know anything." She bit her lower lip. "I wish you were here."

Scott's tone grew more serious. "Abby, you'll do fine. Did you read the transcript of the letter I sent with you? I thought it might put you in the historical frame of mind."

"Letter? What letter?"

"The one our great-great—whatever—grandmother wrote for her kids and grandkids. The other Abigail with the red hair." He giggled warmly. "Who'd have thought my sister would be the red-haired fulfillment of the family legend?" He paused. "I'm so proud of you for going. I know this isn't easy for you, going by yourself and all. But you're really brave making this pilgrimage alone. I have no idea why things turned out the way they have, but somehow God allowed it. Maybe someday we'll figure it out."

She clenched her jaw. "Yeah. Maybe. So where is the letter?"

"I tucked it in your small bag. In the elastic pocket."

She held onto the receiver while searching through her small bag with her free hand. "Here it is. Thanks."

An odd thought popped into her mind. She remembered the conversation in the motel office this morning. "Hey, Scott. Do you have any idea what the first Abigail's name was? Before she married?"

"I'll have to double-check that one. Hold on a sec." He placed the phone down, and she could hear him ask Maureen to bring him a box. After some rustling sounds in the distance, she heard Scott pick up the receiver. "Gillingham. Abigail Gillingham. She married William Carpenter, who was wounded in the war. Abigail Gillingham nursed him back to health. She was a nurse, like you."

Abby clutched the phone cord and shivered. "Weird."

"Why?"

"Well, someone in the motel office this morning asked me if my ancestor's name was Abigail Gillingham. I had no idea, and I told him so. He was a bit strange, and now I feel a little queasy about it all. Why do you suppose he'd know that?"

There was a long silence. "I don't know, Abby." She could hear the nervousness in Scott's voice. "That is weird. Do you think I should come out there?"

"No. You're still recovering. Besides, there's a police officer from London next door in the motel. I think he's watching out for me."

"Are you sure he's legit?"

"Yeah, I saw his ID. Besides, he talks like a cop."

"He's not a psycho maniac type?"

"No, he's far too rude."

"What?"

"Private joke. No, he's fine. I'm just a bit unnerved by this other guy. But I'll be okay."

"Abby, you be careful. I mean it. Do you have the local police number by your phone?"

"Yes, Scott. Look, I don't want you worried about me. I'm fine."

"You call me anytime you need me. Understand?"

She wished she could hug her brother right now. "Yes, Scott, I understand. You rest and get well, okay?"

"Yeah. Love you, Ab."

"Love you back."

She slowly set the phone back on its cradle.

God, why am I here all alone?

Chapter 8

The motel office was less crowded this morning, much to Abby's relief. In fact, all the streets were quiet this morning. The Sunday morning slowdown. The day of rest.

But Abby didn't feel rested. She'd tossed and turned all night and felt anything but refreshed this morning. An earlier glance in the mirror confirmed dark circles under her eyes, the fate of pale skin combined with allergies. Add very little sleep to that genetic mix, and she looked like she belonged in the raccoon family. She had done her best to cover the under-eye damage with makeup.

The motel owner was behind the counter this mist-covered morning. Much to Abby's relief, Ambrose Cardwell was nowhere in sight. As the motel maid prepared to deliver fresh towels to the rooms, she instructed a young man on the use of cleaning supplies.

Mr. Cardwell greeted Abby. "Morning, young lady. Have you met our maid, Liz Tysdale? She's been doing a marvelous job with all the guests staying here. We just hired her younger brother, Gregory, to help keep up with the work. I'm keeping them both on their toes with forty full rooms."

"How do you do, Liz? So pleased to meet you and very grateful for the clean towels. And the clean rooms, Gregory." Abby smiled and shook their hands. Liz's grip was steady and sure. Gregory's was somewhat limp and his speech a bit slow. Some of her favorite patients had mental disabilities, and it warmed her heart to see Mr. Cardwell hiring someone who might have difficulty finding employment. By the cleanliness of her room, Gregory was doing a better than adequate job.

"How do you do?" Liz extended her hand to Abby. "You're Miss Carpenter, Room 20, correct?"

"Yes. You've a great memory. Don't know how you keep us all straight."

"How do you do?" Gregory reached out his hand again, eliciting a maternal smile from Abby. His voice was measured and sluggish.

"Very well, thanks." She squeezed his fingers softly then released his hand.

Abby turned to the motel owner. "Are there churches close by, Mr. Cardwell? I'm used to going each Sunday and feel I'm missing out if I don't."

He pulled out a street map and began putting Xs on various landmarks. "There're all kinds in Saratoga Springs. I'm certain you'll find something to strike your fancy."

"Thanks so much. You've been very helpful. By the way, the diner you referred me to yesterday was delightful. And affordable."

She opened the door and buttoned her sweater all the way to her neck. The morning fog sent a chill through her. *I should have worn pants instead of a skirt.* Lost in thought, she studied the map.

"Good morning."

Abby jumped at the voice behind her.

"Abby, it's only me." Ian walked around in front of her.

She put her hands across her chest and gasped. "Ian. I'm so glad it's you."

"What's wrong?" He touched her arm.

"Nothing. I was just lost in thought, and you startled me. That's all." She held up the map. "I was looking for a place to attend church this morning. I'm not certain where to start."

He took the map from her outstretched hand and perused the landmarks. "Well, let's start here on Broadway and work our way up and across. I'm certain we'll find something suitable."

"We?" She squinted her eyes as a ray of sunlight made its way through the morning mist.

"Yes." He took a step back. "Unless you don't want me to go with you."

She reached out and put her hand on his sleeve. "Oh. Of course I do. I was just taken by surprise. I didn't think …" She dropped her hand to her side.

"You didn't think a London copper would go to church?"

Abby scrunched her face. "Copper? Really? Is that what constables are called?"

He straightened his shoulders. "Yes, Nurse Carpenter. Do you have a problem attending church with a copper?"

She giggled. "Not unless you have trouble attending church with someone who empties bedpans."

Ian waved the map in front of his face and moved away from her. "You've not done so recently, have you?"

"Not recently. You're safe for now." She nudged at his arm in jest and moved closer to him as he stared at the map. "Good thing you're navigating once again."

"Glad to assist you so we can prevent having to file a missing person's report. Don't want to cause a stir in this sleepy town."

"I'm sure it would." It occurred to Abby that she knew nothing about his job as a "copper." "So, tell me about your life as a police officer."

Ian grew quieter as he looked back and forth between the map and the street signs. "Oh, the usual."

"Well? What is the usual? Do you wear those hats that look like black upside-down pots?"

"Upside-down pots? Good heavens. You are speaking ill of the long-standing tradition of the famous bobby uniform. How dare you mock our historic accoutrements."

Abby wasn't sure if he was jesting. "I ... I'm sorry? I didn't mean to offend ..."

He grinned. "No offense. Just teasing." He glanced at her. "I suppose they do look a bit like upside-down pots."

"I wasn't sure if you were serious." They continued walking. "So, do you wear the bobby uniform?"

His face sobered again. "I used to wear it to work. Every day for two years. Until I joined the CID—the Criminal Investigation Department. We wear plain clothes there."

"What's it like in the CID?"

He ignored her question and stopped in front of a modest church building. "What do you think of this church?"

His abrupt change of conversation caught her by surprise, but she looked at the name of the building. It was a small nondenominational church with little information on the outside sign. Just service times and the name of the pastor, Reverend Jacob Moore.

"I suppose it's fine."

He took her gently by the elbow and guided her up the steps into the sanctuary with its simple pews and a red carpet. The service was just starting, and she was delighted that her favorite Maranatha song, "Open Our Eyes, Lord," was being sung by a man with a guitar. They glided into a pew and sat on the hard wooden bench.

Rather than sing along, Abby decided to close her eyes and listen. Really listen. Not just to the words and the melody, but to God's Spirit speaking to her heart.

She poured out her thoughts and worries to Him. Silently and with heartfelt honesty, Abby asked God for wisdom in this situation. Was she worried for no reason? Or did the eyes of her soul need to be opened to understand something? *What is it, Lord? What do You want me to understand?* She pleaded for an answer.

But there was no answer that drifted her way from heaven. Just the words of the song, telling her to reach out and connect with God. He would be there for her.

When the song was over, she opened her eyes and glanced at Ian. To her shock and amazement, he swiped away tears from his face. If they'd not been in church, she would have given him a hug.

Lord, help me to help him. I don't know what to do.

She reached over with one hand and entwined her fingers gently with his. He grasped her hand tightly in return—with the grip of a man clinging to the side of a cliff, lest he fall.

Chapter 9

The after-church crowd at the diner had thinned out, and the waitress had long since removed all the empty plates. Quiet permeated the atmosphere. Ian was so lost in thought over his lukewarm tea that he barely heard Abby speaking to him.

"What time do you want to leave for the ceremonies in the morning? Ian?"

He met her concerned eyes, and when he realized her hand rested on his left forearm, he stiffened. The pain in his arm still reminded him of things he wished to forget. "I'm sorry, Abby. What?"

"You seem a thousand miles away. Or is it 3,000 miles and an ocean away?"

Her smile was sympathetic and beckoned him to bring his thoughts back to the present. "Please forgive me." He attempted a cheerful expression.

Abby released his arm and sat up straight and cleared her throat. "So, what's her name?"

What did she say? "What are you talking about?"

"Well, you're so deep in thought, I assumed there was something troubling you. Perhaps ... someone special?" She lowered her eyes and inspected her teacup with an almost scientific interest.

"Why do you assume there's a bird?" He shook his head. "A woman?"

She shifted in the booth seat. "Well, why else would you be so lost in thought?"

"Why else?" Ian cleared his own throat. "Is it not possible there are other reasons? Does it have to be a woman?"

Abby lowered her eyes and turned bright pink. "Of course it's possible. And I'm sorry. I just wanted to be sure—"

"You wanted to be sure I didn't have someone on the other side of the Atlantic waiting for me."

She turned even redder.

"Well, I don't. But I'm certain you must have someone in California." He rubbed his mouth with one hand and looked away. "How could you not?" Sipping the ghastly tea, he swallowed wrong, leaned forward over the table, and coughed.

"Are you okay?" She reached across and patted his back.

For such a fragile-looking bird, she had wings of steel. "Fine." He gave one last cough before he took another sip to wash away the congestion and smiled for her sake.

She leaned toward him and captured his eyes. "I'm not dating anyone right now. I guess I'm taking a sabbatical from movie nights and dinner dates. But, aside from all that, I want you to know that I'm here for you if you want to talk. I once dated a police officer, and he never wanted to open up and share things with me, even when he was troubled."

Ian avoided her green eyes. "Sometimes officers are bound to keep information private. And sometimes … sometimes things are too difficult to discuss. Even with a friend."

She didn't respond.

He looked up at Abby's warm smile.

"I'm pleased you consider me a friend."

He smirked. "Of course you're my friend. Anyone who puts up with my rudeness has to be a friend."

She chuckled. "Well, there's also that driving agreement we made while you held me hostage."

Her laugh transported him to a depth of relaxation he'd not felt in a long time. "So, once again, please forgive my rudeness, but I don't recall what you were asking me earlier when I was … preoccupied."

She folded her hands together and placed her elbows on the edge of the table. Whispering as if it were top secret, she leaned toward him. "What time do you want to leave for the ceremonies in the morning?"

The subtle shake of her rounded shoulders allured him, even in this brightly lit diner. He wished she wasn't so tidy. *Get ahold of yourself.*

"It starts at nine-thirty, you say? How far to Stillwater?"

"About sixteen miles. Mr. Cardwell says it takes about thirty minutes."

"What about breakfast?" His eyes lit up with a playful grin. "You seem to enjoy a healthy one." He took another sip of the tea.

She swat at his arm, sloshing the liquid in his cup. She put her fingers over her closed mouth. "Oops! Sorry." She barely hid a grin. "I have some fruit and cereal I bought at the market. I'll drink water and just eat in my room. I'll be fine."

"Right. So let's leave about nine o'clock or so?"

"Sounds good." She stirred some honey into her tea. "So, tell me about your family. I know your dad is gone. Do you have any siblings?"

"One sister, Anne. She and Simon have a one-year-old—baby Ian."

Her expression lit up the diner. "Baby Ian! That's so cute."

"Fortunately, he doesn't look like me." He sipped the abominable tea again. "I just hope he doesn't grow up to be a copper."

Abby's face grew somber. "Why not?" When he didn't respond, she asked, "Why did *you* become a copper?"

"I wasn't going to at first. I was at university when Dad was killed. I decided to leave and attend the Peel Centre—that's where they train police officers. It had just been opened by the queen, and I was in the first class." He swirled the remaining liquid in his teacup. "I actually wanted to go into the Army. I was so angry about my dad, I thought I'd get back at the Irish. At anyone who could be so cruel. It broke Mum's heart when I told her. She finally convinced me to take another path, so I joined the police force. She was still unhappy about that choice, but I went anyway."

Poor Mum.

Abby kept her voice low. "How does your mother feel about your decision now?"

Ian covered his mouth and stared out the window for a moment. "I don't know how she'd feel right now, if she were still alive. Mum died of cancer a year later."

I probably made her sick with my decision.

"Ian, I'm so sorry."

He wanted to change the subject. Remorse and anger battled for first place in his mind, and he wanted to talk about anything else but this. Shifting his thoughts into neutral, he forced himself to look at Abby. "So tell me about your family."

There was that sympathetic smile again. She sat up straighter in the booth and seamlessly adjusted to his mood and feelings. He was thankful for that.

"Well, you know about my brother, Scott. He's single." He noticed an almost imperceptible squint in her expression. "So far." She waved at nothing in particular in the air. "Anyway, he works for the county sheriff's office as communications director. He's a nature kinda guy. Always has been. Loves to roam the San Bernardino Mountains." She took a sip of her tea then continued. "Then there's my mom. It's Sunday. I suppose I should call her." She bit her lower lip.

"You don't seem too anxious to ring her up."

"I would be, but ..." She sighed. "She's just so distracted with her new family. When I call, there's always either a stepbrother yelling in the background or my half-brother crying on her lap 'cause he got up from his nap on the wrong side of the bed." Her eyes moistened.

"So she remarried after your dad was killed."

She nodded and looked at him. "Yeah. I guess I thought Dad would always be her one and only love." After taking a hesitant sip of her tea, she settled the cup back in its place on the saucer.

He hesitated before reaching over and tucking his fingers between hers. "Sometimes, when one has known true love, she—or he—wants to find it again. Hopefully, your mum has. Does she seem happy?"

"I guess. Except when she says she doesn't see me enough."

"Well, that's a cue for you."

Abby swiped a finger below her eye. "I s'pose."

"My sister, Anne, found true love a second time."

She tilted her head to the side. "She did? So Simon …?"

"He's her second husband. Her first was killed in a motor car crash after just a year of marriage. I thought Anne would never recover from it. But after a bit, she started seeing another fellow. Then she met Simon. He was so different from her first husband, but Anne became alive again. She's really happy. And now she's a mum." Ian grinned despite himself.

Abby's face lit up again. "I can tell you love the little guy."

"Yeah." He grew thoughtful. "He's a reminder to me that there's good in the world."

Their tender moment of conversation ended abruptly when Ambrose "Travolta" Cardwell strutted through the diner door as if dancing to inaudible disco music. Today, he wore a white suit and a shirt that revealed that ghastly chest hair.

"Well, well. Moving in on my territory, you British b—"

"Excuse me, Mr. Cardwell, but I'd rather not hear your offensive language. Especially in regards to my friend. And I'm certain the

Bicentennial Commission would want all the out-of-town guests treated with hospitality. Isn't that so?" Abby's brash look could tame a bull.

"Hey, I was only joshing my British buddy here. Wasn't I?" He sat next to Ian, making sure to step on his toes with his pointed leather shoes.

He kicked the idiot's foot away. "Right. Actually, we were just leaving. Big day tomorrow." He shoved Ambrose's leg over with his own, forcing the man to the edge of the booth.

This total gorm could brass off a saint. Even Mother Teresa would lose her patience.

Ian stood his full height—grateful he was slightly taller than this nitwit—took Abby's arm and led her to the cashier counter. He paid the bill.

Looking back at Cardwell, Ian recognized an expression in Ambrose's eyes that made the London constable uneasy. He'd seen that look before. It didn't bode well for Abby—or for him.

As they walked the block back to the motel, Abby clung to his arm. She looked back once. "He's not following us, is he?" For all her bravado in the diner, her voice sounded vulnerable—fearful.

He dared a quick glance behind them in the growing autumn dusk. "No." He was still focused on Cardwell's sinister eyes. His copper sense had kicked in full-bore. Mouth drying and gripping her arm tightly while trying to be gentle, he walked faster than normal.

Back at the motel, Abby fumbled in her purse for the motel key as they stood in front of her door. "Thanks for paying for my lunch. You didn't have to." She seemed reluctant to go into her room.

"Would it help if I made sure that all was well inside?"

She breathed a sigh of relief. "Yes. I don't know what's the matter with me. I'm not usually so … ill at ease." She looked around with heightened alert.

He took her key and unlocked the door to Room 20. Standing back so she could go in first, he glanced around outside once more and then shut the door behind them. Abby stood there hugging herself while he checked out the small bathroom, the closet, even under the beds.

He attempted a cheerful report. "All's well."

He stood next to her and was taken aback by a sudden urge to kiss her. He fought the battle and won—with great regret. With his hands in his pockets, he said, "Abby, please be careful around Ambrose. Don't be alone with him."

She tilted her head slightly. "Well, I'd already decided that, but why are you saying it?"

"Call it my 'copper sense.' He's not to be trusted."

"Ian, I've met guys like him before. They're so full of themselves and their minds are—you know—in the gutter." Her eyes narrowed. "But this guy's different."

He swallowed. "I know. Please guard yourself." He looked at his feet then met her eyes. "I once had a friend who was not on guard when she was approached by a similar lout." He raked his fingers through his blondish hair. "It didn't go so well for her."

Abby's eyes widened in horror. "I'll be careful."

"Good. Would you give us a bell if you need me?"

"*Us?* Do you have another Brit or two hiding in your room?" Her giggle sounded nervous.

"It's just how we say it. Would you?"

"Yes. I will. I think right now I'll take a rest and maybe give my mom a 'bell.'"

His face crinkled into a grin. "Sounds like a good plan."

He had not expected her to kiss his cheek. When she did, the warmth of her touch rippled from his face throughout his entire body.

"Thanks, Ian. For everything."

As she went back into her room, she closed the door. He heard her bolt the lock.

"Well done, Abby," he whispered.

His heart raced erratically. Was it fear of more confrontations with the devious, smooth-talking Ambrose? Or was it the fervor growing in his heart for a beautiful woman who lived too far away and deserved so much more than he could offer?

For her sake, he must keep his distance from the alluring Abby Carpenter. Yet he could still feel the warmth of her kiss on his cheek.

And the hair on his neck bristled whenever he thought of Ambrose Cardwell.

Chapter 10

Abby awakened the next morning to the sound of bagpipes.

What?

She threw off the covers and pulled a sweater over her pajamas. Hugging it tightly, she unlocked her door and peeked out. Opening it wider, she stared in awe and stepped over the threshold.

There, in the motel parking lot, three pipers blew into their instruments. One older man with a full beard and two clean-shaven gentlemen were dressed in red and black kilts and military-looking jackets. Long black feathers accentuated their fur hats. The plumes waved in the early morning breeze as if saluting the day.

The instruments were amazing, each bearing three long pipes nestled on the men's shoulders, one pipe much longer than the others. Two smaller pipes were on the underside of the bag. The piper's fingers moved with expert precision on one while he blew with measured force into the other.

At first, Abby found it annoying, especially since she had just woken up. But as the haunting melodies lilted across the quiet morning, a soothing, unexpected calm surrounded her. If she closed her eyes, she could imagine being on a heather-covered field in Scotland.

When they stopped playing, she opened her eyes. Ian stood a few feet away, watching her. He appeared as entranced as she did and seemed pleased that she'd enjoyed the unscheduled concert.

"It's a balm for the soul, is it not?"

She hugged herself, suddenly self-conscious about being in just her pajamas and sweater. "Yes." Her cheeks grew warmer, and she turned toward her room. "I better get ready." Shivering from the early morning chill, she closed the door and locked it.

She needed to get the image of Ian in his nightwear out of her mind. He'd been standing in his doorway wearing shorts like those worn by soccer players. The material barely covered his long, sinewy legs. His long-sleeved T-shirt revealed every muscle in his torso.

She'd better shower.

Thirty minutes later, Abby munched on some granola while she checked herself in the mirror. Her Bohemian blouse from India wasn't new, but it was still one of her favorites. The burnt-orange color of the gauzy cotton was highlighted by embroidery across the scoop-neck bodice. She sniffed the material, always intrigued by the smell of the dye. Wash after wash, the aroma lingered, and Abby found it exotic.

She took out the necklace that Scott had presented to her before she left. Placing the chain over her head, she tucked a pewter button underneath her blouse. After spraying on a few puffs of cologne, she checked the waistband of her floor-length peasant skirt. The outfit was hardly colonial, but it was more befitting the celebration than a polyester dress or blue jeans. Besides, the colonial dress she'd ordered from Miss Swanson wouldn't be worn until the big weekend of October 7. That's when thousands were expected to commemorate what everyone called, "the turning point of the American Revolution." She'd look eighteenth century then.

Today's festivities would be smaller but equally important. This was the commemoration of the first battle of Saratoga—the one in which her great-great-great-great-grandfather had been wounded, according to Scott. She was celebrating her ancestors meeting and falling in love. The war was not romantic, but her heart skipped a beat at the thought of a tragedy turning into a triumphant love story. It was their family's story, and it had grown in its importance for her since arriving in Saratoga.

Abby tucked a strand of her red hair behind her ear. Satisfied with her appearance, she gathered her purse. With her car keys in hand, she glanced back at her room. She should have straightened up. *Oh well.* She hurried out the door.

Ian leaned against the driver's door of the rental car, waiting for her.

"Sorry. I hope I'm not running late."

At first, he didn't answer.

Oh no, he must be angry.

But his expression told her otherwise. "I don't care if we are. It was worth the wait. You look … lovely."

Abby fiddled with the zipper on her purse and stared at her sandals. She never could take compliments well. Especially not from good-looking men. "It's just an old blouse."

"It's new to me. And it's wonderful."

He held the car door open for her, and she slipped into the driver's seat. When he got in the other side, the scent of his cologne distracted her for a moment.

"Anything wrong?" He picked up the map.

"No, nothing at all." She fumbled to click her seatbelt. "Tell me the way, Mr. Navigator."

"I don't think we need the map today. It looks like there are reenactors in that blue car. Their hats make it a bit obvious. We can follow them."

"I hope they're locals. If they drive on the left side of the road, I'll know they're not from around here." She glanced sideways at him.

He snickered. "Will you let an enemy soldier stand by you today at the ceremony? If you have any concerns, I'll be certain to find another spot."

"I think I can tolerate a Redcoat's presence. As long as he's not carrying a musket."

"No guarantees, Miss Colonist. I could be armed and threatening."

"Well, there should be enough colonial soldiers there to protect me." She shot him a teasing look. "Hey, Ian, why do they call this battle 'the turning point of the Revolution?' Scott was going to fill me in on the details but, since he's not here, maybe you can tell me."

"So you'll trust me with telling the story—from the British point of view?"

She nodded. "I think you're trustworthy."

He inhaled a deep breath. "Let's see, where do I start? The Rebels—your people—had been driving our king absolutely *mad* …"

"Enough already. Just the facts, please." She smirked while trying to focus on the road and follow the blue sedan.

"Very well. In short, our General Burgoyne was supposed to meet up with two other generals and combine forces to separate the colonies and weaken them in their rebellion. Divide and conquer, as it were. But sometimes plans go awry, as we all know, and the other generals never arrived. Burgoyne's army had diminished in numbers while the Americans increased. After two terrible battles—combined they're called the Battle of Saratoga—General Burgoyne was forced to surrender. It was the first great victory for the Americans. And because France was so impressed with the outcome, they decided to throw in their hats for the American cause and help your people win the war. Which, of course, finally occurred in 1783."

"Wow. You and Scott would get along great. You both have such a passion for history."

"I'm afraid that's what was mostly discussed at the supper table when I was growing up. If you didn't learn your facts, you didn't get sweeties. And I love sweeties." A smile creased his eyes.

"Me too."

It wasn't long before they'd arrived at the Bemis Heights Battlefield area.

"I thought the first battle was fought at another location." Ian looked around. "Someplace called Freeman's Farm?"

"I guess I'm the wrong person to ask since I know so few details."

Abby parked the car in a designated field following the directions of an attendant. She stepped out into the dried grass and breathed in the fresh autumn air. *No smog.*

Swept up with the movement of the crowd, Abby and Ian walked side-by-side.

They were each handed a program of the day's events.

After taking a position on the field, they were directed to await the Freedom March, a procession of adults and children attired in colonial costumes. The group marched quietly in unison toward the onlookers, a somber parade of citizens silently unearthing memories from the past. The previously chatty crowd of several hundred onlookers suddenly hushed.

Abby's formerly jovial mood turned melancholy. An unexpected sadness overwhelmed her. She may not have known all the facts of this day in history, but she could sense the heartbreak and tragedy. Soldiers wounded and dying. Loved ones lost. Lives changed forever.

As she envisioned the anguish so many endured on September 19, 1777, Ian's hand took hers. She treasured the feel of it. When she glanced at his face, she saw the shadows of the past weighing on his spirit as well.

Distant music interrupted the stillness as drums clicked a beat in unison and fifers blew their high-pitched melodies. Scott had talked about this—the music that stirred soldiers to battle at Saratoga. Abby shivered, and Ian drew her close.

Was he thinking about his grandfather from this war as well? Was there a stirring in his blood, a visceral connection with the ones wounded here? Their ancestors were the lucky ones—they had survived. But so many did not.

While Abby knew she had no physical wounds, pain filled her spirit—the sort experienced for a loved one who has been hurt. Like the pain that tore at her heart when her father died. It did not draw blood—just tears.

Daddy, I wish you were here.

Her lip trembled as she fingered the button hanging on a chain around her neck. The remnant of her great-great-great-great-grandfather, William Carpenter, had been passed down from generation to generation until her father, Michael Carpenter, had given it to his son, Scott. And Scott had given it to Abby to wear on this special day. She wore it proudly.

The sound of the fifes and drums grew louder. The corps of musicians was followed by colonial militia carrying muskets, then women and children dressed in eighteenth-century linen and leather.

Abby was surprised and a bit frightened to see Ambrose Cardwell with the reenacting militia. She shrunk back, hoping the crowd would hide her. But the incessant playboy, seemingly ill-dressed in historical garments, saw her. At first, he smiled, until he laid eyes on Ian, who took a step in front of her. The sinister glance he gave Ian alarmed her.

Abby focused on others in the march. She recognized the bagpipers from this morning's concert, others she'd seen in the Gates Motel office, and Gregory Tysdale, the new custodian.

Gregory found her in the crowd and waved a childlike, frantic wave. She grinned and waved back, glad they let him participate.

Abby glanced at Ambrose one last time, and he winked at her. She pushed thoughts of him to the back of her mind, refusing to let him ruin her day.

Now the musicians stood in formation in front of the grandstand, and the crowd repositioned themselves on the field for a better view. After a brief moment of silence, the bagpipers began their soulful song. Abby glanced at the program and saw it was called "The British March." Ian stood taller next to her, his jaw moving with the emotion of melodies that surged with the heart of England in every note.

For the first time, she felt empathy for the soldiers who had crossed the sea to fight for a cause they believed in. And here, on this battlefield, that cause had become the death knell of their core belief that England would win, regardless of opposition. The song took on the tone of a dirge as if a funeral were being held for the greatness that once was but was no more. Her heart ached for Ian and for all whose passion had died in that place. She squeezed his hand and he shot her a grateful glance.

When the pipers had finished, the Drum and Fife Corp stood at attention and faced two flags: one a modern American flag, one a circle of thirteen stars from the Revolution.

As the musicians began playing "The Star-Spangled Banner," Abby placed her hand on her breast. This was the song celebrating her country—the country her ancestor fought for on this very spot 200 years before. Pride filled her heart as tears welled. William

Carpenter had fought for freedom, been wounded in the fray, and survived to love and see his children become free Americans.

The program continued with more bagpipes performing the national anthem of Great Britain and then the anthem of Poland, according to the pamphlet she held.

Abby's expression must have revealed her confusion because Ian leaned down and whispered, "A Polish soldier, Thaddeus Kosciuszko, came over to join your fight. He helped the Americans win."

"Oh." In the aura of his cologne, she temporarily forgot about historical facts.

The first speaker approached the microphone and spoke about Burgoyne's campaign and the Americans who fought back. "We Americans owe our freedom and democracy to the events that occurred on this very ground 200 years ago. Let us never forget the sacrifices that were made on this sacred earth so that we could obtain our liberty. Although now separated from these brave ancestors by the ages, their blood still runs in the veins of Americans throughout this country—descendants who carry on the blessings of life, liberty, and the pursuit of happiness. May the freedoms bequeathed upon us carry on forever."

Several skits performed by children depicted the events of the battle and the British surrender. Abby squelched a laugh when the child portraying General Gates dropped the wooden sword handed to him by a pint-sized General Burgoyne. Even Ian smiled at that one.

There was more music, then more speakers with inspiring words about remembering the birth of America and the role that Saratoga had played in its beginnings. Abby had never been prouder to be an American. Perhaps she could become a history lover, as well. She smiled, thinking how amused Scott would be if she told him.

The closing ceremony was sobering as the next speaker announced the total number of casualties killed in this field in both battles. The deceased veterans were honored with a cannon salute. The enormous blast of the artillery, with its sonorous concussion, made Abby jump. She could feel the explosion through her bones as she covered her ears from the assault. She watched veterans from other wars honor the fallen with a salute to their fellow warriors as "Taps" was played.

Next, a local minister approached the microphone. He offered thanks to God for helping birth America, for the Colonists willing to sacrifice their all for freedom, and for the unity that had eventually formed between the allied nations of America and Great Britain. It was, in his words, a miraculous transformation that could only be wrought by our Creator.

As the bagpipers played again, the crowd slowly dispersed.

Ian drew her close. "I suppose, since we've been officially declared allies today, that we must no longer consider ourselves enemies."

Abby smirked and held out her hand. "Agreed."

He started to shake her hand, but then a mischievous look crept into his eyes. He took her hand and ceremoniously kissed her fingers.

Her cheeks flooded with a warmth greater than the bright, late-September sun. "Let's find a place to eat. I'm hungry now."

As they headed back through the crowd toward their rental car, Abby heard someone calling her. "Miss Carpenter. Miss Carpenter!"

Spinning on her heels and guarding her eyes from the sun, Abby grinned at Gregory's enthusiasm. He was out of breath as he approached, but he continued to smile with the enthusiasm of a child who couldn't wait to tell his secret. "Miss Carpenter. I … I think I know where your family's cabin is. Do you want to see it?"

"My family's cabin? You know where it is?" She covered her open mouth. "I used to go there when I was little, but I don't remember where it is. Do you know the way?"

"Yes, yes. My … my brother and I used to play there. You're the … only Carpenter I know. Must be your home."

"My ancestors' home, yes." She put her hand on Gregory's shoulder. "Thank you. I'd love to. Perhaps this week."

"Yes. Yes! I'll ask … my manager when I'm off."

"Okay. And thanks."

"Thank you, Miss Carpenter."

Gregory turned around and joined his sister, Liz, who put her arm around him. Abby could hear Liz telling Gregory what a great job he had done as a reenactor.

She wanted to shout for joy. "Ian! My family's cabin!" Covering her mouth with one hand, she squeezed his upper arm with the other.

"Ahh! Abby, please don't."

Her joy died with his pain. "What did I do? I'm so sorry."

They pulled to the side, away from the sea of walkers.

"It's … it's not your fault. You didn't know. I was hurt, but it's getting better."

She looked at him with concern. "What happened?"

"It's nothing, really. Nothing for you to be concerned about."

"But I am concerned. Can't you tell me what happened?"

There was a pause. "Someday. But not today. Let's not spoil this day."

Her nursing persona went into overdrive. "But …"

"No Abby. Please, don't be my nurse. Just be my friend."

She swallowed back the urge to heal him. "All right. I am your friend. I'm here for you, whenever you want to talk."

His eyes moistened, and he reached out and stroked her hair. "Thank you, Abby. I treasure your friendship—and you. I've known you such a short time, yet I feel like I've known you for so long."

"I feel the same." She swallowed her emotion with difficulty. She knew he was going to kiss her, and her heart lurched just thinking about it.

He seemed to change his mind and, instead, took her arm and drew her back into the crowd headed for the parking area in the weeds.

Just as they were unlocking the car door, she looked up and met Ambrose Cardwell's glare. He stood in a colonial militia uniform, holding a musket.

"He's not allowed any gunpowder in that weapon, Abby. Don't let him intimidate you." Ian directed her to get into the car.

She shut the door, pulled on her seatbelt, and shivered despite the heat. Ambrose had the look of a man who didn't need gunpowder to cause harm.

Chapter 11

Oh no. Not now. Abby woke up the next morning knowing this would be a day in bed with a heating pad and pain pills. Thank goodness she'd packed them. At least it hadn't started yesterday, out at the ceremony.

She was supposed to visit the cabin with Ian and Gregory. That was definitely out of the question—for at least a couple of days.

It annoyed her when the older nurses at the hospital reminded her every month that "It's the plague of being a redhead. You might as well go into hibernation for a few days. And watch out when you have a baby …"

Great. Something to look forward to.

She rolled onto her side and sat up. She winced and held her belly before hurrying into the bathroom.

* * *

Ian splashed a little cologne on his neck. He didn't usually wear it every day, but lately, he'd been applying it faithfully. Perhaps he only imagined it, but it seemed to have an effect on Abby. A very positive one.

During his mirror check, he noted his hair getting longer over his collar. He couldn't wear it like that when working, and it was rather nice to look a bit more in style.

He dialed Abby. It rang several times, and he grew concerned. On the seventh or eighth ring, she finally picked up.

"Hello?" It didn't sound like her.

"Abby?"

"Hi, Ian." He heard her catch her breath.

"Are you all right?" Was she hurt? Ill?

"I'll be okay. I'm just not feeling so well."

"Do you need to see a doctor?" He imagined the worst. Food poisoning? Influenza? Was appendicitis contagious? He rubbed his hand through his freshly combed hair, messing it up.

"No, it's just the usual … female thing."

"What? Oh." He felt ill at the thought. Squeezing his eyes shut, he didn't know if he was more shocked that she shared this with him—or touched that she would entrust him in such a personal way. How did women tolerate it?

"What can I get for you? Aspirin? Whiskey?" He was trying to remember his sister's remedies.

She gave a weak laugh. "No. I'll be okay, and I have everything I need. I just want to rest." After a moment, she added, "This is really embarrassing."

He wished he knew what to say. "Please don't feel embarrassed. I'm feeling quite helpless, actually. Kind of like I felt when Anne went into labor."

"You were with her?"

"Yes. Long story." Pause. "Abby, please let me know what I can bring for you. I won't stay long but ... I just don't want you to be alone all day."

"You're sweet. But I'm sort of used to hibernating on a regular basis. I've got books, and I'll listen to the radio here."

"You'll give us a bell if you need me?"

"Yeah. I'll *bell* you—and that mysterious other Englishman you seem to be hiding in your room."

"You always make me smile."

"That's what friends are for."

Ian reluctantly hung up the receiver. A pang of loneliness stabbed him. How had he come to rely on her so much in just four days? *You must be off your trolley, Copper.*

Picking up his tweed jacket, he decided to grab some breakfast. Time to eat and, any road, he'd not had a chance to wander about Saratoga Springs yet. After locking his motel room, he stopped outside of Abby's door. He thought about knocking. He shouldn't do it. She needed to rest. With regret, he forced his legs to follow his logical brain. He'd fully intended to try a new place for breakfast, but his feet seemed to have a mind of their own. Before he could say "tally ho," he found himself sitting at the diner booth he usually shared with Abby.

The waitress who'd served them several times approached the table. She snapped her gum and held her pencil above her order pad. "Wife couldn't come today?"

"No, she's not feeling well. No, wait ... she's not my wife."

The orange-lipsticked waitress grinned and fluttered her lashes. "Coulda fooled me. So what can I getcha?"

Ian looked studiously at his menu. "Soft-cooked eggs, English muffin, and coffee." He looked up at her and with a nod said, "Yes, I'll try coffee this morning."

"Brave man." She snapped her gum again and left with the menu.

Nervousness crept through him as he looked around. This place should have felt familiar to him, but somehow it seemed foreign, empty. Lonely without Abby.

While watching a young couple a few booths down, Ian noticed the way the woman twirled her hair and threw her head back when she laughed. He observed as the man rubbed his leg against hers under the table. She stroked her arms seductively. A few minutes later, as they exited, the man put his hand on her back—very low on her back.

Ian shifted in his seat. It had been a long time since he'd been close to someone. At university, he'd been *too* close to someone. She couldn't understand why he wanted to marry her after his dad died. He knew he needed to straighten his life out. But she just wanted to sleep together. No commitment. Free love. It was the 1970s, after all. Who needed to get married?

I do. I need to settle down. But I'm a broken piece of machinery right now. Who'd want me?

Orange Lips brought him steaming coffee. "You seem deep in thought, mister."

"I've got lots to think about. Thanks for the coffee." He sniffed the dark brew. Pouring in creamer from the small pitcher on the table, he added some sugar. Holding the packet of sweetener gave him an idea.

The waitress came back with his breakfast. "Excuse me. Would it be any trouble if I took a few packets of sugar with me when I leave?"

She waved her hand dismissively. "Take all you want. It'll be fewer sugars I have to clean up from all the teens who come in here after school."

"Thanks. Oh, and, one more question. Are there any shops nearby where one might find a tea set? A ceramic one?"

Putting her pencil behind her ear, she put both hands on her hips and tipped her head up as she thought. "Oh, I know. I bet that shop on Caroline Street might have what you're lookin' for. They carry lots of gifts and stuff." She grinned. "Lookin' for a gift for your wife?" She playfully punched him on the shoulder. Fortunately, it was the uninjured arm.

"Yes. That's who it's for." Why bother explaining again?

He downed his eggs and muffin in record time. The coffee, he sipped more slowly. It would take him time to get used to *that* flavor. He paid the waitress and thanked her for the suggestion.

"No problem," she said. "And I hope your wife feels better."

The sun was out this morning without a hint of fog. The air was still cool from the autumn breeze carried up from the Hudson River. Ian sauntered slowly past several shops and a pub before finding the gift store the waitress had mentioned. Looking in the window, he could see several things he'd like to buy for Abby. But on his constable's salary, he'd have to watch his shillings.

As he entered the shop, a bell rang, announcing his presence to the proprietress. She was a smartly dressed, middle-aged woman with dark hair edged with gray. Her hair swirled pleasantly into a bun crowning her head. She reminded Ian of his mum.

"May I help you?"

"Yes, I'm looking for a ceramic tea set. Do you carry any?"

She placed her hands on her cheeks in surprise. "Why, you're from England! How lovely! My father came from that country decades ago. I was born in America, but I delight in my family roots."

"I do as well." He relaxed in the woman's friendly presence. "How did your father come to be in America?"

"He was a soldier in World War I—they called it the Great War. Anyway, my mother was an American nurse, and she felt it her duty to go and help the brave soldiers fighting for freedom in Europe. My father was wounded and my mother took care of him. When the war was over, Mom had to return home. She said it was the hardest thing she'd ever done, saying goodbye to Dad. Imagine her joy and surprise when he came to America. She said their reunion was the sweetest kiss ever." The store owner blushed and sighed. "The rest, as they say, is history."

Ian was silent, imagining the reunion. "That's quite a story."

"Like a fairy tale, don't you think?"

"Yes, very much so."

"Well, listen to me carrying on. What can I do to help you? You say you're looking for a tea set?"

"Yes—a ceramic one."

She smiled. "Would this be for someone special?"

"Well, yes, as a matter of fact. She's not well today, and I thought perhaps an authentic cuppa might help rally her."

"I may have just what you're looking for. Wait here. I have a new shipment in back."

Ian placed his hands in his pockets and hummed an Elton John song. It was the same tune he and Abby had listened to on the car ride from Albany. Every time he thought of it, he envisioned her green eyes. And now the song was stuck in his head.

The proprietress emerged from a floral curtain that separated the merchandise area from the back room. "I think I've found exactly what she might like."

Placing a medium-sized box on the counter, the store owner lifted the cardboard lid and pulled out a small teapot, decorated with flowers the color of autumn. Lavender asters, orange chrysanthemums, and burgundy carnations were delicately painted on the rounded curve of the china.

Ian's mouth gaped before he finally spoke. "It's extraordinary."

"The perfect one for your lady friend?"

"Yes. These are the colors of autumn. Her hair reminds me of the same."

"Well then, she must be lovely, indeed."

He swallowed. "Yes. Yes, she is."

"Let me wrap it for you. And if you're looking for loose tea and a strainer, there's a shop around the corner that should be able to help you."

"Thank you."

Ian paid for his purchase then visited the tea store where he found sweetly scented Earl Grey, the pride of British civilization. He couldn't wait to make Abby a proper cuppa.

After walking briskly back to the motel, he approached her door. Out of the corner of his eye, he saw Gregory carrying a bucket with cleaning supplies. "Morning, Gregory."

"Good morning ... Mr. Thacker. Miss Carpenter is ... sick today." He looked sadly at the walkway.

"I know, Gregory. But she'll be better soon."

The custodian looked up, squinting in the sunlight. "I don't like it ... when people get sick." Each word seemed like such an effort for him. "Sometimes they die."

"Don't worry, Gregory. Miss Carpenter isn't going to die."

"That's good ... Mr. Thacker." He walked back to the office with his bucket.

Ian hesitated just a few seconds, then gently knocked on the door of Room 20.

"Who is it?" Her voice was sleepy and weak.

"It's me. Ian. I've brought you something." He waited a moment before he heard the door unlock.

She seemed weak and slightly bent at the waist. "Ian. I'm okay."

"I don't normally say this to a lady, but you don't look okay. May I come in?"

Without speaking, she turned around slowly, hugging a sweater tightly around her torso. She climbed into her bed and pulled the covers high. Her face winced with discomfort.

He set to work. "May I wash something out in your sink?"

"Sure." She rolled onto her side.

He washed out the new teapot, dried it with a hand towel, and set everything up on her dresser. He pushed a few toiletry items to one side to give him more room. "I'll be right back. I'll leave something in the door to prop it open so it won't lock."

Moments later, he returned with a kettle of steaming water and poured it over the loose tea leaves in the china. He set the hot kettle near the sink, placed the small lid on the teapot, and carried it toward Abby's bed.

Her eyes were closed until he held the spout near enough that she opened them. "What's that smell?"

"Earl Grey tea—England's finest. The scent of Bergamot to help you get well."

She slowly sat up under the covers and propped her pillow behind her back. Her disheveled hair reminded him of the first day they met at the airport. It was a pleasant memory—very pleasant.

"When I was ill, Mum used to make me tea. She would entertain me by making up stories about the leaves. She said you had to let it brew just long enough to allow them to open up their lovely flavor. Too short a time and the leaves wouldn't open their hearts. Too long a time and they were withered and worn with the life snuffed out of them. Ah, but just the right amount of time and the leaves would open their hearts to love and the romance of the tea would bloom. Sweet. Delicious. Heavenly."

Abby smiled. "Your mother was a romantic."

"She was." Ian's expression sobered. "I'd best check the leaves before they wither." He carried the pot to the dresser and lifted the lid. "Looks like they've opened their hearts."

He poured the steaming brew into the cup while holding the strainer to catch the leaves. Then he added a bit of milk that he'd gotten in the motel office and some sugar from the diner. Stirring it with a straw from the restaurant, he carried the cup and saucer to Abby. "See if this does not bring you comfort."

Pushing herself up higher into a sitting position, Abby adjusted the covers over her lap and accepted the cup of tea from Ian. She looked paler than usual.

He watched her take a sip, and a look of surprise emerged in her expression. "This is wonderful. Thanks so much." She rested the saucer on her lap and put her head back against the pillow. "I can't believe you went to all this trouble."

"No trouble, really. It gave me pleasure. And, it gives me pleasure to see you like it."

"I love it. Thanks." She took a few more sips before her eyelids started to droop. "I think I need to sleep, Ian."

He stood and took her teacup and saucer before it spilled.

She slid below the covers and brought them up to her chin. Her long hair lay across the pillow like a carpet of autumn flowers. Abby was stunning—even in illness.

He set the tea and saucer on her bedside table and pulled the phone closer to sleeping beauty. "Give us a bell, anytime."

"Okay."

Her eyes closed. He leaned over her and gently kissed her brow. "Have a nice kip."

"Kip?" she whispered.

"Rest. Sleep well."

Ian straightened up the dresser, rinsed out the pot, and made everything ready for the next cup of tea that she might want. Whenever she was ready, he would be there for her.

He took one last look at the lovely Abigail Carpenter and quietly closed the door of Room 20.

* * *

"Ian?" Abby was groggy, and the lights were dimmer than she remembered. She started to drift back to sleep, but then she heard it again. One of the drawers in her dresser was being opened. Fear seized her. Throat dry and pulse pounding, she attempted to speak. "Who's there?" Her voice sounded small and raspy.

She shook convulsively, but sheer will helped her push up from her pillow and turn over. She could just make out a figure exiting her door and heard the click of the lock.

Her screams shattered the stillness of the late-afternoon dusk.

Chapter 12

"So you're sure you didn't see who it was?" The police officer held a pencil and pad for his notes.

"No." Abby shivered, even though Ian had wrapped a blanket around her and held her close. "All I saw was just the shadow of a figure leaving—then I heard the click of the door."

"How come your deadbolt wasn't locked?" The officer was intimidating enough in his official blue uniform, and his take-charge voice made her feel like it was her fault.

"That was my fault," Ian spoke up. "She wasn't feeling well, and I brought her a cup of tea. She started to fall asleep. So I cleaned up and made sure I closed the door behind me when I left. She didn't have a chance to deadbolt it. And I thought she'd be safe in the daytime."

"Normally, Miss Carpenter should be. Here in Saratoga Springs, we pride ourselves on our low crime rate. But we've got lots of out-of-town guests here right now. Where did you say you're from, Miss?"

"Redlands, California."

"I'll need to see both your IDs."

Ian stood and brought Abby her purse. The officer glanced at her ID but stared at his for some time.

"So, you're a police officer from London? Why are you here for this bicentennial?" He handed the card back to Ian.

"My distant grandfather fought here 200 years ago. My family takes great pride in our history, and I wanted to come with my dad. But he was killed when in the Army." Ian frowned.

Abby didn't wait to be asked. "That's why I'm here also. Ian and I met in Albany, at the airport."

"So are you two"—the officer looked at the beds—"cohabitating here, as they say?"

"No! We've only just met. And we're not even married." Her face flushed with heat. Her stomach cramps increased with the tension.

"Doesn't seem to stop young folks these days."

She couldn't tell if he was speaking to them or just voicing his displeasure in general.

The officer wrote more on his notepad. Walking over to the dresser, he looked at the teapot then the tin of tea leaves. He opened the container and sniffed. "You don't have marijuana in here, do you?"

Abby's eyes widened. "No! It's tea!"

"I bought it at the tea and coffee shop, just off of Caroline Street. I can't remember the name of the store, but it must be on the receipt." Ian felt his pockets. "I guess I left it in my room." He swallowed.

"And where is your room?" The officer sighed with an impatient look.

"Next door. I'd fallen asleep. Until I heard Abby scream. I ran over as fast as I could."

"Do you have any witnesses?"

"Of me taking a kip? No one was with me." Ian sat down again and put his arms around Abby.

"Officer, there's a man who's been giving me far too much attention since I arrived. He's the nephew of the motel owner—"

"Oh, Disco Johnny. We know about him. Thug. Watch out for him." He pointed his pencil at Abby then toward the dresser. "We'll have to take fingerprints here."

Another officer arrived with a fingerprint kit. She watched him collect samples of nearly every surface of her dresser, even the teapot and dresser handles.

Ian stood. "My prints will be all over her dresser and sink knobs. I made her tea. They're likely everywhere."

"Okay. Our guys will keep that in mind." The first officer looked at her. "Miss, I suggest you bolt that extra lock at all times. Let me know if there are any more problems." As he started to leave, he turned back. "You're sure you weren't dreaming, Miss Carpenter?"

Her lips trembled. "No. It was quite real."

The second officer wrapped up his samples and both policemen left.

The moment they walked out, she sobbed. "He doesn't believe me!"

"Yes, he does. An officer has to cover all possibilities." Ian stroked her hair and held her close. "Abby, you need to eat something."

"I don't want you to leave." She shivered.

"Look. I'll stop in the office and have Mr. Cardwell keep an eye on your door. I'll be back in no time. What are you hungry for?"

She looked up at his face with moist eyes. "A hamburger?"

"There's my hungry girl!" He spontaneously kissed the top of her hair and wrapped the blanket around her. "Stay right here. Don't move."

"Can't I go to the restroom?" She half laughed.

"Oh. Yes. Of course."

He turned before he exited. "I'll be back, two shakes of a lamb's tail."

She smiled despite her distress. After he left, she walked to the door and bolted it. She'd never leave it unbolted again.

* * *

It amazed her how much better food made her feel. Ian poured her another cup of tea and brought it to her as she sat on the edge of the bed.

"Thanks." Despite the trauma of the day, she gave him a mischievous grin. "You didn't put any of that marijuana in my tea, did you?"

He snorted. "I can see the headlines at home. 'London constable arrested for possession of illegal substance in America.' That's just what I need." He shook his head and a smile gradually creased his features. "It's so ridiculous, it's laughable."

Abby took a long sip of the delicious brew. "Do you know who they questioned about sneaking into my room?"

"No. I'm certain everyone in the vicinity, but that doesn't mean they found the one who came in here." He looked around the room and back to her. "Are you sure nothing was taken?"

"Yes, I'm sure. I looked through all my stuff. I didn't notice anything missing." She drank more of the soothing brew. "But it's so creepy someone was looking at my—personal things."

He scowled. "Some sicko, no doubt."

She set the teacup in the saucer and shivered.

He stood and paced at the foot of her bed. "Look, Abby, I mean this in the most gentlemanly way, but do you want me to stay in your room tonight to be sure you're all right? I'd stay in the other bed. Or sleep in the chair."

Her jaw dropped and her eyes grew wide. When she realized it, she quickly closed her mouth. "No. I'll be okay. I'll deadbolt the door. And I have your number right next to me."

"Very well. But ring me if you change your mind."

"I will."

He bent over to kiss the top of her head when they were both startled by a loud knock on the door.

"I'll get it." He strode toward the door. She could hear a male voice as Ian gripped the doorknob. He left the room, leaving the door ajar. She couldn't hear the conversation, but he was obviously distressed. When he stepped back over the threshold, he told the guy, "All right. I'll be right there."

Walking back toward Abby, he rubbed the back of his head. "I have to go with the police officer."

Her throat constricted. "Why?" Her breathing raced.

"They … they want to question me." She watched him swallow. "The only fingerprints they found in here were mine."

"Ian …"

"Abby, you'll be all right. Double lock the door. I'll be back. I'm sure there's been some mistake."

As she watched him leave with the officer, she clutched her teacup.

God, who will watch out for me now? And who will watch out for Ian? Lord, help us!

Chapter 13

"Any coffee, constable?" The American police officer's eyes searched Ian's face.

"No." His insides roiled with nausea. This was the first time he'd been on this side of the interrogation table.

"So, tell me again about what happened earlier today."

Inhaling deeply, he explained the day's events step-by-step—again. He had no idea how irritating this was for a suspect.

Suspect. He couldn't believe it.

"Look, I already told you I had fingerprints all over the dresser area. When the intruder came in, is it so far-fetched to believe he was wearing gloves of some sort?" He swallowed back his irritation.

Maybe the outcome of the American Revolution should have taught him something. Were Americans still suspicious of their former enemies?

And then the real reason for their investigation revealed itself.

"We've been in touch with your London superiors. Tell us about your stay in Brighton."

Ian shifted in the hard wooden chair. "I've been a patient there recovering from an injury I sustained in a riot."

"And the other reason you've been there? And put on temporary leave?"

His throat constricted.

The interrogating officer leaned toward him across the table. "Tell me about the psychological reasons."

* * *

Abby took another pain pill and applied the heating pad to her abdomen. She needed to talk to someone she could trust. She thought of Scott but knew he'd probably get on a plane to protect his baby sister if he knew what was happening. Plus, he was still recovering. She couldn't burden him.

Maureen! She hoped she was home.

Looking at her digital watch, she figured it was only 5 p.m. in California. She grabbed the small notebook with her friends' numbers and dialed Maureen's. After four rings, she picked up.

"I'm so relieved you're home."

"Abby? What's wrong? I can hear it in your voice. Are you okay, sweetie?"

Her lips trembled. "No." She wiped the moisture from her face. "Where do I begin?"

She told Maureen about the events of the last several days. About Ian, Ambrose, the intruder. The details poured out of her like a water fountain with a clogged outlet.

When she finished, she sobbed, "Maureen, I'm so scared!"

"Oh. My. Word. This is not good. Let me pray for you."

Maureen was the best at praying, even over the phone. She didn't mind praying out loud anywhere, even in public. That always made Abby a little uncomfortable. But at the same time, she loved her friend for her boldness. When Maureen finished praying, she was crying too.

"I wish I could hug you right now."

"Me too." She wiped her face with tissues. "Listen, Maureen, you can't tell Scott. No matter what."

She didn't respond right away. "Don't worry about that. I won't be telling him." After another pause, she added, "He's back in the hospital."

Abby's heart leaped. "What? Why? What happened now?"

"Please don't hate me. I think it was the popcorn I made for him on movie night. It kind of didn't settle well after his surgery. But please don't worry. The doc says he'll recover just fine." Maureen cleared her throat. "Just no popcorn for a while." She sobbed into the phone. "You must hate me. I'm so sorry!"

"I don't hate you. You're the best friend I could have." She shook her head in disbelief. "Just not the best nurse. Maybe you'd better stick to being a unit clerk."

"You're right. Just a sec." She could hear Maureen blow her nose then return to the receiver. "Abby, are you sure Ian's safe to be around? What if he did put something in your tea?"

"What? That's crazy. No. I don't know what's going on, but please pray for me." Tears welled again. "I feel so alone."

"Sweetie, you've always got Jesus with you. No matter how alone you feel."

"You're right. Thanks for the reminder."

"Thanks for not hating me. Scott's getting better now. Promise."

"I'll call you tomorrow."

"I'll be home from work by four. Call me."

"I will."

After they hung up, Abby put the heating pad over next to her pillow and turned it off.

She walked toward the dresser and lifted the lid on the teapot. Sniffing the remaining brew that had a few tea leaves still floating on the water, she shook her head.

Guilt at even entertaining suspicion of Ian flooded her with remorse.

Yet the thought kept nagging at her.

She didn't know who she could trust.

*　*　*

"We live in a cruel world, Mr. Thacker."

"Yes." Ian's eyes felt swollen, and he tried to hide his humiliation.

Silence ensued for a few moments.

Then the interrogating officer spoke. "I have a younger brother who fought in 'Nam. Came home wounded, although he survived. He got better physically but never quite recovered in the mind. Kept having nightmares. His wife left him. He took to drinking. Lost everything."

"Trying to make me feel better, Sergeant?" He looked for a window but there was none. He tilted his head up to the ceiling.

Sergeant Walker continued. "I often wonder how my brother would have done if he could've opened up to someone about the experience of war. Talked about the pain. The guilt. The terrible images."

Ian shifted in the wood chair. "I don't know." He sipped water from a glass and avoided eye contact with the sergeant. When he felt the sergeant staring him down, he finally looked up and met him with defiance.

The officer snorted. "Yeah, you've got the pride of the profession all right—the idea that tough cops can and should take anything. We're like strong robots, invincible. But, son, we're not made that way"—the officer pointed a finger at his heart—"inside here. If we were, we wouldn't be human."

"So what's a cop supposed to do? Go home and cry about his day?"

"He needs to find someone he can talk to. Either a fellow officer, a loved one, or sometimes a counselor to get him through the really bad times. There's no shame in that."

He worked his jaw 'til his face hurt. "Then why do I feel shame?"

"For having nightmares? For being human? Perhaps pride. Or fear. Fear that we'll be so wounded in the heart we can't recover. Some folks take comfort in faith. It seems more healthy than alcohol or drugs. Some call it a crutch. I call it a lifesaver."

He folded his hands and stared at his lap.

The sergeant inhaled. "Look, we're finished questioning you—for now. Just don't leave town. We'll be checking out everyone at the motel for their whereabouts or if they saw anything." He paused. "I suspect there's a young lady who might be concerned about you right about now."

The police officer stood and Ian followed suit. "Thanks, Sergeant. I appreciate your advice." He held out his hand and they shook.

The sergeant grinned. "Glad it's not 200 years ago. We might be firing at each other."

Ian wiped his face and murmured, "Can't imagine shooting one of those muskets."

"I'll show you how they fire, if you like. I'm one of the reenactors." He stood proudly with hands on hips.

"I might take you up on that."

On the way back to the motel, he hiked up Caroline Street. He saw the pub he'd passed earlier today and stopped in for some ale. A pint would do him good right now. Approaching the bar, Ian stopped short. A huge map of Ireland stared back at him from the wall. His muscles tensed and blood rushed in his ears.

Blasted Mics. I'll take my shillings elsewhere.

Whipping around, he stalked back outdoors and walked without thinking. He didn't care where, just anywhere to get away from the memory of that map—the place where his father was murdered. He glared at the sidewalk as his hatred for the Irish rippled through every vein.

Suddenly he stopped. He looked upward and noticed the door of the church building that he and Abby had attended the previous Sunday. He tried to keep walking, but a compelling urge to go inside overwhelmed his thoughts of leaving.

Feeling like an idiot—or an intruder—Ian approached the wooden door. He felt like he should knock because it was getting late. But he tried the doorknob and it opened without resistance.

The minister who spoke last Sunday was straightening up. "May I help you?"

He stood speechless for a moment. "Um, I'm not certain."

The reverend walked toward him and pointed a finger. "You were here on Sunday. Never forget a face." He held out his hand in a friendly gesture. "I'm Jacob Moore, pastor of this little congregation."

He shook his hand. "I'm Ian Thacker—a constable from London. I'm only in town for a visit."

Jacob laughed. "You're not here to take America back, are you?"

He smirked. "Doubt I could even if I wanted to."

"Well, sit down, Ian. Tell me about yourself."

The two men spent the next fifteen minutes talking about their professions. He'd never spoken much with a minister before, and he was surprised at how easy it was to talk to Jacob Moore. He just seemed like an ordinary bloke, not a holier-than-thou sort.

During a pause in their conversation, Jacob looked intently at him. "I'm guessing you didn't stop in here to find out about my family or what I do to run a church. Is there something else on your mind?"

He looked down at his hands.

"Well, first tell me why you're here in Saratoga Springs."

"Well, you've probably guessed I'm here for the bicentennial of the battle."

The pastor furrowed his brows. "That's a long way to travel for a battle commemoration."

"Yes. Well, you see, our family history was so important to my dad. Since he couldn't come, I felt I needed to make the journey. In his memory." He fiddled with the edge of a hymnal sitting on the pew.

"So your dad died. When?"

"'71." Ian rubbed his mouth and looked up at the cross behind the pulpit. "He was murdered."

"Murdered?" Jacob leaned forward, one elbow propped on the back of a pew and his hands held together. "By whom?"

"By the bloody Irish." His face inflamed. "I'm sorry. And here I am in church …"

"Don't worry about me. Believe me, I've heard worse." Jacob gave an understanding look. "Tell me about it."

He wrestled to maintain his emotions. "Dad was in the Army, stationed in Belfast. There was a bomb someone set off in a pub. Many customers died." He swallowed. "Within days, army officers, including Dad, went undercover, but someone was an informant—from the other side. First, one British officer died. Then … then they found my dad." Warm tears flooded down his cheeks. He wiped them away as fast as he could.

"I'm so sorry, Ian."

His face contorted and he grit his teeth. "I hate them. Every last one. I know you're not supposed to say that in church, but there you have it."

Jacob's gaze fixed on him. "Do you think God's afraid of your honesty? Telling him your deepest emotions? He designed every part of us. Even the feelings that often fill us with hate. And yet He says to love our enemies."

He flashed furious eyes at Jacob. "Love them?"

"Yes. And forgive them."

"How can I forgive someone who murdered my dad?" Ian's voice rose in volume.

"You can't on your own. But with God's help you can. Only by asking Him to help you can you accomplish that seemingly insurmountable task. You have to remember that God has forgiven us, even when we didn't deserve it."

"I've never murdered anyone. My job is to protect people from that."

"You've never ended anyone's life. But have you ever wished you could kill your father's murderer?"

He narrowed his eyes then averted them to look at the wall. "What if I have? I've never carried it out."

"Well, it says in God's Word that even entertaining the thought of murder in your mind is just the same in God's eyes as actually killing them."

Confusion raced through his mind. "Look, if we interrogate someone at the nick and ask them about a murder, and they say they would have liked to but they didn't do it, we don't charge them." His defiant eyes engaged the pastor.

Jacob grinned. "Well, I guess God's court of law is a bit different than ours. But the great news is that, by confessing those murderous thoughts, we are forgiven. No charges pressed. No time served in jail. Scott free."

He was silent for a moment as he stared at the cross. Then he spoke in a low voice. "Do you ever wonder why there is such evil in the world?"

Jacob stared down at his hands, then looked up. "All the time."

Ian fingered the hymnal. "I watched one of my mates getting beaten unconscious during a riot. We were there to help keep order, but the crowd turned on us. I went to help my mate, and I was stabbed." He stared at the hymnal and stopped fingering it for a moment. Then he looked at Jacob. "I don't remember much else about that day. But I'll never forget the look in that man's eyes as he beat my friend. It was pure evil."

Jacob inhaled deeply and waited a moment before speaking. "Evil has been around since the pride of the evil one brought him to defy God. Evil caused the first murder—and every murder since then. The enemy is not the Irish. Or the crowds in a riot. Or the enemies in war. It's the alliance with evil in men's souls that leads to the pain in this world. But Jesus Himself said, 'I have overcome the world.'"

Ian sat silently. He tried to process all that Jacob had said. He couldn't place the puzzle pieces of the pastor's words together just now, but he hoped someday he could. "I appreciate you taking the time to talk with me."

Jacob held out his hand. "I hope it helped."

"In some odd way, it did. I guess I need to sort it through."

"I'll pray you can."

As he stepped out into the cool night air, he pulled the collar of his jacket higher and hurried back to the motel.

Chapter 14

Abby's eyes shot open when someone knocked on the door.

"Who is it?" She sat up in bed, heart pounding.

"Abby, it's Ian."

Her spirit calmed and relaxed. His voice was the one she knew she could trust. Throwing off her covers, she ran to the door. She unlocked the deadbolt and opened the motel door.

The look on Ian's face caused a flush to creep across her cheeks as she realized she wore her thin, eyelet nightgown. "Excuse me a second." Closing the door, she ran toward the extra bed, grabbed a sweater and pulled it on, buttoning it to her neck. Cringing, she slowly opened the door. "Sorry."

He grinned so wide, she thought his mouth would crack. "No need to apologize. I rather liked the view."

"Hey, I'm already embarrassed enough. Don't make it worse."

"I'll try not to."

She sat on the edge of her bed, and he sat opposite her on the extra one. "Well? Is everything okay?" She tried to smooth her disheveled hair.

"Yes. They asked me a lot of questions, and I hope I answered to their satisfaction. It was rather lengthy, but everything should be all right now."

"You were gone a long time."

"Yes. We visited for a while."

"Police talk?"

"Yes." His voice grew quiet.

"You're not very forthcoming for someone who's so forthright." She tilted her head. "So tell me what's going on."

He lowered his eyes. "I'm afraid to talk about it with you. I'm afraid you might think less of me."

"Less of you?" She stood up, crossed the distance between them, and sat next to him. "Why don't you give me a chance?"

He looked down at his lap. "Because I fear our friendship will fade, if you knew."

"Why don't you test our friendship then?"

"Because ... I want it to last."

She took his hand. "It won't last if there's an ocean of secrets between us."

He was quiet a moment. "Something happened to me a few weeks ago that has been giving me nightmares. Terrible dreams that wake me up in a frenzy of fear."

He paused. She urged him on by squeezing his hand.

"I think I told you I'd joined the Crime Investigation Unit after completing two years as a bobby. I was just getting used to wearing plain clothes again when there was a political uprising between two opposing groups in a borough south of London. They needed extra police to control the riots that threatened to break out. Since it was considered an emergency, and I was fairly new in the CID, I was drafted to don my old uniform and carry a truncheon again."

"A truncheon?"

"A big stick."

"Oh. Okay. Go on."

"We were assigned to keep the opposing sides apart. They gave us riot shields. Several officers came in on horseback. Everything was chaos as more rioters came from every side. At first, the opposing sides were just at each other, throwing broken bottles, bricks, anything they could get their hands on. Then we lost control."

Ian's hand trembled in Abby's. She held it tighter.

"I saw …" He closed his eyes. "I saw my mates being pulled off their horses. Trampled on. Beaten. One of my close mates was being throttled so badly, I raced to help him. Then someone drew out a long knife. I felt searing, hot pain in my arm and fell. There was so much chaos after that."

Her eyes filled with tears. "Ian. That's so horrible. Thank God you survived."

He stared with a blank expression. "After that, the nightmares started."

Unexpected memories of a former patient forced their way into her thoughts. She shuddered. "I've had nightmares."

He turned to look at her. "When?"

"When I took care of a little boy who'd been beaten so badly, he nearly died."

"Who did it?"

"The mother's boyfriend. He was convicted and went to jail. But no jail time could *ever* make up for the pain that little boy endured." She faced him. "I had to go to court to testify about the boy's injuries. I remember … I remember staring at that man on trial and looking in his eyes. It was …" She swallowed back thick tears. "It was the face … the face …"

"Of evil."

"Yes." She burst into tears, and he drew her close.

They clung to each other for a long time, their embrace an oasis of good in a world of wickedness.

Chapter 15

Abby spent the next day resting again. She listened to WKAJ easy listening radio. She read her Bible, then started a Dickens novel she'd brought on the trip. She usually didn't have the luxury of reading such a lengthy work as *Great Expectations*.

But mostly, she thought about Ian. The way his mouth curved upward when he smiled, his blue eyes reminding her of the clear autumn sky over Saratoga Springs. The gentle, yet strong way he held her hand. The way his sandy-brown hair tousled across his collar and always looked a bit unkempt. Those wisps beckoned her fingers to comb through them.

His voice sent her attraction into overdrive. His low baritone with the British accent weakened her at the knees.

Get a grip, Abby. This was ridiculous—the man lived in London.

She remembered the letter Scott had sent, and she removed it from the pocket in her suitcase. The note was the typed transcript of the words written by her great-great-great-great-grandmother, Abigail Carpenter. Abby's grandmother, Sarah Carpenter, had carefully retyped the original message on plain white paper, Scott had told Abby. The original was worn and frail, and their grandmother knew the messages would be lost if they weren't transferred to fresh paper.

She opened the folded eight-by-eleven pages and stared in awe at words written 200 years ago. The formal style of communication astonished her as she began to read:

7 October 1778

My dearest son, Joshua,

As I watch you nurse at my breast, I am overwhelmed by the miracle that you are. Your small fingers envelop mine as you draw nourishment that will begin your journey toward manhood. 'Tis a journey which, I know, will have you reach your destination far faster than this mother would hope or wish for. But for now, you are still a tender babe whose sole interest is to eat and grow. I shall accommodate you with joy.

You may wonder as to why I've begun this letter to you many years before your schooled eyes will be able to read and understand. Yet, if I do not write these thoughts down now, I may forget the tender details which I deign to hand down to you and, Lord willing, your brothers and sisters who may follow.

I met your dear father when he was wounded in the war of the Revolution. We became fast friends ...

Abigail read on, enthralled by the words of her namesake from long ago. Her heart quickened as her grandmother described the terror of the war, the wounds of her future husband, and the eventual marriage of William Carpenter and Abigail Gillingham.

The letter ended with words that confused her.

He rescued me and protected me. He loved me enough to stay with me.

The words struck her as peculiar. What had he rescued her from? And why did he love her 'enough to stay with her'? Why *wouldn't* he stay with her if he loved her?

The letter formed questions she'd not anticipated. But the one sentiment she understood beyond all doubt was that Abigail and William loved each other deeply and with a devotion that sent warmth throughout her.

Closing her eyes, she thought of Ian.

Lord, take away thoughts of this man. He could never stay with me. Even if he loved me.

* * *

Ian had arranged to meet two fellow Brits who were staying at the motel at a Saratoga Springs restaurant. One of them was a reenactor from West Yorkshire, the other a professor from Cambridge.

Although not famished, since he'd recently brought breakfast to Abby and eaten with her in her room, he didn't want to appear unfriendly. He'd manage to swallow a few bites.

The professor, Nicholas Cuthbert, was studying the impact of the War for American Independence on the present-day British economy. Ian listened with polite disinterest.

"It's astonishing to think how economically stable the entire British Isles would be if we had just won this Battle of Saratoga. Just astonishing." Cuthbert sipped his ale.

"Really?" Ian yawned.

"Well, economy good or bad, ya got to admit the birds in America made the American victory worthwhile," Lawton said.

"They'd keep me flying south if ya know what I mean." The well-dressed man, perhaps in his thirties, twitched his eyebrows and licked his lips before taking another chug from his pint.

Ian's eyebrows narrowed. "No, Mr. Lawton, I don't."

"Well, take that bird in Room 20. I saw you with her once or twice. Are you two, you know …?" Lawton made an obscene gesture with his two hands. "'Cause if you're not, I wouldn't mind havin' her."

Ian and Professor Cuthbert both dropped their jaws in astonishment.

"You bloody sot. You keep away from her if you know what's good for you." Ian's voice rose with his anger.

"I just asked, mate. No need to go barmy on me. I've heard how these American women are." He gave a leering grin.

Ian bristled. "Is that so? Well, I wouldn't give a second's thought to that rumor. But I'll tell you one thing." Ian leaned forward and glared into the man's eyes. "You do anything to her or any other American bird, and this copper will haul you into the local nick. You'd have a lot of explaining to do to get your passport back in hand."

Lawton stood up. "Well, I certainly expected a bit more camaraderie from my fellow countryman. Guess I'll drink at the bar, where the company's more friendly." He straightened his tailored jacket and stomped toward the bar.

Professor Cuthbert sat there, speechless. Finally, he closed his lips and swallowed. "I say. Not what you'd call a right cordial chap, is he?"

Ian's eyes stayed glued on the man who was already in deep conversation with the bartender. "Not exactly." He looked at the professor. "He's just off his trolley." He attempted a weak smile of encouragement.

He felt sorry for the professor. Visiting all the way from England for a research project and he's motel neighbors with a bloke on the pull. "What say we spend a day next week walking around Saratoga Springs and visiting the historical buildings? Might help you with your research."

"Say, that's awfully civil of you, Constable Thacker. I'm grateful."

Ian smiled and sipped his lager, but he kept a sharp eye on Lawton. He would keep him closely in his sights—and away from Abby.

Chapter 16

By Friday, Abby was well enough to visit the cabin where her ancestors had lived. According to Gregory, it was in the woods south of Congress Park. It would be less than a mile on foot, and she couldn't wait to get out in the fresh air.

She stood at the mirror and noticed how pale she appeared. White enough as it was, she decided to take an iron pill. No point in becoming anemic too. She brushed her hair back, adjusted the collar of her sweater, and rechecked her eye makeup. Fingering the button that belonged to her grandfather William, she stroked the smooth edges of the pewter piece and held it up in front of her face. "Sixty-two. I wonder what that means? Maybe Ian knows."

A gentle knock on the door announced his arrival. She hurried to answer and grinned at the sight of him. Dressed in a woolen sweater with a horizontal striped pattern, she laughed. "I guess we received the same notification today. Striped sweaters only."

He inspected her outfit. "Well, it certainly is far more attractive on you."

"Thanks. But I disagree." Pointing at the motel office, she said, "We'd better tell Gregory what time we're leaving. Otherwise, he'll wonder where we are."

After leaving a message with Gregory's sister in the office, Abby grabbed Ian's elbow. "Let's go. I'm starving."

"Where do you put that food? Your legs must be hollow."

"Right." She walked faster. "Let's hurry."

Her pancakes and eggs disappeared in moments. After wolfing down the food, she swallowed a large glass of orange juice. She patted her stomach and sat back in the booth. "That was delicious." She fingered the button on the chain.

"What's that?"

"This?" She held it up. "It was a button from my great-great-great-great-grandfather, William Carpenter. It was from his uniform during the war. Scott had it, and he sent it with me so I could wear it for the commemoration."

He looked confused. "May I see it?"

"Sure." She pulled the silver chain over her head, straightening out the hair she'd mussed up with the motion. "Isn't it beautiful? I'm so proud to have it—such a connection to my family, you know?" She lowered her eyes a moment then looked at him. "Before this week, I had never felt so proud to be an American. So proud to be descended from one of the Patriots who fought to bring liberty to America." She tilted her head. "Does that make sense?"

He seemed deep in thought, staring at the button.

"Ian? What's wrong?"

He looked up. "Wrong? Nothing. Nothing's wrong." He handed it back. "Yes. Yes, it's beautiful." He smiled with closed lips.

"You seem quiet, all of a sudden."

"It's nothing. Indigestion, I'm sure." He grabbed her hand. "Are you ready to visit your ancestral home?"

She beamed. "Yes!"

They scooted out of the booth, paid their bill at the counter, and headed back to the motel.

Gregory was waiting for them with a larger-than-life grin, wearing a jacket and a wool hat with flaps that covered his ears and snapped under his chin. "Ready?"

"Absolutely." Abby patted his arm. "Lead the way, tour guide."

The three tromped off south along Route 9, then veered slightly east on a small path toward the woods.

"This is an old road." Gregory walked with plodding steps. "Watch out for burrs on the weeds."

"We will." She looked upward at the canopy of maples and oaks overhead. A red leaf drifted down from the overhanging branches, and she caught it in her hand.

"It's the … same color as … your hair, Miss Carpenter." His smile was rather charming.

"I suppose it is, Gregory." Twirling the leaf in her fingers, she grew more excited the deeper into the woods they traveled.

Ian seemed lost in thought as he stared ahead.

"Ian, aren't these woods lovely?"

"Hmmm? Yes, yes they are." He spoke to Gregory. "Do you know how much farther, Gregory?"

Gregory seemed annoyed by the question. Ian was being rather unmindful of the excitement of this mission, and Abby found herself getting irritated with him as well.

She stopped. "We can go back if you want. You don't seem to be enjoying this trek."

He rubbed his mouth and looked at her with apologetic eyes. "I'm really sorry. I just had something on my mind."

"Well, that's obvious. I just thought you'd be excited for me. Finding this cabin means a lot." She shifted her feet back and forth, trying not to feel hurt.

He stopped walking and put his hands on her elbows that hung limply at her side. "Forgive my less-than-jolly mood. I'm quite anxious to visit this site with you. I'm sorry."

"Okay. Let's go on, then. You must be tired from this week."

"We can't stay too long, Mr. Thacker. I have to … be back to work … later today." Gregory shot him a smile.

"Thanks, Gregory. I appreciate you taking Miss Carpenter and me. I'll try to be more pleasant."

The threesome trudged through the thickening woods until they reached a small clearing. Abby stopped abruptly and gasped. She'd expected to find the cabin she'd played at when she was a small child. She only had vague memories of the visits but vivid recollections of photos taken of her and Scott playing cowboys and Indians there. Instead of a worn-out cabin, she faced the burned-out shell of a home. All that still stood was the old brick hearth.

Gregory stood in front of the skeletal remains. "It burned."

As Ian put his arm around her, she struggled to find her voice. "My cabin." Her eyes burned from the still-shifting ash that swirled in the autumn breeze.

"This fire was not that long ago." Ian's eyes darkened.

"What happened, Gregory?"

"I don't know, Miss … Carpenter. It was here. Now it's gone."

"When? When did this happen?" She shook her head, stunned with disbelief.

Gregory stared. "I don't know. Maybe *he* knows."

"He?" Ian riveted his eyes on Gregory. "He, who?" His voice grew louder.

"The man who … calls Miss Carpenter … a different name. The man who … knows Mr. Cardwell."

"You mean Ambrose Cardwell?" Abby shivered.

"Yes. That's him."

"What do you mean he calls Miss Carpenter a different name?" Ian was in full interrogation mode.

"Ambrose calls her … Abigail Gillingham."

Chapter 17

Sergeant Walker seemed a bit friendlier to Abby this visit, but his message was less than satisfying.

"There's really nothing we can pin on this Cardwell character, Miss Carpenter. And he has an alibi for the day of the fire. He was nowhere near your family's cabin." The smartly dressed officer took a few more notes. "I wish we knew more about that fire, but we've had several unsolved arsons in the last few years. Can't pinpoint a cause or a perpetrator." He scratched his head.

Ian stood at the police station counter and sighed. "Does Cardwell have an alibi for the day someone snuck into Abby's room?"

"He does. He was at his parents' home, according to his mom, playing with his new pong table." The sergeant rolled his eyes.

"But, Sergeant Walker ..." Abby leaned toward the man behind the wooden counter. "His knowledge of my family history is creepy. Combine that with the intruder in my room and his obnoxious behavior toward me—can't you charge him with something?" She exhaled in exasperation.

"I understand your frustration, Miss Carpenter. But unless we can come up with a charge for someone acting like an imbecile, our hands are tied. Until we have more evidence of something, all we can do is keep an eye on him. And if I were you two, I'd keep all four eyes on Cardwell."

"All right. Thanks, Sergeant. Let's go, Abby." Ian put his arm around her shoulders and led her toward the door.

After stepping over the threshold, she stopped and stared into the distance, her arms folded. "Why? Why would Ambrose know my grandmother Abigail's name? Why would he care?"

"I don't know, Abby. But I know one thing." He gave her arm a playful pinch. "This afternoon is far too beautiful to waste thinking about—what did the sergeant call him, the imbecile?" His voice lowered. "Let's stroll toward Congress Park. I've heard it's near some charming houses that would be a nice distraction from your worries. What do you say?"

She met his eyes. "I say, 'Let's do it.'" It was worth agreeing to the walk just to see Ian's relaxed smile. There'd been far too much tension, and they both needed a break.

She allowed the afternoon breeze to sweep thoughts of Ambrose and family mysteries far away from her mind. Instead, she took in the surrounding autumn foliage swaying as if directed by a maestro conducting an unheard and unseen orchestra. The beautiful melody was displayed in the motion of the wind and the ballet of the branches that beckoned an onlooker to dance. She found it refreshing and exhilarating.

The street was lined on both sides by houses of numerous architectural styles. Some had been built over a hundred years ago, but loving care through the years had kept most of them in pristine condition.

Although some of the stately mansions they passed were impressive with their height and grandeur, it was the Gothic cottage on Regent Street that drew her eye and prompted her to stop walking. The deeply set porch instilled visions of a warm summer's day, rocking chairs, and lemonade. The small garden was enthroned with a bower of ancient-looking trees that seemed to protect it from the world around it. It was warm and secure. It looked like the home of her dreams.

She sighed. "I've never seen anything like this in California."

"It's quite peaceful." Ian stared at the two-story cottage. "Would you like to walk through the park or go for some hot chocolate?"

"Strolling in the park sounds enjoyable and relaxing."

They continued their jaunt until they reached Congress Park. Acres of rolling grass, interspersed with flowers and fountains, took her breath away. "This was a great idea, Ian. I needed to be calm and clear my thoughts."

"We both did." He stared at a squirrel racing across the lawn with a large nut in its mouth. "This place could even calm a rodent preparing for winter."

They continued a slow pace, taking in the numerous monuments and markers that explained the history of the springs in the town.

"The motel owner said that healing spring waters drew the first settlers to Saratoga Springs. I hear they still run and are considered somewhat medicinal."

An unusual fountain caught their eyes. It was a rectangular pool with male figures on either side blowing water toward each other. Streams of the liquid nearly crossed in the middle, but they missed connecting by a matter of inches. The spray of each followed its own trajectory, the spouts never intersecting with one another.

It's like Ian and I. Separated by an ocean and unable to connect.
Abby sighed.

He must have thought she was tired. "Would you like to sit by this pool?" He pointed to another rectangular basin of water with a statue of an alluring woman at one end.

"Why don't you sit facing me, instead of that statue?" She giggled.

"I'd prefer facing you. That nymph has nothing on you."

They sat silently for a moment, the sound of bubbling liquid filling the void. He reached out and passed his finger through the hair resting on her shoulder. "Is there anything else you'd like to do today?" He leaned in closer and made firm eye contact.

"Well, I was thinking. We didn't get to that cemetery of the Revolutionary War veterans the other day. What if we drove over to Stillwater and walked through there to see if we could find William Carpenter's grave?"

He glanced downward. "I'm not certain that's such a good idea."

"What do you mean?" His seeming disinterest hurt her feelings. "I thought you liked family history. Or is it just *your* family history you care about?"

"That's not it." He paused. "Are you certain your ancestor, William Carpenter, was an American soldier?"

She half laughed. "Am I certain? Yes. Why on earth would you ask such a question?"

"Look, Abby, I'm not questioning your honesty. But I'm wondering if someone has misled you. Made you think your grandfather was a Patriot, when in fact …"

"What?"

"In fact, he was likely a British soldier in the King's Army."

She stood in a huff, pointing an accusing finger at him. "That's not funny, Ian. Why would you say that? Why would you accuse William Carpenter of being an enemy of the Americans?" She crossed her arms to keep his words at bay.

He stood and fingered the button hanging around her neck. "Because of this. When you showed it to me this morning at breakfast, I was taken aback. My father owned a book with photographs of all the British uniforms and the various details, including the style of button. This button is from a coat belonging to a King's soldier from the 62nd Regiment of Foot. If …" He exhaled. "If this button was worn by William Carpenter, your great-great-great-great-grandfather was a soldier in the King's Army. Like mine was."

Speech eluded Abby. When she finally found her voice, she stuttered. "But … but why wouldn't my father have told me? Or Scott? Something's not right here." She paced as she rubbed the back of her neck. "How could this be?"

"Many of the soldiers in the British Army deserted for one reason or another. They were starving. They were far from home. Abby." He put his hands on both of her arms, stopping her pacing.

"We can't know the whole story. But we mustn't try to form our thoughts of those who came before based on preconceived ideas. You don't know why he might have left the King's Army. Or why he stayed to marry Abigail Gillingham."

She remembered the words in the letter she'd read. *He loved me enough to stay with me.* Would love have drawn him to desert his army and become an American?

"Ian, let's go back to the motel. I need to call Scott."

"All right."

They walked in silence at a brisk pace down the sidewalk heading south. When they arrived at the Gates Motel, Abby took out her key. "If you don't mind, I'd like to speak with my brother alone."

"I understand." He kissed the crown of her hair before she walked inside and closed the door.

* * *

"What do you mean, you thought you told me? That was a pretty important piece of family history, don'tcha think? I feel like a dope, talking about the Revolutionary War hero in our ancestry, bragging about my Patriot bloodline. What if I'd tried to join the Daughters of the American Revolution?"

"Now hold on, Abby. Just because you're all into family history now doesn't fit with your previous laissez-faire attitude toward all things historical. Every time Dad tried to talk about it, you tuned him out. And then when I started to bring it up, you weren't much better. I know I should have told you before you left, to be sure you remembered. But did you really care—before now?"

A pang of guilt raced through her mind. "You're right, Scott." She plopped down on the bed. "I really am a dope, bragging about my ancestor to Ian."

"Tell me about this Ian. Are you sure he's a good guy?"

"Yes, Scott, I'm sure." She nearly started to tell him about the not-so-good guys but thought better of it. "Hey, I'm really sorry. I was just so shocked to find out that button was from a Redcoat. I still can hardly believe it."

"Abby, we don't know why he left the army. But we do know he loved Abigail Gillingham. And it probably cost him dearly to desert, for whatever reason he did it."

"You're right." She sighed. "I guess it's a family mystery. But a romantic one."

"You're such a girl." She could see her brother shaking his head at her.

"Yup. That's what they said the day I was born." She remembered Scott's second trip to the hospital. "Hey, are you doing okay? Maureen told me about your adventure with the popcorn."

He groaned. "Yeah. I think it'll be years before I eat *that* treat again. But I'm feeling lots better."

"Good. I'll let you get back to watching soap operas." She loved teasing her brother, who abhorred daytime TV.

"Right. Hey, call me and let me know you're okay."

"I will."

After hanging up, Abby grew somber again. Looking at her watch, she saw it was almost dinnertime. She wondered if Ian wanted to go eat. A quick phone call brought him to her room in a matter of seconds.

"Well? What did Scott say about William Carpenter?"

She looked at the floor then up. "Well, you were right. He was a British soldier who … apparently deserted the army. Not sure how I feel about that."

He walked closer to her. "He must have had a reason."

"I read a letter from my grandmother Abigail."

"She wrote a letter? Do you have it with you?"

"Yes. It's a copy of the text—not the actual letter. Do you want to read it?"

"Yes. I feel guilty, though, reading yours, since I've yet to read the one my father gave to me. I meant to read it on the flight here, but I fell asleep."

She pulled the letter from her bag and handed it to him.

He carefully opened the typed pages and began to read.

They both sat, and Abby watched his blue eyes scan the words.

He looked up. "Knowing he was in the King's Army explains why she said, 'He loved me enough to stay with me.'" A confused look crossed his countenance. "But what"—he pointed to the letter—"or who did he rescue and protect her from?"

"I don't know. The family mystery deepens."

He folded the pages and handed them back to Abby. She tucked them into the suitcase pocket and closed the lid.

She stood, suddenly self-conscious over the way he looked at her. "So, do you want to go eat supper?"

He stood in front of her and moved closer. "Abby, reading that letter … well, I can understand how William felt about Abigail." His Adam's apple moved slightly as he swallowed. "I wish things were so different—that we did not live so far apart."

She lowered her eyes. "I know. But we do."

He lifted her chin.

Why did he have to wear that cologne?

Abby shivered when Ian's lips met hers. It was slow and warm and wanted. As it continued, she thrilled when his fingers wove through her hair and his hands drew her closer. His embrace threatened to make her forget they were not married—and she needed to remember. She would not make the same mistake twice.

"Ian," her voice came out breathless.

"Abby." He kissed her again.

"Ian, please stop. We're not married."

He paused in his passion and licked his lips. "That seems unimportant at the moment."

She pushed him away with gentle force. "But it is important, Ian. I don't want to have some affair and then long for you after you go back to England. Besides, I made a promise."

His eyes narrowed. "A promise? I thought you didn't have anyone."

She shook her head. "No, I don't have another guy. I promised myself—and God—that I'd not go too far until I was married."

"Truly? Do you not feel for me what I feel for you? I love you. I want you."

"Yes, I feel it. And I want you as well. But there's more to love than feelings. There's a commitment of mind and heart, as well as body. I was taken advantage of once. I'll not be again."

Ian released his strong grip and held her loosely. "I'll not take advantage of you, Abby. You mean too much to me."

"You mean so much to me too."

He kissed her gently then pulled away. He inhaled deeply and raked his hands through his hair. "If I forget your promise in future, please remind me. With a kick, if necessary."

"I will." She kissed him and grabbed her purse.

After leaving the motel room, they held hands as they walked to a restaurant. With every step, Abby prayed silently. *Lord, help me stay true to my promise.*

Chapter 18

Sunday arrived with Abby and Ian choosing to go back to the same church. Abby's eyes widened at the camaraderie he shared with the pastor when they greeted each other. When Ian whispered to her that the two men had talked a few days before, she was taken by complete surprise. She glanced at him occasionally during the service, but he was swept up in the sermon and never returned her glances.

Afterward, they decided to eat brunch at a larger restaurant, for a change. Abby hugged her thick sweater tighter against the chill in the air as they walked toward the charming eating establishment adorned with colorful Tiffany lamps. She was grateful when they arrived and she could get out of the cold. They were seated right away, and the waitress served them hot coffee.

"You probably think I'm a wimp, being so cold here. We're quite spoiled where I live, temperature wise. Of course, there's the smog we have to contend with." She contorted her face and faked a cough.

"Well, in London, we have cold *and* wretched air. When I was a bobby doing traffic duty, my face was nearly black after directing traffic at a busy intersection."

"Wow. That's almost as bad as smoking cigarettes." She sipped her coffee and added more cream to it. "So, I don't mean to pry, but what did you and Pastor Moore talk about last week? I must admit, I was taken aback by your friendliness this morning."

He stared at the coffee that he'd doctored with a lot of cream and sugar. "Many things. I'm not quite ready to share those with you just yet." He took her hand. "I hope you understand."

She squeezed his fingers. "Of course. Sometimes we all need to find someone to talk to about the deeper things. I'm just happy you were comfortable enough with him to open up."

"I hope you know how comfortable I am with you." He lifted her hand to his face and kissed her fingers. A moment later, he turned red and looked down at the table. "And I want to apologize for being so … familiar … with you the other day. I'd no right to touch you like that. And I'm sorry."

Her face warmed. "I didn't exactly resist at first. I enjoyed it far too much, but …"

"I know. I think it may be safer if we spent less time together in your motel room. I am far too attracted to you to trust myself, and I respect you too much to push the limits. And no guarantees I would not get carried away."

No guarantees she wouldn't either. "Okay. Can we at least be seen in public?"

He grinned. "I certainly hope so. Just be aware of my hands at all times."

"I'll be watching you, Constable." She grinned and sipped her coffee.

* * *

The next day was the first fitting for the colonial costumes. Miss Swanson had scheduled the appointments the week before, and Abby looked forward to seeing herself in eighteenth-century clothing.

She and Ian walked to the Frederika Inn through a morning mist. Upon entering, she was astonished again by the warm, glowing atmosphere in the large lobby. It felt safe and warm, even cozy, despite the vast foyer and huge chandelier. Whoever had designed it was obviously an expert in illumination.

Ian saluted her as he headed toward the men's fitting area. "Headed for the King's Army, m'lady."

She laughed and peeked into the women's area.

"I'll be right with you, Abby." Miss Swanson was adjusting the fit of a ball gown on the same brunette Abby had seen the week before.

"I'll wait out here." She smiled pleasantly, but her nerves carried away the image of the buxom brunette with the striking décolletage. She hoped hers wasn't so low cut. She crossed her arms over her chest and stopped near a brown, upholstered chair for a few moments as she contemplated sitting down. But as she glanced around, she strode toward the portrait of the baroness, remembering that Ian had described her as having been a great lady.

Ian had told her that the Baroness gave food to the starving troops. He respected her great kindness, apparently. And then she remembered the softness in his eyes as he compared the lady's ginger tresses to her own. He had gazed at Abby with such admiration, she shivered with pleasure at the memory.

After a few moments, the brunette exited the dressing area with a sway in her hips. Abby noticed that every male head in the room turned her way.

"Ready for you, Abby." Miss Swanson's friendly grin greeted her. "I think you're going to like the dresses."

She smiled like a schoolgirl, rubbing her hands together in anticipation. "Would you like me to write you a check now?"

"No. Wait for the final fitting next week." Miss Swanson closed the door to the lobby.

Abby undressed.

"I know you're modest, but you'll need to take nearly everything off."

"Oh." She nodded and removed the next layer of clothing.

"Colonial women wore what they called 'stays,' instead of bras. They're kind of like a corset and hold everything in and upward."

"Oh." That explained the cleavage on the brunette.

A nightgown-like piece of clothing slipped over her head as she held her arms up. Miss Swanson placed a corset-like binder around her torso and breasts. She firmly tied up the strings that tightened the undergarment.

Looking in the full-length mirror, Abby gasped. "Oh, my." If she felt warm before, it now felt like full sunlight had seared her whole body. Blotches of embarrassment appeared on her neck. She swallowed. "Does it have to show so much?"

Miss Swanson inspected her. "It's not too much, for the style of the day. That's what they wore." She grinned at Abby. "You're just not used to having your curves accentuated. You look beautiful."

"Yeah, but … I don't want to be … tempting someone."

A wide grin crossed the seamstress's countenance. "Would that someone be getting fitted next door with the tailor?"

"Is it that obvious?" She turned toward Miss Swanson. "It's not that I don't want to look nice. I just don't want to give the wrong impression." Beads of sweat trickled down her hairline. "You see, he lives clear across the ocean. I'd love to get closer to him, but there's no possible way we could get married. And, I don't want to seduce him if we're not man and wife."

Miss Swanson looked at her and sighed. "You are a rare treasure these days. It seems most don't care about sleeping around with whoever. I work in Hollywood. Believe me, I know. I could tell stories …" She shook her head and exhaled.

She picked up the blue linen gown and slipped it over Abby's corset and shift. Adjusting it and securing it with clasps, Miss Swanson pointed Abby toward the mirror. "Look."

She gasped at the sight.

"Even the simple dress of a working woman looks lovely on you."

Her décolletage still showed too much for her comfort, and Abby tried to adjust to the new look. She'd always been a bit uncomfortable with her womanly curves and tried to keep them less noticeable. Apparently, in colonial America, they advertised their assets.

"Now, let's try on the other gown. I can't wait to see it on you." Miss Swanson swept the linen dress over Abby's head and hung it on a hanger. "I'll get this sewed with permanent stitching this week. Now …" She carried an abundance of green silk toward

Abby as though carrying crown jewels. "Here is your gown for the ball, m'lady. Close your eyes while I secure it."

Abby did as she was told and felt Miss Swanson pull, tug, and adjust what felt like a mountain of soft material.

After what seemed like several minutes, she stopped and sighed with pleasure. "Exquisite. You can open your eyes."

It was a Cinderella moment. "This can't be me."

"Ah, but it is. Your gentleman friend? I don't know what his circumstances are, but if he doesn't get swept away by your beauty and want to marry you? Well, I don't know what to say."

"Ian is a police officer in London. And I work in California. Miss Swanson—that's 6,000 miles of separation." She reddened once again, staring at the abundance of skin showing thanks to this gown. It made the first dress look like a nun's habit. "I feel like a seductress!"

Miss Swanson placed a hand on her shoulder. "You'll not be seducing him. Merely giving a hint about what he might miss if he leaves without you. Sometimes a hint can be our greatest ally." She winked at Abby.

"I hope you're right." She bit her lower lip. "Miss Swanson, thank you. I hope you don't think I'm ungrateful because of, you know, this low neckline." She traced the silky material with her fingertips.

"No, dear. I think you are wise to withhold the milk when he's not bought the cow, as my mother used to say." She grinned.

"I haven't heard that one in a while."

Miss Swanson helped pull the dress over Abby's head and hung up the gown.

"I heard it at my house all the time."

They both giggled.

"Thanks. You've been so helpful."

"See you next week, Abby."

Chapter 19

The days seemed to pass quickly for Abby and Ian, touring the historical sites almost on a daily basis. Abby could sense the excitement building within the communities of Saratoga Springs, Stillwater, and Schuylerville as they anticipated the big weekend that would start October 7th. Each town planned on participating in the bicentennial in one way or another, whether with parades, reenactments, or speakers. Or all three.

Despite the towns' excitement, she began to worry about seeing Ian so much. The more the bicentennial approached, the sooner they would be bidding each other farewell—perhaps saying goodbye forever.

Abby tried not to think about it. They would keep in touch, he'd assured her. Perhaps next summer they could visit. Of course, they'd have to arrange for more vacation time from their jobs.

She realized that staying in touch with her would become burdensome for the busy copper. He might even become resentful of her need for him. Almost more painful than the thought of saying goodbye was the expected, gradual ending of their friendship. Each missed phone call, each note they forgot to answer would hammer one more nail in the coffin of their relationship. As this awareness grew, she determined to protect herself by erecting emotional barriers. The thought of him pulling away from her was more agonizing than she could bear.

As they wandered through the park later that week, Abby inhaled deeply. "Ian, I think we need to see less of each other." Even as she spoke the words, she nearly choked on them.

He frowned. "Can't we spend as much time together that we can? Shouldn't we treasure the moments that are available to us here and now?"

"I can't, Ian. I know once you leave, our friendship will change. I can't bear the thought of you slowly forgetting me." She fought back the tears while she and Ian strolled through Congress Park.

He stopped and held both of her arms. "Abby, how could I forget you? You've no idea how I've wrestled with this myself. My heart aches for you. Every part of me aches for you. But I can't stay. I don't know what to do." He stared at the ground.

"I need time to think. This is too hard. I need to go rest." She walked away and left him standing near a fountain—the same fountain they had sat near on the day he kissed her. She covered her mouth and held back the tears as long as she could.

* * *

Ian stood and watched Abby run back to The Gates Motel. The ache and loneliness he'd felt on the plane to New York couldn't compare with the emptiness and hurt compounding his despair now. How could she not see how much he cared? How much he needed her? What was he supposed to do?

God, why have You brought this woman into my life? My heart is more tortured than ever with these feelings.

He knew he needed to do something that Pastor Jacob had talked about in last Sunday's sermon. He needed to seek God in all this mass of frustration. What was it Jacob had quoted? "God is not the God of confusion but of peace."

Well, there's not much peace in my soul. I can tell You that, God.

Running swift fingers through his hair, Ian put his hands in his pockets and walked somberly back to the motel. As he walked past Abby's door, her sudden scream jolted him out of his misery.

He pounded on her door. "Abby!"

Fear gripped him as adrenaline raced through his bloodstream. His throat constricted as he again thrust a forceful fist onto the wood that separated him from Abby.

He heard a click as she unlocked the door. Her face was frozen in fear as she hugged her arms tightly. She didn't speak but stood back so he could come in.

"What's wrong?" He searched the room with widened eyes while his heart pounded. "Abby, what happened?"

She stood mutely, pointing toward the bathroom at the far end of the room. He hurried over and gasped.

Written on the mirror were two words: Abigail Gillingham. Below the name was a heart shape. But this was no Valentine's heart. There was a knife stabbing it, and drips of blood were drawn with red lipstick.

His stomach churned with nausea. He turned as he heard a female voice ask, "What's happening?"

Ian tried to swallow past the lump in his throat. "Don't touch anything, Liz. We need to call the police. Can you call them from the office?"

Liz saw the mirror and gasped. "Dear heavens, what is happening here?"

"Please, Liz, go call them."

The motel maid was near tears. "Of course." She looked at Abby. "Mr. Thacker, take care of her."

He glanced back at Abby, who'd sunk onto the edge of the bed. He hurried over and wrapped his arms around her. She still didn't speak.

"Are you hurt? Was anyone in here?"

She rested her head on his shoulder and held onto him tightly. He gripped her in his embrace, afraid to let her out of his sight.

Chapter 20

"Perhaps you should go to the hospital, Miss Carpenter, and see a physician. You've had quite a shock." Sergeant Walker stared at her. She'd hardly spoken since he'd arrived.

"I think she should as well." Ian tucked a strand of her hair behind her ear.

"No." She sat upright. "I need to tell you something else. I … I thought perhaps I was imagining it."

"Abby." Ian lifted her chin. "Something else happened? Why didn't you tell me?"

"Because I wasn't sure. I thought maybe I'd misplaced them or forgotten to pack them. But after this …" Her lips trembled.

The sergeant sat on the opposite bed and looked at her with fatherly concern. "Miss Carpenter, I'm so sorry to have to question you when you've been through such a shock. But I must have all the facts so I can help you. We want to find who's been harassing you."

She looked at him with reddened eyes. "I thought it was nothing. But … This is so embarrassing." She shook her head. "A personal item is missing from the dresser. I noticed it yesterday after Ian and I returned from sightseeing."

"Why didn't you tell me?" Ian rubbed the back of his neck, attempting to massage away his near panic.

"A personal item?" The sergeant had stopped writing.

"Yes." She looked downward. "A pair of my pantihose." She looked at the sergeant. "Can you understand why I didn't report that? I might have just misplaced them, or—"

"Or they might have been stolen." Sergeant Walker sighed. "Miss, I don't like the way this is going. I think we need to station someone at this motel. In the meantime, please don't go anywhere alone. Is that clear?"

Abby's voice was small. "Yes."

The sergeant turned toward the two men taking photographs and gathering more fingerprints. "Are you fellows finished gathering evidence yet?"

"Just wrapping up." They collected their tools of the trade and exited without looking at her.

The sergeant gave his attention to her. "Look, Miss Carpenter, you shouldn't be staying in this room tonight."

"She can stay in mine." Ian intruded into the conversation as quickly as he could. "I can stay in here."

Shock etched across Abby's eyes. "But it may not be safe for you."

He stroked her cheek. "I'll be fine. I can handle myself." He smiled. "You can sleep on the far bed. The sheets are still clean."

The sergeant tapped him on the shoulder. "Can I speak with you outside?"

"Of course." He looked at Abby. "I'll be right back."

Ian stepped outdoors, and Sergeant Walker motioned him away from the open doorway. He kept his voice low as he watched the door.

"I'm getting concerned about this perpetrator, whoever he is. I'm sending detectives over to interrogate Ambrose Cardwell. And we'll interview every person that came near this motel while you two were gone. You say you were out walking in the park. About what time?"

He could barely remember what time they took their walk. All he could recall was her hurtful declaration to him. "I think it was about three to five, or so. Really not certain. I know dusk was starting, but that's about all." He stared into the distance, battling the rage in his mind. He wished he could have this criminal under his fist right now.

"Constable, I think you know what I'm concerned about."

"You don't need to tell me, Sergeant. I've followed a few psychopaths in my brief career as an officer. And their intent is usually quite clear."

Sergeant Walker patted Ian's upper arm. "Don't worry. We'll catch him. But stay with her." He turned and left.

Although the knife that had stabbed him had left its mark over a month ago, Ian's nerve endings seared as though it was happening all over again. And the thought of someone stabbing Abby firmed his resolve.

He would protect her from harm. Or he would die trying.

Chapter 21

Abby crawled into the unused bed in Ian's motel room. She knew an armed officer was right outside her door, keeping watch, but she still had trouble getting to sleep.

Whenever she closed her eyes, she envisioned that horrid message on her motel mirror. Opening her eyes was no better. Everything in this room seemed strange and foreign to her, except the aroma. It was the scent of Ian's cologne.

Sitting up on the edge of her bed, she glanced over at the disheveled covers on the bed he usually slept in. Although there wasn't anyone there to disturb, she quietly rose and tiptoed to the bed. She picked up Ian's pillow and held it near her face, inhaling the spicy, musky essence that brought his presence to life for her. She slipped back under the covers and cuddled the pillow. The sweet fragrance of the man she loved calmed her. It was the last thing she recalled that night before drifting off to sleep.

* * *

"Abby. Abby, I've made you some tea."

Was she dreaming? She was enveloped by a sweet field of flowers and the heady perfume was exhilarating. She rolled onto her back.

"Abby."

Her eyes opened wide. A man stood over her. She nearly screamed, but a familiar, calming voice broke through her confusion.

"Abby, it's me." Ian's blue eyes searched her face. "Are you all right?"

"What? Yes. Where am I? Why are you in my room?" She sat up, rubbing her eyes.

"Well, actually, you're in my room. But you needn't fear. I was in yours."

Then she remembered. She held the pillow close like it was a fortification against fear.

He spoke again. "I'm so sorry I had to awaken you, but today you have an appointment with the seamstress. I can bring you breakfast from somewhere if you like."

His sweet concern nearly made her cry. She remembered the hurt in his eyes when she declared they should see less of each other yesterday. "You're being too kind, after what I said."

"We can talk about that another time. We have other things to be concerned about today. Here. Why don't you have a proper cuppa?" His eyes drew together as he looked at her lap. "Is that my pillow?"

"Um, yes. I needed another one, so I borrowed yours. I hope you don't mind."

"Mind? No." He took the pillow and tossed it onto his bed. "Liz came early this morning and cleaned your room. She cleaned up … everything. I thought you'd rather get ready in there. While you do, I'll wait outside, guarding your door. The other officer had to leave."

"Okay." She sipped the tea and closed her eyes, the rich flavor of the brew energizing her and bolstering her spirits. "This is heavenly. Thanks." She swallowed the rest and handed the cup back to Ian.

He picked up her sweater. "Here you are, Miss Carpenter. I'll escort you to your room, and you can prepare to go see Miss Swanson." He held the sweater up with a gallant flourish. As she slipped her arms into the sleeves, he bowed. "At your service."

She was genuinely surprised at his playfulness. But when he stood up from his bow, he wore a more serious expression.

"And I will be at your service all day and night if you need me. Sergeant Walker still has no suspects, but he and his staff are working on it. I want you to know, I'll protect you. No matter what."

Abby wanted to throw herself into his arms but thought better of inciting emotions better left undisturbed. "Thank you, Ian." She walked ahead of him out the door and waited to go into Room 20. He insisted on checking out her entire room before declaring it safe.

"Thanks again." She hurried inside.

* * *

"Did you sleep well, Abby?" Miss Swanson touched her arm in a maternal manner. "You seem somewhat drawn. Is everything okay, honey?"

"Not exactly. Can we talk for a moment?" She'd been cautioned by Sergeant Walker to avoid discussing the incident in her motel room. But she needed to talk to someone about Ian. She needed a woman's insight and felt she could trust Miss Swanson.

"Of course." The seamstress moved a bolt of fabric off a chair and motioned for Abby to sit, then she sat across from her. "I could tell something was bothering you the moment you walked through the door."

Unbidden tears rolled down Abby's cheeks, and she flinched with embarrassment.

"Oh, Abby." The seamstress leaped up to find a box of tissues and handed it to her. "Please, dear, tell me what's wrong."

When Abby could control her tears for a moment, she blew her nose and spoke. "I don't know how to deal with my feelings toward Ian. I want him so much, yet I know he's leaving next week." She inhaled convulsively. "So I told him we should see each other less. It hurts too much to be close to him, knowing he's going away. I know I've hurt his feelings, but I'm trying to keep us both from getting wounded in the long run. I know our relationship can't last."

Miss Swanson got up and poured a glass of water for Abby. She handed it to her and sat again. "First of all, you don't *know* it can't last. You're *assuming* it won't last. But one never knows what the future holds."

She wiped her eyes with a fresh tissue. "How can it possibly last?"

"Well, I don't know the how. But obstacles can be overcome if true love is willing to adapt." She paused a moment. "I was like you once. I'd fallen for a man who lived in the Midwest. I was busy managing my new career in Hollywood and couldn't possibly see a way to make it work. He wanted me, but I let circumstances push us farther apart. I told him he should forget me." She lowered her eyelids. "I don't know if he forgot me, but I heard he married someone else."

Thinking of Miss Swanson's loss filled Abby with sadness. "That's heartbreaking."

"Yes, it is. I've never forgotten him. I pushed him away, rather than follow my heart. I never gave it a chance. I never gave *him* a chance." She leaned over and took Abby's hand. "Do you love him?"

"With all my heart." Tears welled again.

"Have you told him you do?"

"No. I'm afraid to."

"Has he told you he loves you?"

"Yes."

Miss Swanson sighed. "Perhaps he will be more encouraged to find a way to make it work if he knows he holds your heart. Men fear being rejected as well, you know."

"I suppose I thought he would know how I felt."

"Well, honey, unless he's a mind reader, that's likely not the case." Miss Swanson squeezed Abby's hands with hers. "Now, let's wipe those tears away and begin to think positively. How does that song go? 'God will make a way ...'"

Abby's red eyes brightened. "'When there seems to be no way.' You know that song?"

"We sing it at church quite often. It's one of my favorites."

"Mine too." She took a deep breath. "I've kept you far too long in conversation. I know you're busy."

"I'm never too busy for a friend in need. I'll say a prayer for you, Abby."

"Thanks. That's the best thing you can do for me."

* * *

Ian was quieter than usual at lunch. He sat across from her in the booth, stirring his coffee and staring out the window.

She couldn't stand the silence between them. "How was your fitting with the tailor?"

He glanced at her briefly then looked at his coffee. "It went well."

When he didn't add anything, tightness gripped her stomach. She laid her sandwich down. The thought of eating chicken salad suddenly seemed nauseating.

"You're not hungry?" Ian wiped his mouth with a napkin.

"No."

Have I completely blown my chances with Ian? Will he ever forgive me for pushing him away? How do I get past this terrible strain between us?

He broke the silence. "Look, I know you don't want to be with me. But for safety's sake, I hope you can put up with me. Sergeant Walker doesn't have enough officers to provide twenty-four-hour protection. So, hopefully, you can tolerate my presence as your bodyguard."

"Ian, you don't understand—"

"I think I understand quite well. You've been tolerant of me because I paid for your rental car and we've had a lark together. You've felt safe with me, but you're ready to move on. And now you're somewhat trapped with me, due to this maniac on the loose." He chewed another bite of his sandwich then paused before he swallowed. "I'm terribly sorry that I'm the only one available to protect you. I hope you can bear my presence until you go home."

She reached across the table and put her hand on his arm. "Ian, you have this all wrong."

He pulled away. "Do I?" The pained expression in his eyes was unmistakable. "I've thought about what you said yesterday, and I think I understand your meaning quite clearly." He lowered his eyes to look at the table. "But I want you to know, I will do everything in my power to keep you safe."

His name choked in her throat. "Ian …"

He motioned to the waitress. "May I have the bill, please?"

Dread and pain infused Abby's heart—and she knew it was her own fault. What had she done?

Chapter 22

The long-awaited commemoration for the final Battle of Saratoga was about to begin, but it held no celebration for Abby. Regrets of what she had said to Ian pierced her spirit like an emotional bayonet.

Visiting the battlefield would be like a visual confrontation with the unseen wounds of her heart.

The drive in the rental car from Saratoga Springs was fraught with tension. The only time Ian voluntarily spoke was when he discussed the ball later that evening.

"I bought tickets a couple of weeks ago for us. If you still wish to go, you needn't feel compelled to dance with me. I'll attend as your escort. But you may dance with whomever you choose. I'll not force my presence upon you, other than to make certain you are not bothered by anyone."

After he had spoken, he'd turned toward the car window and stared at the autumn fields between Saratoga Springs and the national park, where the events would occur.

Try as she might, Abby was unable to engage him in further conversation. It was the longest thirty minutes she could recall.

Now Ian stood beside her in the crowd as they awaited the speakers and musical presentations. Hundreds of visitors to the park began arriving via shuttle buses set up for the event. Soon hundreds turned into thousands.

Dignitaries from the countries that had participated in the battle took their places on the platform, shaking each other's hands and laughing jovially. The contrast with the atmosphere that must have existed 200 years ago struck Abby as ironic. A representative of France greeted a counterpart from Great Britain. A German Consul of Affairs shared firm handshakes with the Americans. Former enemies now friends.

Did Ian think of her as his adversary? An antagonist who'd bruised his heart? She couldn't bear to contemplate that. It occurred to her that, in trying to defend her own emotions from being wounded, she had inflicted suffering on his. Would he ever forgive her?

She gently touched his hand, only to feel him draw it away. He folded his arms across his chest but continued to look around the crowd for any danger. Her spirits despaired that their hearts could never reconnect.

Some things could not be mended—like broken hearts. She supposed the song was right.

Abby tried to focus on the events beginning on the dais. The Master of Ceremonies, a local television personality, welcomed the crowd to this historic occasion. He introduced a choir from a local college, and a hush fell over the crowd as the singers began the national anthem.

Abby automatically placed her hand on her chest. She glanced sideways at Ian, trying not to let him know she was watching him.

His expression confused her. It held a mixture of sadness and tenderness with a tinge of anger. What could he be thinking?

After the patriotic song finished, a local rabbi opened the ceremonies in prayer. Abby was stirred by the heartfelt words the rabbi lifted before God as he acknowledged the birth of the United States of America, with gratitude toward God, Who divinely interceded in the victory for liberty.

Several other speakers arose and encouraged the crowd to remember, once again, the battle that had turned the British Empire upside down.

A highlight of the events was the appearance of Tom Brokaw from TV's *The Today Show*. His rousing words filled her with renewed patriotism—a fervor now strengthened by the knowledge that her ancestor, whom she had assumed was American, had chosen America as his new home.

"As we have seen, without the victory at Saratoga, we would not have won the hearts and minds of the French," Brokaw said. "Without the French alliance, the Americans would not have won at Yorktown. They would not have gained independence.

"But the significance of Saratoga goes beyond the question of freedom for the United States. Abraham Lincoln, much later, said it best. 'I have often inquired of myself,' he said, 'what great principles or idea it was that kept the colonies so long together. It was not the mere matter of the separation of the colonies from the motherland, but that sentiment and the Declaration of Independence which gave liberty, not only to people of this country, but I hope to the world for all future time.'"

Abby's eyes welled with tears, and Ian sniffed. She longed to hold his hand, but his arms were still crossed.

The morning television host then read from diaries of soldiers from both sides of the conflict in 1777, detailing the difficulties suffered by so many to obtain liberty for the United States—and for the world.

There were few dry eyes in the crowd as the benediction was given by a reverend from Stillwater. When "amen" was said, the crowd responded in kind. The inspiring event had the aura of a church service.

Ian unfolded his arms. "Shall we get something to eat? There are food tents over there."

"Sure."

He drew her toward the outdoor restaurants, but there was little intimacy in his touch. It was merely a guiding hand to get her through the masses, who all seemed intent on following their noses to the ethnic food offerings.

Abby was hungrier than she cared to admit. Chinese spices toyed with her nose and Polish sausages sizzled to capture her attention. But it was the Greek food that drew her eye and her appetite. "I love Greek food, Ian. Can we stop there?"

"Of course."

She chose a gyro—a folded sandwich of lamb and beef with a smothering of yogurt sauce. She wrinkled her nose at the raw onions and pulled them out with her fingers. "I love Greek food. Except for raw onions."

Ian tried one as well. "This is delicious." He had yogurt smeared around his mouth after the first bite.

Abby used her napkin to wipe it off.

She didn't realize that she apparently wore a similar mess, as Ian wiped off her cheek with a gentle stroke of his napkin.

"Oops." She grinned. "Thanks."

"You're quite welcome."

To her disappointment, he went back to being serious. "When we've finished, we should go back to the motel to rest. If you want to go to the ball, that is."

She wrapped the leftovers. "Of course I want to go." She put her hand on his arm and looked him in the eye. "I want to go with you."

He looked to the side and around the crowd as if searching for someone. He inhaled a deep breath. "All right. Shall we take the shuttle bus back to the car?"

The gyro twisted uncomfortably in her stomach. "Sure."

She threw the garbage from lunch into a trash receptacle nearby and walked back toward the shuttle stop with her head down until shouting in the distance drew her attention. "What's happening, Ian?"

His eyes were glued to the location of the shouting. "I don't know."

They quickened their pace. When Abby saw a red-faced Ambrose Cardwell shouting with Sergeant Walker, a chill rippled through her veins. "It's Ambrose." As they drew nearer, she gasped. "Gregory's on the ground, crying."

Her nursing instincts prompted her to race toward the weeping young man sitting in the dry weeds. "Gregory, what happened?"

"He … he wanted … to hit me."

Liz appeared. "Gregory! What happened? Are you hurt?"

Abby thought Liz would burst into tears, so she placed a hand on her arm. "Let me check him out, Liz, to make sure he's okay." A quick assessment for cuts and bruises assured her that Gregory was upset but not physically injured.

Sergeant Walker handcuffed an enraged Ambrose. "Looks like you'll be spending a bit of time in the clinker, Mr. Cardwell. Threatening bodily harm is not permitted, according to the law."

The sergeant led Ambrose toward his police car while Abby and Liz helped Gregory get to his feet.

"What happened, Gregory? Why was Ambrose threatening you?" Abby wiped dried grass off of Gregory's arm.

"He said … I caused … trouble for him." He wiped his wet nose off with his sleeve. "He said … I told the police … about the fire." He started to cry again. "Ambrose … said he'd kill me. I don't … want to die."

Liz put her arm around Gregory. "Let's go home, Gregory." She looked at Abby. "Thanks, Miss Carpenter. You've been so kind."

As the brother and sister walked away, Abby watched them leave. "There are no words for people like Ambrose. Threatening that poor boy." She shook her head and fought back her own tears.

For the first time that day, Ian put his arms around her. "Let's go, Abby. At least Cardwell will be in the nick for a time. Perhaps the rest of the weekend will unfold without incident."

His arm felt warm and protective as they walked to the shuttle waiting area. Was there a touch of tenderness in his gesture? Abby prayed she wasn't just imagining it.

Chapter 23

Abby dressed for the ball in a room designated for the ladies at the casino. Miss Swanson had placed all the gowns in there and, one-by-one, she transformed each participant into a vision of silken beauty.

Abby had yet to see the ballroom, but everyone who had been there before assured her that it was a room straight out of a movie. A fairy tale setting come alive. Her nerves tingled with anticipation.

As she waited for Miss Swanson to tighten her stays, her mind drifted back to her conversation with Liz at the motel that afternoon. Liz had taken Gregory home for a rest before she returned to clean rooms. The motel maid's distress was obvious.

"Are you okay, Liz?" She had placed a gentle hand on the maid's arm as the worker carried a bucket.

Liz paused in her work. "I'm so worried about Gregory. He's always had such a tough time understanding things. But he's still recovering from our brother's death a year ago. He's just not been the same." Liz looked down at the sidewalk in front of Abby's motel door. "I don't know how to help him. And frankly, life has been more peaceful since Greyson died. But Gregory … he took it hard."

"I didn't know your brother died. I'm so sorry."

"Thank you, Miss Carpenter. You've been a great help. And I'm so sorry about all that has happened here to distress you. I've never seen anything like it before. You take care now."

Liz went back to work, but that conversation played over and over in Abby's thoughts. She inhaled deeply and closed her eyes.

I will think about this ball. And I will pray I say the right words to Ian so he knows how I feel about him. Lord, please help me. And please—help him forgive me.

* * *

The other ladies in the casino dressing room had not exaggerated. The ballroom was indescribable by human standards. Abby was transported to another world when she walked through the double doors.

Her eyes were drawn to the Greek columns in each corner, curved in such a way to draw the eye toward the ceiling. She gasped at the display of stained-glass windows in geometric designs. Each fenestrated section was a piece of fine art. The shiny floor glistened as she smoothed a slippered foot across the canvas of parquet. She hesitated to mar the appearance yet eagerly awaited the chance to leave her mark while dancing.

She looked across the room and saw two men dressed in eighteenth-century military clothing—one in British red and one in blue wool trimmed in white—speaking earnestly to each other. Ian and Sergeant Walker. Sergeant Walker looked dashing, but it was Ian who stole her breath. She reminded herself of Miss Swanson's advice: "Give him a chance, Abby. Don't push him away." Abby inhaled as deeply as she could with the corset constricting her. Lifting her gown off the floor a few inches, she floated across the ballroom toward Ian. His back was to her, but Sergeant Walker saw her and pointed Ian to look her way.

He spun around on his heel and stood speechless as he stared at Abby. She stopped walking toward him, feeling self-conscious, and lowered her gaze to the floor.

In a few seconds, Ian's shoes stood in front of her. She lifted her head, smiled, and curtsied as his eyes swept over her from head to toe.

"Abby." He put both hands tentatively on her arms. "I didn't expect …"

"What? You didn't expect me to come?" Her heart beat faster.

"No, I was hoping you'd come. I didn't expect to feel this way. About you."

The announcement that the orchestra was ready to play rescued him from stumbling over his words.

Abby's stomach knotted. "What were you and Sergeant Walker talking about so intently?"

"Oh." He shook his head. "Nothing really. Actually, it is something you need to know." He sighed with disgust. "Cardwell was released on bail."

"What?" She scowled. "How?"

"His parents. They didn't want their son spending a night in the nick. I guess they thought he needed to sleep in his comfortable bed." Ian's voice dripped with sarcasm.

When she didn't speak, he changed his tone to a gentle one. "Look, Abby, I don't want you worried. The sergeant is here, as well as a couple of other officers."

She looked around and only saw colonial-clad guests. "Where?"

He smiled and whispered. "They're in disguise. Quite a few reenactors around."

Abby couldn't help but grin. The opening foot-tapping song was over, and the orchestra geared up for a slower melody, announcing that this next number was dedicated to lovers of history, as well as lovers of love.

Ian glanced around the room then shyly met her eyes. "I know you want to keep me at a distance, but would you allow me to dance this number with you? We've only a few days left together." He adjusted the cravat at his neck.

Apparently she wasn't the only one having difficulty breathing. "I'd love to dance with you."

He put one arm around her waist and held her other hand up in the air. Their hands entwined in a perfect fit. He swayed her across the floor, careful to avoid stepping on the full skirt of her ball gown. The melody of "You Are So Beautiful" toyed with her heart as Ian swept his eyes across her. He closed the distance between them slightly, just enough that she could whisper near his ear.

"Ian, please forgive me for pushing you away. I was so afraid of being hurt. I …" She swallowed back tears. "I drove you away before you could hurt me."

"I wasn't going to hurt you, Abby." He pulled back just enough to make eye contact. "I love you."

Inhaling deeply, she whispered the words in his ear she had feared saying. "I love you so much, Ian."

"Abby." He drew her closer.

His gentle kisses along her face sent ripples of pleasure through every part of her. She felt his pounding heart as she placed her arms behind his neck and rested her head on his shoulder. His gentle grip with both arms revealed that any barriers they had each forged in their hearts were dismantling, one tender touch after another. Holding Ian was like finding her way home.

The song ended after just a few moments, but a lifetime of love together suddenly seemed possible. They pulled back and, still holding hands, stared at each other, each apparently afraid to break the spell that seemed to surround them.

Ian fingered his cravat and glanced toward the refreshments. "Can I get you something to drink?"

"Yes. Thanks."

He held her hand for as long as he could, stretching out his arm until only their fingertips touched. He went to the bar for some punch.

Abby stood near the double doors, away from the guests dancing to the next song. Someone opened a door, and the wind outside sent a shiver through her.

"You two make a lovely couple."

She jumped, and now goosebumps joined the chill running up and down her body.

"But I know something about you, Abigail Carpenter, descendant of Abigail Gillingham."

As he spoke into her ear from over her shoulder, her fear increased. The scent of whiskey sickened her. "You're drunk, Ambrose."

"Well, that may be so, Miss Carpenter. But aren't you interested to know how I know about your grandmother from the Revolution?" He circled around from behind and now faced her, far too close.

"Not really." She did want to know but didn't want to engage a drunken slob.

"Well, I happened to find out that my grandfather, in 1777, was engaged to your grandmother … many times removed. But funny thing happened. She married someone else."

Abby was shocked, but Abigail Gillingham's refusal of Ambrose's ancestor didn't surprise her. She took a step back and sought Ian but couldn't find him in the room. "And how does that concern me, Mr. Cardwell?"

He breathed alcohol-drenched breath in her face. Ambrose stared at Abby's low-cut ball gown and grinned. "I thought you might want to make amends for Abigail Gillingham's betrayal. Perhaps, for old time's sake, as they say." He stroked a thick finger over Abby's curves, and she backed away in horror.

She could see the rage on Ian's face as he threw the drinks at Ambrose. Then the fists began flying. Ambrose may have been inebriated, but it didn't stop him from throwing powerful punches.

Abby gripped her stomach and stumbled toward the doors.

Dear Lord, protect Ian.

She stepped outside and breathed erratically as her stays seemed to tighten with her nerves.

"Are you … all right … Miss Carpenter?" Gregory had come to the ball wearing a coat of the King's Army.

Dizziness overwhelmed her. "Not really." She fought back dry heaves.

"Can I … help you back … to the motel?" His look of concern comforted her.

"Yes, I'm not feeling well." He put his elbow out for her, and she held onto him. The fresh, cool air helped calm her stomach. "Thanks, Gregory."

"Thank you … Miss Carpenter. You've been … so kind to me."

They walked slowly through Congress Park, but instead of turning toward Broadway and the motel, they kept heading south, toward the woods.

"Gregory, I think we took a wrong turn. The motel is over there."

"I know it is."

"Then why …"

Abby looked at him, and the grin on his face sent chills through her.

"Gregory, take me back to the ball."

"I don't think so, Abigail."

"What? Take me back now."

Panic seized her as he tightened his grip.

He didn't say a word.

Her mind raced. *Maybe if I talk to him.* "Gregory." She swallowed with extreme effort. "Why don't we go back to the ball?"

Silence. He gripped her arm so hard, she knew it was bruising.

"Gregory, why don't you answer me?" Her voice rose in alarm.

He stopped abruptly and stared at her with dark eyes. "Because, I'm not Gregory."

Abby's heart raced so fast, she didn't know how long she could stay alert and not faint.

Talk to him, Abby.

"What ... what do you mean, you're not Gregory?" She barely recognized her own voice.

He paused a moment, the fog from the river swirling around them. "I'm Greyson, Gregory's brother. Gregory is dead." Even in the ghostly mist, she could see the evil in his eyes. "Gregory was such trouble, interfering with me all that time. So one day, I just happened to lure him to a cliff. Everyone thought it was an accident. And since we were twins, I told them it was me who died and Gregory who lived." He cackled. "After spending a lifetime hearing his pathetic voice, it was easy talking like him." He began to imitate his brother. "Isn't ... that right ... Miss Carpenter?"

Abby shuddered as queasiness gripped her. Even in tense situations as a nurse, she could keep her head. But this wickedness was something she'd never dreamt, even in her worst nightmares. She wished she could wake up and find it was a bad dream. But Greyson's voice in her ear and his painful grip while dragging her through the woods told her otherwise.

Dear God, help me.

* * *

Sergeant Walker finished talking to Ian about the fight as another officer took Ambrose away in handcuffs.

Ian's jaw ached where Ambrose had landed a punch. He rubbed it and was startled to realize he couldn't find his date. "Where's Abby?"

The sergeant looked around. He approached a man who stood nearby holding a tray of hors d'oeuvres. "Did you see a redhead in a green gown near here?"

"She went outdoors, Sergeant. She looked like she didn't feel too well when the fight started."

Together they ran out the double doors and looked around. Abby was nowhere to be seen. Several men were standing nearby, chatting and laughing. "Excuse me. Did you see a woman with red hair and wearing a green dress leave here?" Ian tried not to panic.

"Yeah, that hot chick? I thought maybe she'd had too much to drink, 'cause she looked a bit sick. But that guy from town—you know, that simpleton—came and offered to take her back to the motel. That's probably where she is now."

Ian released a huge breath then started walking to the motel until Liz came running toward him. "Mr. Thacker! Sergeant Walker!" She was out of breath and near hysterics. "Where's Miss Carpenter?"

"Those men said Gregory took her back to the motel. I'm heading there now."

A look of horror darkened Liz's countenance. "No. You've got to find her. She's in terrible danger. Look! I found this in Gregory's room!" Liz's shaking fingers handed a paper to Ian. It read, "Tonight is our night, Abigail Gillingham."

Cold, raw fear worked its way through Ian. "We've got to find her."

Sergeant Walker looked at the note. "Ian, we don't have much time." He looked at Liz. "Where might your brother have gone?"

"I don't know." Liz covered her mouth and cried.

"I think I know. The cabin." Ian took off running.

"I'll get the other officers here."

Ian didn't wait. He raced through the mist toward the path they'd taken the day they visited the cabin. He knew what psychotics could do. As he ran, he fought the nausea that threatened to stop his quest. Stumbling in the darkness, he prayed as never before. The thought of losing the woman who had just revealed her love for him spurred his feet faster. He tripped and fell more than once on the uneven terrain, but he rose again, determined more than ever to find her.

A scream in the distance stopped him cold.

Dear God, no!

Whipping around, he sought to determine where the call for help had come from. The trees and fog seemed to conspire against him. The sound echoed everywhere, confusing the location of the plea for help.

Another scream.

Dear God, help me. I must find her. Please.

He gripped an ancient tree and leaned his forehead against the trunk. His fingers touched the thick bark and moved across an unusual groove. Lifting his face, he saw a deep notch that appeared manmade. Was that an arrow?

If it was or wasn't, Ian didn't know, but he had few choices before it was too late. He followed the direction of the arrow. When Abby's next scream drew closer, he knew he was on the right path.

As he finally reached a clearing, his throat constricted. He saw Gregory with a knife, holding it near Abigail, whose arms were bound behind her back.

"So, the hero has arrived. You'll not take Miss Gillingham away from me this time."

"Gregory?"

Before he could contemplate the shocking change in the man's voice and demeanor, Gregory lunged at him with the weapon.

Ian jumped out of the way and scanned about for anything that might help him defend himself. Gregory came at him again. This time, Ian felt a familiar, searing pain across his side.

Abby screamed.

His adrenaline kicked in further, and he grabbed the other man's arms and twisted them around his back. Gregory dropped the knife and began cursing Ian. The experienced officer was shocked at the strength of the man who had appeared so fragile and vulnerable—until now.

Shouts in the distance told Ian the other officers were nearby. "Over here!"

Sergeant Walker and two others dressed in colonial costumes appeared with very modern-day weapons at the ready. One grabbed a set of handcuffs from a hidden pocket and tried to put them on Gregory.

Ian thought things were under control and plopped on the ground, grabbing his bleeding side.

But the strength of the man surprised the officer with the handcuffs, and Gregory wriggled free and lunged for the knife on the ground, sweeping it up with his hand.

Sergeant Walker aimed his weapon. "Put the knife down if you know what's good for you."

A look of enraged madness crossed Gregory's face, and he lunged toward Ian with the knife.

Sergeant Walker fired, and the knife-wielding madman fell to the ground.

Ian pushed himself up with difficulty and stumbled toward Abby, whose arms were still tied behind her back. "Abby." His eyes were wet. "You're safe now." His hands shook as he untied the pantihose that held her wrists together. Fear shivered through him when she didn't respond but stared into the distance. He placed trembling fingers on her cheek. "Abby!"

Sergeant Walker approached. "She's in shock. Let's get her to the hospital." He looked at Ian's bloody side. "Let's get you there as well."

Chapter 24

Ian winced when the nurse started the IV in his arm. The glass bottle hanging on the hook overhead made him feel trapped.

"Look, I need to go see Abby." The stitches in his new wound tugged as he moved. "Can't you do this in her room?"

"As soon as we get everything set up with the antibiotic, we'll wheel you in there, Mr. Thacker. But two knife wounds in one month are two too many. We don't want a nasty infection starting." The nurse gave him an understanding smile. "I'll be quick. And your girlfriend is resting comfortably. She'll be okay."

She left him alone with Sergeant Walker, who looked at him with furrowed eyebrows. "Are you doing all right? That could have been a grave wound."

"Hardly hurts at all." He gave a wry expression. "Well, perhaps smarts a bit." He paused in thought, watching the IV fluid drip. "I still can't believe it. Gregory. Or rather, Greyson. I didn't even know there were twin brothers."

"Well, you weren't the only one fooled. Even Liz couldn't tell. She'd always said Greyson was the complete opposite of Gregory. Poor girl. The thought that her favorite brother was killed a year ago and she never knew it." Sergeant Walker shook his head and sighed.

Ian combed his fingers through his disheveled hair. "But I don't get the connection with Abigail Gillingham." He readjusted his position in the wheelchair and winced when he tugged on his new stitches.

"According to Liz, Greyson became obsessed with family history—especially the saga of an ancestor named Elizabeth Pomeroy. Mrs. Pomeroy wrote diaries after an apparent rape by a British lieutenant. She blamed Abigail Gillingham for the rape—and ended up pregnant with the lieutenant's child. According to the diaries that Greyson read day after day, Abigail Gillingham was the source of all her woes, including the shame of an illegitimate child and her subsequent poverty." The sergeant inhaled a deep breath. "In his twisted mind, the source of their family's troubles all traced back to one woman—Abigail Gillingham. When he heard that the descendant of Abigail was here in town, well …"

"His sick mind wanted revenge." Ian covered his eyes with his free hand. "To think how close I came to losing her." His mouth trembled as a terrifying concern arose. "Was Abby interfered with?" His nostrils flared and he gripped the arm of his wheelchair.

"Interfered with? Do you mean raped?"

"Yes."

He felt the sergeant's hand on his shoulder. "No, Ian. She wasn't. She'll be fine." He paused. "'In the world you will have tribulation. But take heart: I have overcome the world.' One of my favorite Bible verses." Sergeant Walker wiped at his eye. "Must have gotten something in my eye."

The nurse returned with the antibiotic to add to the IV solution. "This may burn a little, but it's better than getting a nasty infection."

Ian sat up straight in the wheelchair and swallowed. His eyes widened. "I agree with the burning assessment." He breathed in and exhaled slowly.

She patted his good arm. "When your girlfriend wakes up, she can kiss it and make it better." The grinning nurse left, no doubt to torture the next victim.

"So, you ready to go for a ride?" Sergeant Walker pushed the chair forward.

"Only if you know how to drive this thing. And only if you know where Abby is."

He watched anxiously along the hallway for any sign of Abby. At the end of it, the sergeant turned the wheelchair into a private room. She lay sound asleep on the bed. She also had an IV running, and she appeared to rest peacefully.

"You two are a matched set." The sergeant grinned. "I'll leave you alone."

Ian didn't want to wake her, so he worked his legs until he could get up close to the bed. Her hand without the needle in it lay closest to him. Grasping her hand gently, he kissed her bruised fingers. Seeing the discoloration of her skin elicited warm, unbidden tears.

He rested his head on the edge of her mattress and closed his eyes.

* * *

"Ian. Ian."

Am I dreaming?

He lifted his head from a white sheet. Light filtered through a sheer curtain covering an unfamiliar window.

"Ian." Abby stared at him with groggy eyes. "Ian, I feel so strange."

A nurse walked in and checked Abby's vitals. "How are you doing, Miss Carpenter? We've given you a sedative, so you might feel a little dizzy."

He felt the bristle of his unshaven face. "Nurse, will she be all right?"

"Of course, Mr. Thacker. She'll be fine. I hear you're the hero of the day, rescuing her." She smiled and looked at Abby. "I hope you're planning on keeping him around."

She gave a sleepy smile and touched his day-old beard. "Oh yes."

The nurse left.

He stood and stroked her cheek. "Are you truly well? Abby, I've been sick with worry."

Her face grew serious and tears brimmed on her eyelids. "He had the face of evil, Ian. It was so terrifying."

He gripped her hand. "I know." Once again, he fought back a surge of anger and fear. Then he remembered his prayer last night. And he remembered finding the arrow on the tree. "But he didn't win. Evil did not triumph. God did."

She smiled and closed her eyes, the sedative helping her relax.

He kissed her fingers again before resting his head next to her. He closed his eyes, and an unfamiliar and comforting peace washed over him.

* * *

A few days later, Ian insisted on driving them back to the airport, considering all that Abby had been through. Had it only been three weeks since they'd arrived? It didn't seem possible. It seemed a lifetime ago.

As they drove, he occasionally reached over to squeeze her fingers, which elicited a smile from her and then fresh tears. The thought of saying goodbye was tearing them both up.

"I'll ring you up as soon as I arrive in London."

"Okay." She put her hand up to her mouth and stared out the car window.

God, please help us both.

"Now, Scott and Maureen are picking you up at the airport in California, correct?"

She nodded. "Yes."

He took their exit and drove into Albany airport, looking for the car rental return sign. Abby was silent as they dropped off the car that had transported them to a different time and place. One where they'd fallen in love and would never be the same.

He carried both bags into the terminal and checked them in at the airline counter.

"Are you traveling together?" The agent's smile was charming but the question painful to hear.

"No. Not just yet." He wiped a finger against his nose and turned away.

"Well, here's your ticket, sir." She gave Abby a sympathetic look as she handed her a ticket. Abby's eyes were almost as red as her hair.

He drew her to a quiet corner. "You don't need to go with me to see me off." He gripped her hands.

"No. I'll go. I want to be with you as long as I can."

They walked without speaking until they reached the gate. Passengers were just beginning to walk out on the tarmac and climb the stairs into the short-hop airplane to New York City. There, he would catch his flight to London.

"I'll be speaking with my superiors to see what my options are. Until then, please know that I'll do everything I can to get us together as soon as possible."

She responded with a brave smile. "I know. I'll wait to hear from you."

He set her bag down and held her in his arms. "My heart is breaking, Abby."

"No more so than mine." She cried on his shoulder and all he could do was hold her. An elderly lady walking past handed him a couple of tissues. She looked with sympathy at the lovely young lady weeping on his tweed jacket before she boarded the same flight.

Abby pulled away, and he handed her the tissues. She wiped her eyes. "You need to go, or you'll miss your flight." Her beautiful smile almost made him change his mind.

"I'll ring you up." His leaden feet refused to move.

"I know." She waved a finger and gave a contorted smile that edged on trembling. "You need to go."

It took every ounce of his will to kiss her goodbye one last time. As he turned away, he wished he had saved a tissue for himself.

He couldn't look back because he knew he'd turn around and run back to her. He trotted up the steps leading to the small prop jet and bent low as he approached the narrow aisle. He looked at his ticket and plopped into his assigned seat, grateful to be sitting alone.

Ian stared at the ticket a moment, sighed, and placed it in the inside pocket of his jacket. He felt a bulge in that same pocket and pulled out a thick envelope—a typed transcript of a letter his father had long saved for him. It was a letter written by Ian's great-great-great-great-grandfather after the Battle at Saratoga. Ian and his dad had always planned on reading it together during the bicentennial ceremonies. Before Ian's mum died five years ago, she'd reminded him to take it with him in 1977, in memory of his dad. Ian had nearly forgotten it.

He opened the worn pages that looked like they'd been typed at least thirty years before. At the top of the letter, it explained that this message was meant to be read by all the sons in the family.

Better late than never.

Ian began to read the content, written by his ancestor who fought at the battle of Saratoga:

To my most beloved son, Jonathan,

This missive to you, my only son, has been written with the understanding that I am not long for this world. It is a heartfelt sentiment and desire for your happiness in life that prompts me to put these words into writing.

My own happiness in this life has not been realized. I suppose it will have to be experienced in eternity with my Savior, Who has graciously forgiven my many sins. But, I pray you will heed this instruction before it is too late for you.

I am quite certain that you know of the unhappiness your mother and I experienced in our years together before she died. Indeed, you are the sole blessed joy of this otherwise unhappy union.

It is my hope and prayer that, when you hear my story, you will understand why I heartily entreat you in this, my own desire for you: Marry the woman who holds your heart.

When I was a young man in my third decade of life, as you are now, I met a woman named ...

Ian stopped reading and gasped. He fumbled to undo his seatbelt and tucked the letter back into his pocket. He headed back toward the open door. "I've got to get off this flight."

"But sir, we're almost ready to leave." The stewardess narrowed her eyes.

"Please, I've got to get off."

She stepped aside, and he raced down the steep stairs as quickly as he could. Running back into the terminal, he searched the area, desperate to find her.

*   *   *

Abby's head hung low as she sat in a booth and mindlessly stirred hot coffee. She focused on the swirls of cream blending into the dark brew. As each dollop disappeared, she added another and repeated the process.

She stopped stirring when she thought she heard a familiar voice.

My imagination must be on overdrive. Ian's on his flight back home. Without me.

Sighing, she poured more cream into her coffee. As she finished stirring the dollop into the much lighter brew, she figured she should drink it.

Someone slid into the seat opposite and touched her leg with his.

She jerked her head upward and stared at him. She didn't know whether to cover him with kisses or throw her purse at him. "Are you toying with my emotions, Ian, or prolonging the agony?" Regardless of his intent, she was exhausted.

He didn't speak at first. Instead, he dunked a tea bag into the cup of hot water he'd ordered at the counter.

"You're bruising the tea."

"It's quite odd, you know, the things you discover in letters. Especially old ones."

"Ian, are you all right? You have the strangest look on your face."

He finally looked at her, his blue eyes smiling in the light streaming from a nearby window. "I'm quite all right. Truly, I'm better than all right. I've decided to follow my grandfather's advice—my grandfather from the American Revolution, that is." Ian slipped out of the opposite seat and slid next to Abby. He draped his arm around her and scooted closer.

Abby swallowed nervously. "And what advice is that, Constable Thacker?"

"Well, my grandfather apparently loved your grandmother, Abigail Gillingham."

Her jaw dropped in disbelief. She shook her head. "That's not possible. How can that be?"

Ian pulled out the letter. "It's all in here. The secret love he carried with him his whole life, yet it was never fulfilled. *He* was never fulfilled." He handed it to her.

She opened the crinkly pages and scanned the words. Her eyes widened. She stared at him. "This is too unbelievable."

He took the letter from her and set it down. He placed his hands around her face and stroked her cheeks. "Abby, I have no idea how we can work this out, but I know one thing. I will not live without you and regret it my whole life, like my grandfather did. Please marry me. I want to love you. To caress and hold you. To make babies with you and grow old together."

Her giggles turned into laughter. As a joyous burst of happiness filled her every pore, she leaned in and kissed Ian with unrelenting passion.

He returned her kiss for a few moments before he pulled back and looked at her. "Well, will you marry me?" He kissed her again.

"Anytime, anywhere. Yes."

"Then let's find someone to marry us so we can start our honeymoon."

"I can hardly wait."

Chapter 25

One Year Later, October 7, 1978

"Where have you been? Dispatch has been trying to reach you for hours." Sergeant Walker grabbed his car keys and motioned for Ian to follow.

"What do you mean, where have I been? You know I was doing duty on loan at the Schuylerville parade. I wasn't near enough to hear dispatch." Ian scratched his head. "Where are we going?"

"To the hospital, Daddy."

Ian's knees weakened as his stomach dropped. "That's not possible. The baby's not due 'til next week."

Sergeant Walker shook his head in disgust while unlocking the door. "Didn't you learn anything in that baby class? Kids come whenever they want. Now get in."

Ian plopped into the passenger seat and pulled the door shut. "This isn't good. I promised Abby I'd be there."

"We told her you'd be on your way as soon as we got ahold of you, Constable."

He jerked his head toward the sergeant. "When will you stop calling me that? It's Officer Thacker now."

His superior grinned. "You'll always be that constable guy to me." Ten minutes later, they pulled into the hospital parking lot. "Here we are. Good luck."

Panic seized Ian. "Aren't you coming with me?"

"You are pathetic. Come on, son." The sergeant got out and steadied Ian as he leaned against the car.

"I don't know if I can do this."

"Imagine how Abby feels. Come on." Sergeant Walker half-dragged Ian as they followed the signs to maternity.

He tasted salt in his mouth and stopped a moment. "I think I've had too much sun."

"Here." His friend pulled a can of soda out of his pocket, opened the lid, and handed it to him. "I brought this in case you needed it."

Ian guzzled several swigs. "Thanks." He took a few slow breaths.

"Contractions going better now?"

He glared at his boss. "Very funny."

"Come on."

As they approached the maternity wing, a woman let loose a deep guttural groan that Ian recognized. It was the same sound Anne made when her son was born.

"Oh, no. It's coming." He leaned against the wall and closed his eyes. If he could have spared Abby from this, he would gladly do so. As it was, he was experiencing his own labor pains.

"Buck up, Papa. Your wife needs you."

"I know." Ian forced his eyes open, stood tall, and walked with determination into the delivery room.

His beautiful wife held a small, blond infant wrapped in a blanket. She was smiling and crying all at once.

"Abby. I'm so sorry I didn't make it sooner."

She reached her empty arm toward him. "I'm so glad you're here."

He crossed the room in two seconds flat and kissed her. "I'm so glad you're all right."

"Congratulations, Officer Thacker. You have a son." The nurse grinned and left the room.

"Abby, he looks like you." Ian kissed him on the head.

"He has your hair. Look." She stroked her fingers through disheveled wisps that stuck out in the back.

He kissed her slowly, tenderly. "I suppose someday we might try for another one. Perhaps he or she might carry on the red-haired legend."

She laughed. "I suppose so. But not today."

"No, not today. I can wait. As long as I know you'll be in my arms, I'll always wait for you."

* * *

Abby knew that, as soon as she had a moment, she would begin writing Thomas Michael Thacker a letter. She would tell him how she met his father and how much she loved him. She would tell their son that his father rescued and protected her. And loved her enough to stay with her.

Letter from Thomas Salyer to his son:

To my most beloved son, Jonathan,

This missive to you, my only son, has been written with the understanding that I am not long for this world. It is a heartfelt sentiment and desire for your happiness in life that prompts me to put it in writing.

My own happiness in this life has not been realized. I suppose it will have to be experienced in eternity with my Savior, Who has graciously forgiven my many sins. But, I pray, you will heed this instruction before it is too late for you.

I am quite certain that you know of the unhappiness your mother and I experienced in our years together, before she died. Indeed, you are the sole blessed joy of this otherwise unhappy union.

It is my hope and prayer that, when you hear my story, you will understand why I heartily entreat you in this, my own desire for you: Marry the woman who holds your heart.

When I was a young man in my third decade of life, as you are now, I met a woman named Abigail Gillingham. I was the surgeon's mate in the war camp at Saratoga in the colony of New York. Abigail was a Colonist, a nurse who helped with the wounded soldiers.

I was mightily drawn to her, soul and body. She had been brought into the camp by a most cruel uncle who forced her to tend the wounded. He spoke untruths about her situation. While ensuring *she could remain in camp by claiming she had a consort away at war, Abigail was, in truth, not married.*

Although I felt a strong attraction to her from the start, I battled my own natural inclinations toward her, allowing that she was aligned with another. Due to unforeseen circumstances, I discovered the true state of affairs.

Not wishing to disappoint my father again after choosing my lowly profession, I had promised I would marry his choice for me. I had, therefore, intended to save both heart and loins for your mother. But I fear my heart was not sheltered from loving Abigail. After expressing my desires to her, she was offended by my impetuous lack of chivalry because she knew I would return to England.

She refused my advances, recognizing my lack of intent to marry her. I was crushed and heartsick, yet ashamed of my base desires for her with no thought for her future. I never intended to stay behind in America.

But I had never foreseen leaving my heart behind with Abigail.

May God bless you with the treasure of your heart.
Your most humble servant and loving father,
Thomas Salyer, Esq.